WHERE LOVE LEADS

WHERE LOVE LEADS

by

Erin McKenzie

2017

WHERE LOVE LEADS
© 2017 By Erin McKenzie. All Rights Reserved.

ISBN 13: 978-1-62639-991-4

This Trade Paperback Original Is Published By
Bold Strokes Books, Inc.
P.O. Box 249
Valley Falls, NY 12185

First Edition: June 2017

CREDITS
Editor: Ruth Sternglantz
Production Design: Susan Ramundo
Cover Design By Melody Pond

Acknowledgments

I'd like to extend a huge thank you to Sandy Lowe, Carsen Taite, and Radclyffe for accepting my pitch and making this dream come true. To my editor, Ruth Sternglantz, you're a one-woman master class on writing romance, and your insights are much appreciated. Hugs to my friends Tricia, Shelly, and Lauren, for being first readers and very encouraging cheerleaders. Many thanks to my kids, for hugs, kisses, and being quiet when I need to write. Debbie, your unwavering support means everything. Pat, thank you for instilling in me a love of books from a very early age and for always loving me unconditionally. And finally, thanks to my sixth grade teacher, who told me when I was twelve that I'd be a writer someday…this may not be what you had in mind, Sister Carla, but I did it!

Dedication

To my wife Debbie and our three beautiful children, Kenzie, Sierra, and Matthias...love you to the moon and back!

CHAPTER ONE

Even after all these years, Sarah still got the jitters on the first day of school. Though she had graduated from student to staff member years ago, early September still conjured up childhood memories of freshly sharpened pencils, squeaky-clean sneakers, and a brand-new box of sixty-four Crayola crayons.

"You are such a dork, O'Shaughnessy." Sarah chuckled at her reflection in the bathroom mirror as she put the finishing touches on her freshly cut auburn hair and tucked a wayward strand behind her ear. Her usually fair complexion still carried a bit of a summer tan, making the freckles scattered across her nose more prominent. Her eyes were wide with anticipation.

Back in her bedroom, Sarah gave her outfit a final check. The late-summer weather was still quite warm, and Sarah had chosen tan linen capris and a sleeveless white blouse. The open collar of the blouse revealed a jade teardrop pendant that perfectly matched her eyes. Sarah frowned, acutely aware that her pants were fitting a bit more snugly than they had before. She made the familiar vow to go for a walk later, then headed downstairs.

As she filled her travel mug with freshly brewed coffee, Sarah thought about the day ahead. Although she and her fellow school counselors had spent much of August at work, cleaning up class schedules, triple-checking senior graduation requirements and preparing for the students, it wasn't until opening day that the school came to life. With the pleasant anticipation of seeing the kids and facing the challenges of a new school year, Sarah grabbed her keys and bag, gave her cats a farewell chin scratch, then headed out the door.

❖

Lauren Emerson was making breakfast when she heard the panic-stricken voice of her daughter calling her.

"Mom? Mom!"

"Oh no," Lauren sighed, having fully expected this. She found Kat in the bathroom, sitting on the edge of the tub. Her long dark hair hung in a curtain around her face, and she was sobbing into her trembling hands. Without a word, Lauren took her daughter into her arms and held her close. She fought to keep her own worried tears in check, needing to be strong for both of them. After a few moments, Kat sniffed and looked at her mom. Her pale face and anxious blue eyes telegraphed clearly to Lauren how nervous she was, and it seemed a distinct possibility the poor kid might throw up all over her new school outfit.

Lauren certainly understood the cause of Kat's anxiety. The two of them had left everything Kat had ever known and moved to Easton, a small lakeside city in the Finger Lakes region of New York, in June. They were pretty well settled in the house they'd rented, but now Kat had to face a much more daunting change. It was the first day of her senior year, and she didn't know a soul at Easton High School. She'd be the new kid, and though they'd talked about how she could make a fresh start here, Lauren knew the pain and fear of Kat's horrific junior year had followed her. Kat was terrified the people here would find out her secret and be just as awful to her as her so-called friends back home had been.

"Mom, I can't do this," Kat whispered through her tears.

Lauren's heart broke for the millionth time. "Baby, everything is going to be okay. This is a fresh start, a chance for us to make things better." Lauren took Kat by the shoulders and looked her in the eye. "You are a strong, amazing young woman, Kat. Show them the person you want to be. No one will know anything you don't choose to share."

Kat dropped her gaze, and Lauren tipped her chin back up with a gentle finger. "Remember, Kit Kat, I went to school at Easton many moons ago," she said, earning a flicker of a smile from her daughter at the familiar childhood endearment, "and even back then, Easton was a much more open and accepting place than what you're used to. Those were four of the best years of my life. We're not in Alabama anymore, sweet pea. You're going to like it here." She watched Kat take a deep breath, steeling herself for what was to come. Lauren prayed her words would not be a lie.

CHAPTER TWO

H ey, Ms. O," hollered a group of boys as they laughed and
jostled their way past the counseling office.

"Hey, boys. Welcome back." One of the boys stopped to de-
liver a high five, then continued on with his friends. Sarah and Jamie
Gibson, her colleague and close friend, were in the hall watching
and greeting the steady stream of teenagers arriving at school.

"Joey looks happy to be here," Jamie said, indicating the boy
who had slapped Sarah's hand.

"He does. Let's hope it stays that way." Joey had been one
of Sarah's toughest challenges last year, a sullen, angry boy with
lousy attendance and a lousier attitude. His parents had been going
through a nasty divorce and putting Joey in the middle. He had shut
down, not knowing how to deal with it. To help him, Sarah walked
the slippery slope of talking to the parents about how the circumstances were affecting their son, both educationally and emotionally. Thankfully, the parents realized their mistake and cared enough
about their son to tone down the negativity, and after a while, Joey
turned the corner and started to improve. He was one of Sarah's success stories, and she was proud of him.

"I've got him with you for English 10, so keep an eye on him
for me, okay?"

"Will do. I wonder who your pet project will be this year?"
Jamie said with a wink.

Sarah smacked her in the arm. "Just get to your room, missy. The homeroom bell is going to ring any minute."

"Yes, ma'am. See you for lunch?"

Sarah scoffed. "Since when do I ever get time for lunch in the first week of school?"

"Poor baby," Jamie teased, and headed down the hall to her classroom.

❖

Kat stared anxiously out the window as her mom pulled into the bustling parking lot of the high school. They had a meeting with the school counselor to make sure everything started off smoothly. Kat hadn't said a word on the drive over, and thankfully her mom had left her with her thoughts, which had been whirling around with such intensity her head hurt. No matter how many deep breaths she took, her mind kept returning to one thought: *What if this school isn't any better?* Well, she couldn't back out now. It was time to go in and face the day.

"C'mon, sweet pea, let's go meet this Ms. O'Shaughnessy. I spoke with her on the phone, and she seems very nice."

Kat grunted, feeling miserable, but forced herself to get out of the car.

Easton High School was huge compared to Kat's previous small-town school in Alabama, which had been all one level, with a total of maybe three hundred and fifty students. She'd had eighty-four kids in her entire grade, and she'd known them all since kindergarten. The school before her now had three floors, seemingly thousands of kids, and Kat had no idea how she was going to find her way around. After stopping in the main office for directions, she and her mom made it to the third floor counseling office in time for their meeting.

"Good morning. May I help you?" asked a harried but smiling secretary. The woman reminded Kat of Cinderella's fairy god-mother, with her silver hair and plump, friendly face.

Kat looked at her mom, who replied, "Yes, we're here to see Ms. O'Shaughnessy. My daughter is a new student."

The secretary moved with surprising quickness around her desk. "You must be Katherine. Welcome to Easton."

Kat was a little taken aback at the greeting, and it must've shown on her face, because the woman smiled encouragingly.

"I'm Mrs. Hayden, the counseling office secretary. I know the names of all the new students we're expecting today. You see, the six counselors each have a portion of the alphabet, and you happen to be the only new arrival in *D* through *F*." Mrs. Hayden pointed to the second door on the right. "Go on in. Ms. O'Shaughnessy is expecting you."

Kat felt like her head was about to explode. *Six counselors? How many freaking people are in this place? I am so not going to make it through the day.*

❖

Sarah stood and smiled as the new student and her mom peeked in her door. "Hi there. I'm Sarah O'Shaughnessy, and I'll be your counselor," she said, offering her hand to the student first. The girl's cold, clammy fingers gave away her anxiety. Then the mom shook Sarah's hand, her warm, firm grip matching her smile. The woman's incredible blue eyes made Sarah do a double-take, and she saw a flash of worry in her gaze. The woman quickly looked away and placed a hand on her daughter's shoulder.

"Hi. I'm Lauren Emerson, and this is my daughter, Kat."

Sarah turned her attention to the student. "I bet you're nervous, starting a new school for senior year." Kat nodded silently. "Well, we'll get you settled in as quickly as we can. I've created your schedule based on what you still need to graduate. Often when students transfer from out of state, they also have a bit of catching up to do with our good old New York State assessments."

Mrs. Emerson spoke up then. "I warned you about Regents exams, didn't I, Kat?" The poor kid's expression could only be described as a grimace. Her mom went on. "I graduated from Easton back in '96, but the building looks a lot different."

"Wow, we were students here at the same time. Class of '98, at your service," Sarah said with a mock salute. "They've done a lot of renovating in the last few years. In fact, our office suite here used to be classrooms."

Noticing her discomfort with the adult chit-chat, Sarah smiled again at Kat. "So, you'll need to take three exams in January, in Algebra, US History, and English. But you've had solid grades so far in high school, and I've worked time into your schedule to help you prepare. I'm sure you'll get through them just fine." Again, Kat just nodded. *This girl looks scared to death,* Sarah thought. Undaunted, she went on. "I also need you to choose a couple of electives to round out your schedule. What are your interests? We have classes in Art, Journalism, Business, Technology, Drama, and Music."

Kat glanced up, but didn't respond right away. Mrs. Emerson, seemingly uncomfortable with her daughter's reticence, jumped in. "You've always liked your art classes, haven't you, honey?" After laboriously drawing out the course choices of Advanced Drawing and Photography from Kat, Sarah thought she'd better bring in the big guns if she was going to move this girl along.

"Okay, Kat, here's a copy of your schedule. When new students arrive, we usually arrange for a student tour guide to show them around and walk their schedule with them." Sarah didn't miss the panicked look Kat shot her mother. She turned to pick up her phone. "Mrs. Hayden, has Bridget arrived yet? Great. Could you please send her in?"

Bridget James was frequently Sarah's go-to girl when she needed a tour guide. She was the most outgoing kid Sarah had ever met; seriously, the girl could befriend a rock. She was the kind of person who accepted everyone for who they were and was true to herself as well. If Bridget couldn't make the new girl feel comfortable, no one could.

Bridget bounced into Sarah's office, all smiles, including everyone in her whirlwind gaze. "Hey, Ms. O." Turning to the new girl, she said, "Hi. You're Kat, right? I'm Bridget. You ready to learn how to navigate this place?" Then, with a reassuring smile, she addressed Mrs. Emerson. "Don't worry, Kat's mom, I'll get her all situated in no time."

Sarah had to stifle a giggle at the looks on her new family's faces as they took in Bridget, from her pink-tipped spiky blond hair, to her black T-shirt emblazoned with *Chicks Rule*, to her pink and gray camo pants and combat boots. Bridget had rounded out the ensemble with a sparkly pink nose stud.

"Pink's the color this semester, eh, Bridget?" Sarah said with a smile.

"Yes, ma'am. Are we all set to go?"

"Just one more thing." Sarah turned her attention to her anxious new student, and gently said, "Kat, here's a map of the school. I've highlighted where all of your classes are, and Bridget will show you how to find everything. I think you two have the same lunch, so you'll have someone to sit with in the cafeteria." Sarah glanced at Bridget, who nodded.

"Absolutely, Kat. You can join our table at lunch."

To Mrs. Emerson, Sarah said, "Well, shall we let these girls get on their way?"

Mrs. Emerson stood, gave Kat a hug, whispered something in her ear, and then said aloud, "Have a great day, honey. I'll pick you up at three." Kat looked like she wanted to bolt, but she couldn't escape the irresistible force that was Bridget.

When the girls left, Mrs. Emerson surprised Sarah by dropping back down into her chair. A wave of emotions came flooding across her features, as she ran a shaky hand through her dark hair, letting it fall again to her shoulders in waves. The abrupt change in the woman's demeanor made Sarah lean forward in concern, and she was immediately aware of the emotional toll it had taken on Mrs. Emerson to be upbeat for her daughter. Something wasn't quite right, beyond the usual new student issues, Sarah was sure.

"Thank you for being so kind to Kat. She was so nervous about starting school today."

Sarah nodded. "I could tell. Starting at a new school is tough, but at least she's here on day one with everyone else. I think once she gets the lay of the land she'll be fine."

With a skeptical look, Mrs. Emerson said, "Look, I just want you to know—Kat had a very rough time last year. We've been through a lot, and I moved back to New York to give her a chance to heal. I had a good childhood here, and even though my parents have both passed, I needed to come back home."

Sarah's compassion stirred as she looked at Mrs. Emerson's distraught face, but her curiosity was piqued as well. "I'll do whatever I can to help Kat settle in, and I'm here if she needs anything at all. I don't mean to pry, but if you find Kat is struggling, I can help you find a therapist in the community to help her."

"Oh, I don't know," Mrs. Emerson replied, shaking her head. "Kat doesn't trust anyone right now. I'm not sure she'd want to speak with a therapist."

Not wanting to push the issue, Sarah said, "I understand. Just a thought to keep in mind should you need it. Let me know, and I'd be happy to make a referral. In the meantime, I'll keep an eye on Kat, Mrs. Emerson."

The other woman looked relieved. "Thank you. You know, I don't remember you from high school, but since we're fellow alums, please call me Lauren." She smiled. "I have a feeling I'll be checking in with you quite often."

"No problem whatsoever, Lauren. I'm happy to help."

With that, Sarah shook hands with Lauren again, and she took her leave. Sarah looked after her for a moment, a long-dormant part of her noticing the woman was very beautiful.

Dang...put her in a Wonder Woman costume and ka-zowee!

Surprised and embarrassed by the sudden uptick in her libido, Sarah gave her head a shake and went back to work.

CHAPTER THREE

Sarah collapsed on her couch as soon as she walked in the door. Fiona promptly jumped up on her lap and commenced purring and kneading Sarah's thigh. Kira, on the other hand, puffed up her gray fur and gave Sarah her best *you'd better feed me now* look.

"Hold your horses, cat," Sarah told her. "I'm pooped."

True to form, the first day of school had been hectic and exhausting. Although her workday officially ended at three p.m., it had taken Sarah until four thirty to get through all the schedule changes that had to be addressed before tomorrow. That was nothing new. She flipped on the TV and half listened to the tail end of *Ellen* while she waited for the news to come on. As she relaxed, her mind drifted back to the events of the day. She'd spent a lot of time at her desk, checking schedules, sending emails, and answering phone calls. She never understood why parents waited until the first day of school to request things Sarah could've handled two weeks earlier before the rush. Whatever. It had been great to see the students and staff after a two-month summer break, and several kids had popped in just to say hi. That was why she loved her job, chaotic days notwithstanding.

After watching the news, Sarah got up to fix supper. She was starving, having only had time to scarf down an apple and a granola bar throughout the day.

"And Jamie thinks I'm kidding when I say I don't have time for lunch," she mumbled to herself.

As she bit into her sandwich, Sarah thought about the teasing comment Jamie had made about pet projects, and her mind immediately went to her new senior, Kat. Something about the girl really tugged at her. There was a story there, Sarah knew, but the mother hadn't been willing to share many details. The mother...*hmm*. Curious, Sarah went to her bookshelf and found her old yearbooks. She chose the one from sophomore year and flipped through the seniors, looking for an Emerson. The only one she found was a Trent Emerson, a big brawny-looking guy. As she continued scanning the pages, she found the class superlatives. Under Class Couple was the same Trent Emerson and a pretty dark-haired girl who looked to be a younger version of Mrs. Emerson. Sarah checked the name. *Lauren Clark.*

High school sweethearts, Sarah mused. They must've gotten married, but she never mentioned a husband in the picture. Sarah's brain went into super sleuth mode. She read the words under Trent Emerson's senior picture. *Varsity football captain, Varsity lacrosse, Dave Matthews show with the boys, thanks to all my buds—never stop the party. I'm going to 'Bama, baby! All my love to L.C., mine forever.* She tried to remember him, but Sarah had been busy with band and writing club in school. She hadn't really hung out with athletes or gone to many games. No doubt other sophomore girls had probably been all googly-eyed over those senior football players, but Sarah hadn't been one of them.

She then flipped to Lauren's senior picture. Her hair had been longer and darker then, but Sarah recognized the rather startling blue eyes she had seen today, eyes she had passed on to her daughter. *Varsity cheerleading, Prom Committee, Art Club, yearbook photographer, camping trip with K.C., J.W., M.F., best time ever. L.C. + T.E. forever.* No wonder Sarah hadn't known Lauren back then; she had hung out with the completely opposite side of the teenage social spectrum.

Memories surfaced of Sarah's high school experience. She had been a band geek, an honor roll student, and most of her friends had been the fringe kids. Her brothers were older, and she hadn't really followed in their more popular footsteps. She remembered how cliquey high school had been then, and the drama that erupted when the cliques collided. Even worse had been watching the kids who desperately tried to be someone they were not; it rarely ended well. Sarah had been raised to be friendly to everyone, and she had become an observer of human nature early on. Little had changed in the complex social world of adolescents. That was probably one of the most compelling reasons she had become a school counselor. Every kid deserved to have a supportive person in their corner, especially if they felt they didn't fit in. But Lauren seemed to have been one of those kids who had it all, and Sarah couldn't help but wonder what, if anything, had changed.

Kira pounced on Sarah's shoulder, startling her out of her reverie and reminding her she hadn't yet fed the cats. "All right, already…I'm coming."

Lauren had given Kat some downtime before asking about her day. Now, as they sat down to eat dinner, she inquired, "So, how'd it go?"

"Okay," Kat replied, then silence.

"Did you eat lunch with Bridget?"

"Yep."

"How were your classes?" Lauren persisted.

"Fine," came the reply.

"Jeez, help a woman out here, kid. Do we have to play Twenty Questions?"

"Sorry, Mom." Kat sighed. "Everyone was nice. Bridget introduced me to her friends. My classes seem like they'll be okay, and the teachers were pretty cool." She paused then, a frown forming.

"But?"

"But it's so weird to be in a new place after seventeen years. The school's so big, and being around so many people made me feel kind of like everyone was staring at me, you know?"

Lauren smiled sympathetically. "That's fear talking, baby. I know you're worried and it feels overwhelming now, but you'll be surprised how quickly you'll get used to things. Sometimes a big school is a good thing. At least everybody doesn't know everyone else's business."

"Yeah, I guess," Kat conceded. "Bridget helped a lot. It's like she could tell when I was getting anxious. And we have two other classes together, not just lunch."

"She certainly seemed friendly and is nothing like the kids you used to hang out with."

Kat made a face. "Thank God," she said bitterly.

Reminded of that terrible time, Lauren remembered what the school counselor had said. "Honey, we've taken the major step of getting away and starting fresh. But what happened last year," she said, watching Kat carefully, "isn't just going to disappear from your memory, and you don't have to pretend that it doesn't matter. We may still have work to do on the emotional stuff." Kat shrugged but didn't respond. Lauren pressed on. "How would you feel about finding a therapist to talk about it?"

"I don't wanna talk about it, Mom," Kat cried, jumping up from the table. "Talking won't change what they did to me."

"You're right. The past is done and can't be changed. But both of us could benefit from learning how to keep last year from affecting our future. I have a lot of hurt and anger, too, kiddo, at those kids, at your father, and at myself."

"But you didn't do anything wrong, Mom. You were the only one who stood by me." A tear spilled from Kat's eye. Lauren got up and went to her daughter, her own eyes moist.

"I didn't get you out of there sooner, but that's my own guilt to bear. You were completely innocent, and I love you too much to watch you carry this burden. Moving was only part of the healing process, but I don't think it's enough." Lauren gathered her daughter into her arms, and they both had a good cry.

A few minutes later, Kat sniffled and said, "I guess I could talk to somebody, as long as you're there with me."

Lauren smiled. "Deal, sweet pea."

CHAPTER FOUR

Sarah was perusing the transcript of a new transfer student when Mrs. Hayden rang in on her line.

"There's a parent here to see you, Sarah."

"I don't have any appointments scheduled." The chaos of the first few weeks of school had finally calmed. "Who is it?"

"It's Mrs. Emerson. Shall I send her in?"

"Yes, please."

Lauren Emerson popped her head in the door. "Hi there. Kat forgot her lunch, so I'm making a delivery." She held up a brown paper bag. "Your secretary said she'd call her up when the bell rings."

"We've got a few minutes, then," Sarah said. "Have a seat." In the back of her mind, she noted how attractively Lauren was dressed, in dark, curve-hugging jeans, an embroidered cream peasant blouse, and brown boots, with her hair pulled back in a loose ponytail.

"I wanted to thank you for your suggestion last time we met. I mentioned seeing a therapist to Kat, and she wasn't thrilled with the idea." She gave Sarah a rueful smile. "But she finally agreed, as long as I go with her."

"Great. It's amazing how helpful it is to have a sounding board to help sort out all the stuff going on in our heads."

Lauren nodded. "Yes, I hope so. We've waited three weeks to get in at Mental Health. The therapist is a woman named Sharon something-or-other."

"Oh, that's Sharon Keller. She's fantastic. I think you'll both like her," Sarah said. "She's especially good with adolescent girls, and she specializes in anxiety issues, among other things."

Lauren looked relieved. "I hope Kat takes to her, because there is no shortage of anxiety in our house, and it's very hard for Kat to trust people."

"May I ask what happened?" Sarah asked gently. She didn't miss the guarded look that immediately appeared on Lauren's face. What the hell had made her so fearful?

"Oh, Kat just had a bad experience with other students," Lauren said vaguely.

Sarah could see the topic was still off-limits, that maybe Lauren wanted to leave the past in the past, so she changed the subject. "Forgive my curiosity, but how in the world did a born and bred Central New Yorker end up in Alabama?"

Lauren seemed more at ease with this line of questioning. "I would not in a million years have thought I'd move to the Deep South, but circumstances made it necessary at the time." She looked at Sarah, who was listening with genuine interest. "About a month after graduation, my parents were killed in a car accident on the Thruway."

"Oh, I'm so sorry. That must've been very difficult for you," Sarah said. No stranger to loss herself, she felt the old familiar punch in the gut as she saw her own grief mirrored in Lauren's eyes.

"Yes, it was quite a shock. My parents were in their forties when they had me, and I was an only child, as were they. My grandparents had all passed by then, so I was literally alone in the world."

"Wow." Sarah shook her head in sympathy. "Wasn't there anyone to help you? Friends?"

"Well, my boyfriend's parents took me in," Lauren replied. "He was heading to the University of Alabama, so I quickly changed my college plans and looked into the community colleges nearby. We moved down to Alabama together. My parents had left me a sizable inheritance, a portion of which I could access at eighteen, so I got an apartment and a job, and started school in the spring."

"Hell of a lot of responsibility for an eighteen-year-old," Sarah said, rather impressed at the story she was hearing. "You must've been very strong and mature to handle so much."

Lauren shrugged. "I don't know about strong, but I was pretty mature for my age. My parents had raised me to be independent, thank goodness, and that certainly helped. The next year, though, I found myself pregnant, so Trent and I got married."

"Ah, so you did marry Trent Emerson," Sarah said, then immediately felt her face flush. At the questioning look on Lauren's face, she confessed. "When you said we went to Easton at the same time, I kind of pulled out my old yearbook and looked you up."

"Oh," Lauren said, laughing.

"Sorry for being so nosy," Sarah said, still a bit embarrassed.

"No worries." Lauren smiled, finding Sarah's chagrin endearing. "Trent and I had been dating since we were sixteen, and he was really all I had after the accident. Moving to Alabama with him seemed to be the best option for me. His whole family were die-hard Crimson Tide fans, so Trent didn't even consider going anywhere else."

"Well, you obviously stayed after college."

Lauren thought back to the way things were then, to the girl she'd once been. Seemed like a lifetime ago…someone else's lifetime. "Trent's cousins lived close to Tuscaloosa, and one of them got him a job in corrections. He works at a maximum-security facility down there."

Before Sarah could ask anything else, the bell rang, signaling the end of the period.

Startled at the too-loud noise, Lauren jumped. "Well, I guess that's my cue to get up and do something productive with my day," she said with a smile.

Sarah stood, too. "Thanks for stopping in."

"And thanks for the chat. It's nice to have someone to talk to. I don't really know anyone around here anymore."

"My pleasure. I'm sure we'll see each other again. Stop in anytime." As Sarah watched Lauren walk away, she sincerely hoped their next meeting would be sooner than later.

Jeez, where did that come from? Sarah asked herself, surprised at the unbidden thought.

CHAPTER FIVE

It was the first Wednesday in October, and Sarah was waiting outside of Jamie's classroom for the end-of-the-day bell to ring. Jamie let the Gay-Straight Alliance use her room for meetings, and Sarah was the club advisor. This would be the first meeting of the school year, and Sarah was always curious as to who would show up.

Sarah stepped aside as Jamie's ninth period class streamed out the door, then went in to see her friend.

"So, how's life in the world of tenth grade English?"

Jamie groaned. "We're supposed to be on the second scene of *A Raisin in the Sun*, and I swear half of them haven't even read scene one. God, when I was their age, you could barely get my head out of a book. The love of reading seems to be dying a slow, miserable death." She dropped into her chair in frustration.

"They're fifteen, honey," Sarah soothed. "All they care about is checking their phones every five seconds to make sure they're not missing anything." Jamie laughed. "I can promise you're instilling a healthy love for the printed page," Sarah continued. "My seniors tell me all the time that you were one of their favorite teachers, and you made English fun. So just keep doing what you're doing, girl. Those kids are taking in more than you think they are."

"Thanks, Sarah." Jamie brightened. "So, first meeting today, huh? What's on the agenda?"

"Well, we'll see who attends and give everyone the rundown of what the group is all about. Then we need to begin thinking about the Sweetheart Dance. It's our club's turn to host it this year, and February comes quickly." Sarah was thrilled that Easton not only accepted the GSA as a club, but allowed it to host the biggest event of the year.

As if on cue, five students strolled in for the meeting. A minute later, another six came in, with Bridget bringing up the rear. To Sarah's surprise, she had Kat with her.

"Hey, Ms. O, Mrs. Gibson," Bridget greeted brightly, as the students settled into the seats, chatting quietly. Moments later, without needing to be asked, she took charge. "Welcome to True Colors, Easton's Gay-Straight Alliance, where you don't have to be gay, just very, very cool." The other kids laughed. Bridget had such a gift for putting people at ease. The other group members had unanimously voted Bridget in as club president, two years in a row. She was a natural leader, and she made Sarah's job as advisor infinitely easier.

Bridget went on. "We have a few new faces among us, so let's do intros. First, thanks to Mrs. Gibson, who lets us crash her room every Wednesday." Jamie waved with a smile. "And this is Ms. O'Shaughnessy, school counselor and advisor extraordinaire." Sarah inclined her head, grinning.

The students took turns telling their names, what grade they were in, and the best thing that had happened so far since school began. Answers ranged from *I made the varsity soccer team* to *I finally don't have to take another day of French class with Mrs. Clump*, which elicited several giggles and a lighthearted chastising from Sarah.

The last two students to speak were Bridget and Kat. Bridget went first. "The best thing that has happened so far is I made it to senior year, alive and relatively sane." Chuckles all around. "And," she continued, "I made a great new friend." Bridget smiled at Kat.

Sarah noticed the blush that crept up Kat's cheeks. It was her turn to introduce herself. "Hi, I'm Kat," she said shyly, a lovely Southern lilt to her voice. "I'm a senior, and I just moved here. The best thing that has happened to me is meeting Bridget. I don't think I would know a soul here still if it wasn't for her."

The other students said, "Awww!" and Kat's blush deepened.

Well, whaddaya know? Sarah thought, watching the two girls with interest. *Didn't see that one coming.*

Forty-five minutes later, the kids had discussed what True Colors was all about—advocacy and support for not just LGBTQ kids, but for anyone who felt different and needed a safe place to be themselves—as well as the main events and projects the group hoped to accomplish before June.

At meeting's end, the students said their good-byes and left, but Kat and Bridget stayed behind.

"Good job running the meeting, Bridget," Sarah praised. "The new freshmen seemed comfortable and interested."

"Thanks. Their counselor told them about True Colors at the junior high, so they had already planned to join."

"What about you, Kat?" Sarah asked. "Were you in a GSA in your last school?"

A shadow crossed Kat's face, and she looked at the floor. "No, we didn't have a GSA there."

"Kat was telling me about her school in Alabama," Bridget jumped in. "Guess it's way different down there than it is in New York."

Sarah imagined so. She was an avid reader of her *Teaching Tolerance* magazines from the Southern Poverty Law Center, and she knew Alabama was in the top ten of most homophobic states. She had suspected this kind of group was a new experience for Kat. "As I've told you guys lots of times before, Bridget, not everyone is as lucky as we are to be out safely at work or school."

At this new revelation about her counselor, Kat's head shot up. "You're gay?" she whispered, incredulous. "And people know?"

"Well, I don't shout it from the rooftops"—Sarah chuckled—"but yes, my colleagues and several students know I'm gay."

"Until I got here, I don't think I'd ever seen a gay person other than on TV. If you're gay in Alabama, you sure as heck don't say so." Kat was stunned, and it showed.

Sarah was beginning to see a glimpse of what Kat's trouble might have been last year.

"Were all those kids gay, too?" Kat asked, referring to the club members.

"Some may be, but students join True Colors because they're interested in educating their peers about diversity issues. We make it a point to not ask about anyone's sexual orientation, but if they choose to share, it's safe to do so," Sarah explained.

Bridget was watching Kat closely, concern written all over her face. "It doesn't matter, Kat. It doesn't matter if you're gay, straight, or somewhere in the middle. Okay?"

"Bridget's right," Sarah said. "True Colors is all about letting you be whoever you are without judgment. Confidentiality is very important."

Kat nodded, eyes bright with unshed tears. "Okay," she whispered, and Sarah's heart hurt for the obviously wounded young woman before her.

❖

Lauren waited in the parking lot for Kat to come out of school. She had said she was staying after for a club meeting, and Lauren was cautiously optimistic that Kat might begin to make new friends. A flash of bright pink caught her eye, and she turned to see Kat walking with the girl she had met on the first day of school. Their heads were close together as they walked slowly toward the car, seemingly in deep discussion. Lauren rolled the window down as they approached.

"Hello, Bridget. How are you doing today?"

"Hi, Mrs. Emerson. I'm good. You?"

"Fine, thanks. Hi, sweetie," she greeted Kat.

"Hi, Mom," Kat said quietly.

Lauren heard Bridget whisper, "Are you sure you're okay?"

Kat nodded. "I'll text you later."

"'Kay, bye." Bridget waved to Lauren and walked to her own car. Kat threw her backpack in the back seat, then slid into the front. Her eyes looked red, as if she had been crying.

"Honey, what's wrong?" Lauren asked with growing concern.

"Bridget's gay," Kat blurted, seemingly as surprised as Lauren was.

"Okay..." Lauren paused. "Is that a problem for you?"

"No, it's just...can you believe there are gay kids here, and nobody cares?"

Lauren could see where this was going. "Kat, New York is a whole different world than Alabama when it comes to stuff like this. Not everyone is against homosexuality. That's one of the main reasons I wanted to bring you here. I wanted you to feel safe to, you know, figure things out."

"But back home, they made my life a living hell just because they *thought* I was gay. And remember the kid that used to be in my class, Freddie Simmons? The boys were so awful to him. He just dropped out of school and never came back."

Lauren nodded sympathetically, but inside, her anger started to rise. "Those kids did terrible things because nobody taught them any different. And even though I'm sure others didn't agree, they were afraid to stand up to them."

Kat nodded. "This club I went to today is called True Colors, and the whole point of the group is to celebrate diversity. I mean, some of those kids are gay, and they aren't even afraid of others knowing." Lauren simply listened, knowing Kat needed to talk about this without fear of a negative reaction. Kat told her all about the meeting, then said, "Oh, and my counselor is the advisor."

Lauren's ears perked up. "Really? Well, that's good. She's very nice."

Kat opened her mouth like she was about to say more, but then simply said, "Yeah," and turned to look out the window.

❖

Kat couldn't stop thinking about Bridget being gay. Bridget was the total opposite of Kat; where Kat was quiet, Bridget was outgoing, and where Kat was insecure, Bridget was self-assured. Bridget had been her lifesaver from day one. She hadn't just played tour guide and left Kat to go it alone. Rather, she had befriended her and taken a real interest in her. She had helped Kat adjust to her new life. But Kat also noticed how she was hyperaware of Bridget when she was around, and how she missed her when she wasn't. She thought back to last year and how her friendship with her supposed best friend Amber had ended in disaster. And she was afraid.

With all this going through her head, Kat was almost oblivious to the fact she hadn't heard a thing in Economics class, or that the bell had already rung. Her teacher, Mr. Johnson, tapped her shoulder, startling her. "Everything all right, Katherine?" he inquired.

Kat flushed and stood up quickly. "Yes, sorry." She hurried off to lunch.

Bridget had already gotten through the lunch line and was sitting at the table. "Hey, Kat. How come so late?"

"Um, I had to stop at the bathroom."

Bridget just nodded and smiled, her deep brown eyes watching Kat.

Why the hell can't I stop blushing? Kat thought, feeling the heat creep up her neck to her cheeks. Just then, Natasha and Jordan plopped down in their seats with their lunches, rescuing Kat from her discomfort, at least for the moment.

"So," Natasha said, "I'm throwing a Halloween bash this year. I bugged my parents about it until they gave in just to shut me up."

Bridget clapped. "Well done. Persistence pays off."

"Right? So, as you are my good friends and fellow True Colors members, I thought maybe we could have a group costume theme. I'll now take ideas." Natasha sat back with a grin.

"Well," Jordan contemplated, "what about cheerleaders?"

Bridget groaned. "A definite no. Maybe we could all dress in drag?"

Kat's jaw dropped as she stared at Bridget, sincerely hoping no one agreed to *that* idea.

Natasha rolled her eyes. "Okay, crayons."

"What?" Jordan and Bridget asked in unison.

"You know, those Crayola crayon costumes, but in all the rainbow colors. If we stood together, we'd look like a human Pride flag."

"I kinda like that idea," Bridget said. "Not immediately obvious, not too gross, and relatively easy to find. What do you think, ladies?"

"I'm good," Jordan agreed.

Kat smiled at Bridget. "Me, too, but I call blue."

"Awesome." Natasha grinned excitedly. "We'll have to recruit two more people to round out our rainbow."

"Don't say *recruit*," Bridget said in mock horror. "Westboro will crash your party."

Kat didn't understand the reference.

Apparently noticing her confused look, Bridget explained, "Last year, we researched antigay groups and hate crimes. Westboro Baptist Church is one of the worst. They show up all over the country, picketing events and holding *God hates fags* signs."

"Wait, I've heard about them. My dad got mad once because they were picketing a soldier's funeral. He said they should stick to harassing homos." Realizing what she had just said, Kat's cheeks flamed yet again. "Sorry. That sounded bad." Kat hadn't meant to offend her new friends by talking about her asshole father and his bigoted big mouth.

Bridget frowned. "It's okay. Your dad?"

Kat quickly recognized she had never mentioned her father before. "Yeah. He still lives in Alabama. Long story."

"Oh," Bridget said.

Kat immediately retreated into herself, no longer listening to the other girls as they threw around party ideas. She felt Bridget's eyes on her and took a deep breath, trying to hide the pain she was feeling. Several minutes later, Kat suddenly stood up. "Hey, I'm going upstairs to my locker. I forgot something for my next class."

"Mind if I come with?" Bridget asked. Bridget had noticed the look that had crossed Kat's features at the mention of her father. She saw how Kat shut herself away, as clearly as if she had drawn a curtain. She wondered what the long story was all about. "I need to go to the bathroom, and I'm always late if I try to go between classes."

Kat shrugged and gathered her stuff. "See you later," she said to Natasha and Jordan, then went to sign out of the cafeteria.

Once in the hallway, Bridget stopped Kat with a hand on her elbow. "Are you okay?"

"I guess."

"I didn't think you had a dad in the picture. You never mentioned him."

Kat sighed. "I haven't spoken to my father in months. He and my mom are separated, and he stayed in Alabama when we came here."

"Do you miss him?"

"I don't know. Like I said, it's a long story." Kat paused. "I mean, he was a colossal ass to my mom and me. Some crazy shit went down last spring, and he wasn't there for me at all."

"Wow…that sucks," Bridget said, shaking her head.

"Yeah, well, it is what it is." Kat checked her phone for the time. "We'd better go—bell's gonna ring."

Bridget was getting used to Kat closing the door on difficult conversations. "Okay," she said, and headed up the stairs behind Kat. *God, I so want to know what makes those gorgeous blue eyes so sad.* There was a vulnerability about Kat that made Bridget want to protect her from the world, to hold her until the sadness went away. *Get a grip, idiot. Do you want her to really freak the hell out?*

At the top of the stairs, Kat turned. "See you in English, okay?"

"Yep," Bridget replied, and watched her walk away. Maybe someday Kat would trust her enough to let her in.

Chapter Six

W hat a shitty way to end the day," Sarah mumbled.
She'd just had a very contentious conversation with a parent which made her blood boil. Although not even a parent of one of her students, the woman had been transferred to her line anyway. Almost immediately, the woman launched into a tirade about why a *homosexual group* should not exist at the high school. She did not want her children exposed to such a thing, and in her opinion, the school was irresponsible to allow this club. Sarah had needed to pull out every ounce of self-restraint she could, when what she'd really wanted to do was let the bitch have it.

"Mrs. Anders," Sarah had said in her most neutral professional tone, "our job as a school is to provide an environment where all students feel safe and welcomed. The Gay-Straight Alliance has as much a right to exist as the Youth Prayer Group or any other student organization."

Mrs. Anders continued to protest, at which point Sarah said, "All student groups are voluntary, and no one has to be involved if they don't want to be. If you have any further concerns, please contact our principal, Mr. Stephens."

Mrs. Anders still had her panties in a twist. "Fine, but this isn't the last you'll hear about this. I know lots of other parents feel the same way I do."

"Thank you for calling. Have a good day." Sarah disconnected, then sat at her desk, her ears still hot as she stewed. Was this nasty woman going to make trouble for her club? Sarah had always felt very lucky to work in a school with people who accepted her and didn't make her sexuality an issue. She knew, although surely Mrs. Anders didn't, that there were other lesbians in administrative roles in the district, and at least two gay teachers. She also trusted her principal, Jack Stephens, would handle this woman and calm her down. Still, it pissed Sarah off that some people continued to have such an archaic and mean-spirited worldview.

As Sarah locked her office and headed toward the door of the counseling suite, Mrs. Hayden appraised her quizzically, hands on her ample hips.

"Okay, spill it."

Sarah sighed. She tried to be good at hiding her emotions, but Joan Hayden, who was like a second mom to her, could always tell when anything was even the slightest bit amiss.

"I just got a call from a Mrs. Anders."

"Oh Lord," Joan said, rolling her eyes. "What's she on the warpath about this time?"

"You know her?" Sarah asked in surprise.

"That woman calls here at least once a week to complain about something or ask ridiculous questions. She's one of Tom's parents"—she nodded toward another counselor's office—"and he knows her number by heart. Just lets it go to voicemail so he doesn't slip and tell her off."

Sarah smiled, knowing her colleague Tom Daniels had a bit of a short fuse when it came to what he referred to as *time-wasting stupidity*.

"I'd like to know who patched her through to me," Sarah griped. "She was complaining about the abomination known as the Gay-Straight Alliance."

"Oh, brother," Joan said with a scowl, shaking her graying curls. "That shrew isn't happy unless she's got something or someone to hate on. What did you say to her?"

"I told her the GSA had every right to exist, right along with the Youth Prayer Group and every other club, and to take any further concerns to Jack."

"Good for you, honey," Joan said. "Hope he shuts her right down. And you know, it was probably an innocent thing she was transferred to you. You *are* the advisor and the go-to gal for all things gay around here."

"Yay for me," Sarah said with a snort. "Hey, maybe I should invite Mrs. Anders to the PFLAG meeting on Wednesday."

"Yeah, right," Joan said, laughing. "She'd go with you when hell freezes over."

Sarah was invited to be a guest speaker at the Rochester chapter of PFLAG in a couple of days. She would be giving a presentation on youth suicide prevention, and would focus on the significantly higher rates of suicide among LGBTQ youth. The statistics were sobering, but Sarah felt information and education were the best preventative measures, and she was passionate about sending a message of hope for struggling youth.

"Speaking of that," Joan said, "your flyers and handouts came back from the print shop this afternoon. They're in the box by the copier."

"Thanks. See you in the morning." Sarah shifted her bag's strap to her other arm, then hefted the box onto her shoulder and headed out the door.

As she approached the parking lot, Sarah saw a blue SUV idling at the curb. When she got closer, she realized the driver was Lauren Emerson. Feeling a tingle of pleasure, she smiled. Just then, she stumbled on an uneven piece of concrete and dropped her box of papers as she unsuccessfully tried to break her forward fall. Her handouts spilled all over the sidewalk.

"Shit. This day just gets better and better." Sarah felt her cheeks warm as she saw Lauren get out of her car and rush over with a look of concern. *Real smooth, O'Shaughnessy,* Sarah thought with a grimace.

"Oh my goodness. Are you all right?" Lauren asked, squatting at Sarah's side.

"Yeah, I'm fine." Sarah groaned. "Just call me Grace."

"Oh, stop," Lauren said with a laugh. She stood and offered a hand.

As Sarah shifted up onto her knee, she flinched. "Ouch." Looking down, she saw a sizable spot of blood had soaked through her thin khaki slacks. She took Lauren's hand and stood, then rolled her pant leg up to assess the damage.

"Hold on. I've got a first aid kit in my car." Before Sarah could protest, Lauren had trotted off to her vehicle. She came back with an antiseptic wipe and a bandage. Sarah had meanwhile righted her box and was gathering the spilled papers.

"Here, let me get those," Lauren said, handing Sarah the wipe and bandage. She finished packing the papers back in the box, put on the lid, and instructed Sarah to sit on it.

"Lauren, I'm fine. I can take care of this," Sarah said, slightly embarrassed but also pleased with the attention from this gorgeous impromptu nurse.

"Sit," Lauren commanded again.

Sarah sat with a grin. She watched Lauren's lovely hands as they gently lifted the pant leg and examined the cut. She gingerly dabbed the wound with the antiseptic wipe. Sarah hissed at the sting.

"Hang on, you big baby." Lauren finished her ministrations and straightened up. "I think your pants are history," she said, showing Sarah the tear in the fabric at the knee. "You must've fallen right into the edge of the sidewalk."

"It sure feels like it. Thanks for patching me up, Doc," Sarah teased, standing.

"My pleasure." Lauren's blue eyes sparkled.

Sarah felt her heart skip a beat and quickly turned to pick up her box and tote bag.

"What've you got there, anyway? What's *P-F-L-A-G*?"

"It's PFLAG," Sarah corrected. "Parents and Friends of Lesbians and Gays."

"Oh," Lauren said, her expression unreadable.

"I'm giving a presentation on youth suicide prevention at their meeting on Wednesday. It'll be a long day, since the meeting is at six thirty p.m. and I have to drive to Rochester. Takes about an hour from here." Sarah didn't know why she was babbling on about it.

"Mind if I take one of those flyers?"

"Not at all," Sarah said, wondering why she'd want it. Did Lauren know that her daughter might be questioning her sexuality?

Both women turned as Kat headed out of the school and toward her mom's car. She saw them and waved.

"Well, guess I'd better go," Lauren said. "Are you sure you're okay?"

"I do believe I'll survive," Sarah answered with a smile. "Thanks again for the excellent medical attention."

"What can I say? I'm a woman of many talents."

Sarah raised her eyebrow, and Lauren blushed.

"See you later," she said, and hustled back to her car.

Sarah watched the SUV drive away with a stupid grin on her face, wondering about Lauren's choice of words. Part of her thought she had no business wondering about the many talents of a straight woman, especially a parent of one of her students. But the rest of her remembered the touch of those gentle hands.

"Holy hot damn," Sarah mumbled.

CHAPTER SEVEN

Wednesday afternoon found Sarah driving west toward Rochester and the PFLAG meeting. She'd headed out right after work, wanting to get to Rochester early so she could get a bite to eat and settle her nerves before her presentation.

She stopped at the nearest McDonald's and ordered a grilled chicken salad, ignoring the part of her that really wanted a cheese-burger and fries. The salad was a safer bet, considering Sarah's gen-erally lousy luck; she had dressed up today in her black tailored dress pants and pearly gray silk blouse, and she couldn't risk getting a blob of ketchup on her shirtfront. She found a seat as far from other people as she could get and sat down to eat.

Sarah barely tasted her food or paid any mind to her sur-roundings, because her thoughts had inevitably turned to Tommy. It happened every time she did a presentation like the one she'd do tonight; actually, whenever she heard the word suicide, his face crossed her mind.

Tommy had been a student of hers, back when she was a new counselor, fresh out of grad school. A beautiful, kind, and fragile boy, Tommy was acutely sensitive to the world around him. Whereas others could ignore or push aside the pain and horror of the human condition that flashed across their consciousness, Tommy could not. An ASPCA commercial about animal cruelty, a video about the Holocaust, a news story about a toddler beaten to death for crying— these things caused excruciating emotional despair for Tommy. He had no way to filter the pain, and by the time he was fifteen, the world was just too much for him to bear.

Sarah loved that boy, loved his compassion and gentle soul, but those things were seen as weaknesses by his peers. They mocked him for his goodness, tormented him for his quiet, somewhat effeminate ways. Sarah tried to help and did all she could, along with Tommy's parents, to keep him safe. Ultimately, Tommy made the choice to end the pain he felt he couldn't escape. Sarah had never fully gotten over his loss. Tonight was for him.

Nearly an hour later, when she found her destination and pulled into the parking lot, Sarah was surprised at the number of vehicles already there. She took a couple of deep, shaky breaths, slung her messenger bag over her shoulder, picked up the box of handouts, and walked to the building's entrance.

At the door, Sarah was greeted with a smile and a handshake from Martha Tanner, one of the organizers of the event.

"Ms. O'Shaughnessy? Come in, come in, and welcome. Thank you so much for coming out on a weeknight to speak with us. I know your schedule must be very busy."

Sarah pushed down her nerves and smiled in return. "Oh, it's no trouble at all, and please, call me Sarah. Thanks for having me. Suicide prevention is such an important topic, and I wouldn't want to pass up an opportunity to educate folks."

"My feelings exactly. Can I help you with that?" Martha said, nodding toward the box in Sarah's arms.

"Yes, thanks. These are handouts of the PowerPoint presentation."

"Then I'll just put them here for folks to grab as they come in. The projector you requested is on the cart over there," Martha said, pointing to the front of the room. "Is there anything else you need?"

"I should be all set. Thanks."

Martha nodded. "I left you a bottle of water on the podium. I've got to handle a couple of last-minute things, so I'll leave you to set up. You're on in fifteen minutes."

Sarah busied herself preparing her PowerPoint and reviewing her notes. Then she made a quick trip to the restroom, checking in the mirror to make sure her hair was neat and she didn't have lettuce in her teeth. Popping a mint in her mouth, she headed back out to the podium. She took a deep breath, steeling herself for what would likely be a very emotional evening.

Most people had taken a seat and were chatting quietly. Martha then came up to the mic. "Welcome, everyone, to PFLAG of Rochester. We're so happy to have such an excellent turnout for tonight's program. We'll begin with a presentation on suicide prevention, then hear from our teen panel."

As Martha introduced her, Sarah noticed a flurry of activity by the door, and a latecomer hurried in. She felt a rush of surprised pleasure when she saw the latecomer was Lauren. Sarah smiled broadly as Lauren met her eyes, gave a thumbs-up, and settled in the back row.

What in the world is she doing here? Sarah wondered.

"So without further ado, I give you Sarah O'Shaughnessy." Martha's closing statement brought Sarah back to the moment at hand.

"Thank you, Martha, and thanks, everyone, for coming out on this chilly October night. The topic of suicide prevention is extremely important, especially in light of several recent youth suicides in New York State. While the data you'll hear tonight is sobering, prevention is possible, and there is hope."

Sarah launched into her presentation, beginning with a quiz to warm up the audience and gauge their knowledge of the topic. She shared myths and facts about suicide, as well as risk factors and warning signs. She presented the latest statistics, focusing on the increased risk for LGBTQ youth. Then she gave her listeners several tools they could use to help people who might be struggling with suicidal thoughts. She spoke about the importance of GSAs, PFLAG, and other resources that were available to LGBTQ youth, and that the need for such support was higher than many people realized. As Sarah spoke, she was acutely aware of Lauren, who was leaning forward in her chair, listening intently.

"The key to prevention is bringing the topic of suicide out of the dark, to no longer think of it as a taboo thing to be whispered about or hidden. Every one of us has been to a dark or painful place in our lives, and it's nothing to be ashamed of. We need to support one another, and it is okay to ask the tough questions, like *Are you safe?* or *Are you thinking about hurting yourself?* Most people in pain just want to stop hurting, and if they're alone or isolated, they may convince themselves that death is the only way to end the pain."

Sarah paused, swallowing the lump in her throat and thinking once again of Tommy. "Our job is to show them there are alternatives to suicide, and to be with them and support them when we see the warning signs. There is always hope, and together we can help prevent suicide. Thank you."

At the burst of enthusiastic applause, Sarah dipped her head, pleased her presentation had been well-received and equally glad it was over. Martha came to the mic. "Thank you so much, Sarah. We will now take a fifteen-minute refreshment break. Our teen panel will begin at seven thirty."

A few people gathered around Sarah, to thank her or ask a question. One woman, a short but aggressive sort, with beady eyes and sharp features, quickly commandeered Sarah's attention and began talking nonstop. Sarah glanced around, looking for Lauren and trying to politely disengage from the woman monopolizing her, who clearly had an issue with respecting personal space.

"Don't you think it was wrong of them to do that to me?" The woman was ranting on about a personal issue, actually clutching Sarah's wrist. Sarah took a step back and bumped right into someone.

"Oh my goodness, what a klutz I am." Lauren bumbled behind her. "And look, I spilled water on you. I'm so sorry. Here, let me dry that up for you." The wrist-clutcher dropped Sarah's hand and stared, effectively silenced by Lauren's dramatic display. "Come, there are more napkins on the table over there," Lauren said, taking Sarah's arm.

Sarah nodded a thank-you to the other woman, who looked quite put out, and allowed herself to be led away. They had barely made it across the room when Sarah burst out laughing, trying to stifle it behind her hand. "What was that all about?"

"You looked like a trapped puppy over there. I had to rescue you," Lauren replied with a grin.

"Good Lord, the woman was giving me the unabridged version of her life story, including things I did not need to know. I was trying to be polite, but sheesh."

"Hence the rescue operation. Here, have a cookie," Lauren said, eyes twinkling.

Sarah appreciatively took the proffered Oreo. "Wow, you really know how to help a woman out. That's twice now you've rescued me, and you give chocolate, too. Keep this up, and I'll have to be eternally indebted to you."

"I aim to please, and chocolate fixes everything," Lauren replied.

The remark was innocent enough, but Sarah felt suddenly warm. *Good Lord, those eyes*, she thought, holding Lauren's gaze longer than was probably wise. "Thanks for coming tonight," she said, suddenly finding the cookie in her hand very interesting. "It was great to see a familiar face—helped settle my nerves."

"What nerves? You looked cool as a cucumber up there."

"Only because you couldn't see my insides shaking. I always get that way when I give presentations." Sarah didn't mention it was the topic more than the public speaking that had tied her stomach in knots. Or that her insides were shaking for an entirely different reason at the moment.

"Well, you're a good speaker. The stats are kind of frightening, though."

"Yeah, they are, but that's why I do this. I can't stand the thought of kids taking their own lives because they can't cope. They need to be supported, accepted, and taught, and unfortunately for many, it just isn't happening."

"Well, thanks to people like you, they've got a much better chance," Lauren replied sincerely.

Sarah flushed at the compliment. "Thanks. I truly appreciate that." Sarah realized that what Lauren thought was really beginning to matter.

"You're welcome. Here, let's sit. Looks like they're starting." Indeed, Martha had assembled five teenagers in chairs at the front of the room and was at the mic.

"If I could draw you away from the cookies, please, we're ready to begin," Martha announced. Chuckling, the people gathered their snacks and beverages and settled into their seats. Martha continued, "With us tonight are five amazing young people who have important stories to share. They've each been through a great deal, and they can teach us much about strength and resilience. So I'll get out of the way and let them introduce themselves."

She handed the mic to the first young man on her left. He was thin and pale, with a shock of black hair over his eyes.

"Hi, I'm Troy, I'm eighteen, and...yeah," he said shyly, eliciting a few sympathetic giggles from the crowd. He handed the mic to the young woman on his left, who sported a killer manicure, four-inch heels, and was showing a fair amount of her lovely brown skin.

"Hi, I'm Juanita, I'm sixteen, and you better believe these nails are real," she said, flashing her hands and a sassy grin.

Next was a petite girl with super-short blond hair and multiple piercings, wearing a retro bowling shirt, long shorts, and work boots. "Hi, I'm Dale, I'm fifteen, and I can vouch for the nails. I helped do 'em." The quip earned her a laugh from the audience and a high five from Juanita.

To Dale's left was a burly African American young man who had the physicality of Michael Strahan but the demeanor of a giant teddy bear. "Hello, I'm Jonathan, I'm eighteen, and I'm glad you all came here tonight," he said in a soft, deep voice.

Last was a young woman with long strawberry-blond hair, lightly freckled skin, and huge green eyes. She reminded Sarah of a faerie, with her delicate features and luminous eyes. "Hi," she said quietly, "I'm Tori and I'm seventeen." She smiled and handed the mic back down the line to Martha.

"As we heard from Ms. O'Shaughnessy's presentation, bullying is a major risk factor for LGBTQ youth. One of our goals here at PFLAG is to offer support and a safe space for our youth, but school can often be a different story for them." She turned to the teens. "Would any of you like to share about your experience in school?"

Dale gestured for the mic and spoke first. "Kids used to mess with me, mostly about my clothes. My mom used to dress me up all girly when I was younger, but by the time I was eight or nine, I kept raiding my twin brother's closet all the time. I'd throw a hissy fit if my mom came at me with a dress, so she eventually gave up." Dale grinned at a woman in the front row, who nodded emphatically in agreement. "In middle school, a few kids started calling me a dyke. I had already figured out I was gay, and my family and good friends were cool with it. I also had a couple of awesome teachers who looked out for me. Because of their support, I guess I just didn't let the bullies get to me, and by the time we all got to high school, they had pretty much stopped." She held up the mic, and Juanita took it.

"You all might have noticed I'm kind of outspoken," she began, and her fellow panelists all rolled their eyes with a loud *mm-hmm*. "Whatever," she said to them in mock disgust. "Anyway, my mama raised all six of us kids to be independent and strong, so I don't play if anyone gets in my face. People know I'm transgender, and I'm happy to educate them if they have an issue. So people don't really mess with me."

"Maybe they're just afraid of your shoes. Those heels are a deadly weapon," Dale threw in, chucking Juanita on the shoulder affectionately. Everyone laughed.

"Oh, please, girl, you know I'm like five-foot-nothing. If I don't wear these shoes, I can't see what's going on." More laughter. "Seriously though, I'm blessed to have so much support, from my mom, my family, my girlfriend." She clasped hands with Dale. "Not everyone's so lucky."

Juanita looked at Troy and touched his arm. After a moment, Troy nodded and reached for the mic. "I used to love school when I was little," he began, "but around fourth grade it started to change. Kids started to make fun of me, because I was skinny, or my clothes were old, or I was bad at sports. In junior high, they started calling me faggot and homo, running into me in the halls and stuff. I put up with that crap for a really long time, but I never said anything." Troy sighed and pushed his hair out of his eyes.

"Last year, it seemed like a few guys were making it their mission to target me. It was always in the locker room or on the bus. One Friday when I was in PE, someone took all my books and notebooks out of my bag and wrote FAG on them in huge black letters."

Audible gasps came from the audience. Sarah glanced at Lauren and saw her own shock and sadness mirrored in Lauren's expression. She touched her hand, and Lauren looked at her, eyes moist.

Troy continued, "I don't know why, but I just kinda snapped. I'd had enough, and I told the teacher. I wanted him to find out if the security cameras outside the locker room caught who might have ruined my books. He said he'd let administration know, but unfortunately, he also called my mom. Then the shit really hit the fan." Troy shifted uncomfortably in his chair, and Juanita squeezed his hand.

"See, my dad and I never got along much. He's an over-the-road truck driver, so he's only home on weekends. Usually he'd come home, get drunk, and pick a fight with me. I begged my mom not to tell him what had happened at school, but she's like his little puppet, and she told him anyway. He put me up against the wall and got in my face about being gay. I'd never given my parents any reason to suspect I was gay, but I knew I was. My dad started screaming he always knew something was wrong with me, and that no faggot was gonna live in his house. For the first time, I lost it."

Sarah noticed that the shy young man who had begun talking had transformed before her eyes; there was a fire in him, a more confident lift to his chin. Sarah marveled at his strength.

"So I shoved him away from me," Troy went on, "and yelled that yeah, I was gay, but I wasn't the one who had a problem. He backhanded me and kicked me out the door, and told me as long as I was an effing faggot, I could not come back." Tears tracked down Troy's cheeks. "I spent the two scariest nights of my life at the men's shelter, then went to school Monday morning. I was a mess, but I went to the counseling office to ask for help. My counselor called in the social worker, and together they called my mom. She told them it would be best for me not to be around my dad, so she called my cousin John, who agreed to take me in."

Troy ran his hands over his face. "You know, I wasn't surprised my dad acted that way. What really hurt was my mom didn't do a damn thing to help me. I guess, getting back to the question, bullies hurt me a lot, at school and at home, but the bystanders who let it happen hurt me just as much. Thankfully, my counselor also hooked me up with the youth group here, and with their support, I'm finally okay." Troy took a deep breath and flushed as the audience applauded him, then passed the mic down the line.

"Wow," Lauren whispered. "These kids are amazing." Sarah nodded in agreement.

Jonathan had taken the mic. In his soft, deep voice, he began to speak. "I've got a different side of the bullying thing to share. I haven't really experienced bullying myself too much—I mean, look at me." The audience chuckled, thankful for Jonathan's attempt to lighten the mood.

"I've known I was gay since junior high, but I was a football player long before then. I made varsity in ninth grade, and I've been team captain for the last two years. I've been around the stupid locker room humor for a long time, but I never said much, just kept to myself unless we were talking about football. But last year, a couple of guys on my team started messing with this freshman kid, real bad. We had different PE classes but were all in the locker room at the same time. They would shove him, put his stuff in the toilet, and call him sissy boy. Then one guy decided it would be funny to grab the kid, you know"—Jonathan pointed to his crotch—"then ask him if he liked it."

Jonathan paused and shook his head, clearly upset at the memory. "I knew the kid was humiliated and scared shitless, and I didn't do anything. One day, I was late to class and everybody had already gone up to the gym. But then I heard someone in the bathroom, crying. I went in there and asked if everything was okay, but he wouldn't answer. I could see under the stall door that he had red Chucks on, but I didn't know who it was, and I ended up just going to class.

"The next day, I saw my teammate harassing the freshman again, and this time, I noticed he was wearing the same red shoes. Something kinda snapped in me. I went over, put the asshole up against the lockers, and told him if he or anyone else ever messed with the kid again, I would make 'em pay. I told the kid I was sorry, and I wouldn't let it happen again while I was around."

A few people in the audience clapped. Jonathan, still looking very serious, nodded once and continued. "A week or so later, the kid came up to me in the hall and asked if he could talk to me. His name's Chase, and he told me the day I stuck up for him was the day he had planned to go home and kill himself. He thanked me and was looking at me like I was a superhero or something." Tears slid down Jonathan's cheeks as he spoke. "I'm no damn hero. I let that kid get bullied to the point he wanted to die. I'll never forgive myself for that, but I'll also never let it happen to anyone else if I can stop it."

Jonathan wiped his eyes and straightened his shoulders. "Actually, he saved me. After all that happened, I went to football practice and told my team I was gay. They about fell over. I told them I was sick of listening to all their homophobic bullshit and expected them to knock it off. A few of the guys were really supportive. Even my coach said he respected what I did. The guys who were doing the bullying never talked to me again." He shrugged. "Small price to pay."

Dale gave Jonathan a hug while the audience applauded the young man's story. Sarah's stomach hurt, and she was trying desperately not to cry.

Lauren looked at Sarah, shaking her head. "Jeez, this is heavy stuff," she said quietly. "Those kids are breaking my heart. Do you deal with things like this at work?"

Sarah half shrugged. "I've heard stories, yeah."

"I feel emotionally drained just listening to these few kids. I can't imagine how you handle it all the time. It must be hard not to take it home with you."

"I try not to," Sarah replied, "because I need a mental and emotional break when I'm home. But sometimes it's impossible not to carry it with me." *If you only knew.*

Lauren nodded, and they turned back to the panel, where Tori had taken the mic.

"I just moved here last year, but before that I went to a really small school in Kansas. Everybody knew everybody, and even lots of our parents hung out together. I guess you could say I was in the popular crowd, even though I'm pretty quiet. There isn't much diversity where I come from, so people were sort of hyperaware of anyone different. I had wondered about my sexuality for a while, but I never went there, because I was scared."

Tori stopped for a minute, gathering her thoughts, her eyes staring as if seeing something far away. "I had a major crush on my best friend Taylor, who happened to be going out with the captain of the football team. You know football's a seriously big deal in Kansas, right? He was like a celebrity, but he and his friends were jerks. He and Taylor thought I should hook up with his buddy, and they kept setting up double dates and stuff. I didn't like the guy, but I always wanted to hang out with Taylor, so I went along."

As she spoke, Tori's pale skin flushed and her green eyes seemed huge in her delicate face. She played with a ring on her finger, twisting it round and round. "One night, we all went to a party. The guys and some of the girls were drinking a lot. Taylor's boyfriend, Jake, kept pushing his buddies on me. They were obnoxious, trying to grope me and stuff. Taylor was drunk and thought it was funny, but the guys were getting kind of aggressive, and I was scared. Jake's best friend got me up against a wall and kept asking me why I wouldn't go out with him. He tried to kiss me, and I just shoved him and yelled something like, I don't wanna be with any of you guys. By Monday, it was all over Facebook that I said I didn't like boys and must be an effing dyke."

Tori, looking agitated, glanced at Martha, who smiled and nodded encouragingly. Tori's knee was bouncing, and Jonathan reached over and gave it a gentle squeeze.

She gave him a slight smile, took a deep breath, and continued, "So once it got all around school, the harassment got worse and worse. The most terrible part was my supposed best friend, Taylor, didn't stand by me. She and the other girls sort of distanced themselves from me, and even joined in the bullying. I felt completely alone. And then I started to cut."

Tori's hand went to her wrist, which was encased in a dozen rubber bracelets and plastic bangles. "A teacher noticed cuts on me and told my counselor, who told my parents. I told them about the bullying, and they did try to help," she said, eyes brimming with tears, "but I think all those guys got was a slap on the hand. They were football players, the untouchable Golden Boys, you know? My parents were friends with many of their parents. It just got…weird." Tori sighed. "So my parents decided to send me to New York to live with my grandparents and finish high school, and here I am." She attempted a smile. "Juanita found me with her freakishly accurate gaydar, and her mom has kind of adopted me, too. I miss my parents, but things are a lot better for me here." This time, Tori's smile was genuine and grateful.

The audience stood and applauded, and Sarah, touched deeply by Tori's story, joined in. She glanced down at Lauren and started. The woman beside her looked like she'd seen a ghost, and tears coursed down her cheeks. Sarah's heart plummeted at the sight of her distress. She sat down quickly and grasped Lauren's arm. "What's wrong?"

Lauren just looked at her with pain in her eyes. "My God," she whispered. "She just told Kat's story."

Sarah rubbed Lauren's arm, giving her a chance to compose herself. After taking a couple of shaky breaths, Lauren met Sarah's eyes with an almost pleading look.

"Wanna go somewhere and talk?" Sarah asked. Lauren nodded.

CHAPTER EIGHT

S arah blew on her mocha latte and waited for Lauren to get settled.

They were silent for a few moments as Lauren studied her cup, apparently deep in thought. Finally, she looked up and met Sarah's eyes. Her almost imperceptible nod told Sarah she had come to a decision.

"So, Tori's story was so similar to Kat's, it was scary. A girl questioning her sexuality in a small-town school, bullying by the athletes, the best friend betrayal...everything."

Sarah nodded. "You said she had a difficult time last year, and I wondered, because she was so nervous when she came to school the first day."

"I was lucky I got her there. She had a panic attack that morning. The situation at her old school really did a number on her."

Several more silent moments went by, and Sarah was unsure if the conversation would continue as she watched a multitude of emotions cross Lauren's face.

Then Lauren spoke again. "I felt like a total failure, like I let my daughter down." Her voice caught in her throat.

"Oh no...why?"

"I had no idea Kat was being harassed at school, and it went on for weeks. How could I not see it?" Lauren was clearly still beating herself up.

Sarah sighed. She'd known so many parents who didn't seem to give two shits that they were hurting their kids, who never took the blame for anything. Yet here was this incredible, attentive mom, berating herself when she hadn't done anything wrong. Sarah wanted so badly to ease her pain and guilt. She reached across the table and briefly touched Lauren's hand.

"I'm pretty sure Kat worked very hard at keeping you in the dark. She probably felt like she had to deal with it on her own."

"But why couldn't she talk to me?" Lauren's eyes filled with tears. "I didn't have a clue until I found her in the bathroom with a bloody wrist."

"Did you ask her why?" Sarah asked gently.

"Yeah. She said she didn't want to worry me. Maybe she knew it would hit the fan if her father found out, and boy, was she right," Lauren said bitterly.

"What happened, if I may ask? Of course, if you don't want to share, I completely understand." Sarah wanted to give Lauren an out from this obviously painful conversation.

"No, I want to tell you, Sarah. You've shown me more care and kindness than anyone has in a long time. I've held this in long enough and haven't confided in anyone. But I think what those kids said earlier is true. Telling your story can be healing."

"Indeed it can, and please know I will keep your confidence. It means a lot that you trust me enough to share."

"I do," Lauren said, meeting Sarah's eyes. "I feel very…comfortable with you, and I could use a friend."

"Well, hon, you've got one." Sarah smiled warmly and Lauren nodded before continuing.

"So anyway, Kat was right to worry about what her dad would say. I don't remember it being much of an issue when we were younger, but after being down South for a while, Trent really seemed to change. He became so negative and closed-minded. I didn't like that he hung out with his cousin and a few of the other COs, because they were a tough-talking, hard-drinking bunch. Trent used to come home and say really derogatory stuff about inmates, especially the ones in the Alternative Lifestyle unit."

"There is such a thing?" Sarah asked, surprised.

"Yep. They house all the gay men and transgender folks together, mostly for their safety."

"I bet. Wow."

"Anyway, I used to get into it with him, because I didn't want him spewing all that crap around Kat. He just thought I needed to lighten up because, after all, he was the one who had to, quote, deal with the deviants all day. His words, not mine. I finally told him to leave work at work because I didn't want to hear it. So then he started going to the bar with his buddies instead of coming home. Things were definitely tense around our house."

"Sounds like it was pretty difficult for you," Sarah said.

"Yeah, it was no picnic. When everything went down with Kat, he was off at a two-week training at a different prison. Kat and I finally had a break, but little did I know things were worse for Kat at school than at home. After I found Kat bleeding in the bathroom, she told me what was going on. I had to take her to the ER, and the social worker got even more of the story." Lauren paused and rubbed her forehead, as if thinking about it hurt her head.

"It was just like that girl's story tonight," she continued. "Kat's best friend Amber was dating a star baseball player, and one of his teammates kept bugging Kat to go out with him. Amber and her boyfriend were pressuring her to hook up with this kid, too. Kat said she kept rejecting his advances, and finally told him off one night at a party. Almost immediately, he and others posted stuff online, calling Kat all sorts of nasty things. She put up with that, and worse, for weeks and never said a word."

Sarah shook her head, anger rising at the thought of the damage cyberbullying could do. "What did you do when you found out?"

"After I cried my head off, you mean? I marched right up to the school and spoke to the principal about the bullying. The worst part for Kat was that one of the main culprits was Amber's boyfriend, and ultimately, Amber sided with him instead of Kat. She felt so betrayed." Lauren shook her head, tears threatening again. "Initially Kat didn't want to say anything, but I told her it wasn't fair for her to have to be so miserable while they got away with it. Finally, she agreed to talk to the principal. We were able to show him Facebook messages and texts Kat had gotten from those kids, and a couple of the boys got suspended for harassment."

"Good for you, reporting it," Sarah said. "So many people never do, and then the bullies just keep on doing it."

"Yeah, well, I'm glad the kids got suspended, but she lost her friends over it, and it was ultimately what blew up in our faces with Trent. Turns out he's good buddies with the father of one of the boys, and they were at the same training together. I was going to tell Trent about it all, in my own way, when he got home, but his buddy beat me to it. Of course, he heard their side of the story, and the one thing he fixated on was the rumor Kat was gay. So doesn't he come home and get right in her face? It was unbelievable. Even when I told him she had cut herself, he blamed her for bringing it on herself and creating drama to get those boys in trouble. He didn't once listen to her side." Lauren blew out a frustrated breath.

"That's awful. The poor kid."

"Yeah, I know. Kat and I are very close, but she's always been kind of intimidated by her father when he's mad, so when he was grilling her, she just cried and couldn't look at him. He took her silence as an admission of guilt, no matter what I tried to say."

"I'm so sorry," Sarah said. It always broke her heart to hear stories like this. Home was supposed to be a child's safe place, where they were accepted and loved no matter what. When parents didn't provide that, it was one of the worst kinds of emotional neglect.

"It was a night from hell, for sure." Lauren sighed. "Trent and I really got into it afterward. He kept saying he was embarrassed Kat had gotten his friend's son in trouble, especially because he was an athlete and had to miss games. I was so pissed at him. I said I couldn't believe he didn't care that his own daughter was being bullied to the point of hurting herself. He said she was just overreacting, and I was babying her. I don't think I've ever been so angry at anyone in my life. There were probably sparks shooting out of my eyes."

"If it had been me, I'd have had smoke coming out my ears, too," Sarah said in solidarity.

"Right? It was just the last straw, you know? I haven't been happy in my marriage for quite a while, but I stayed for Kat. I didn't want to uproot her. But after it all went down, I just wanted her to feel safe, and I knew we both needed a break."

"You showed a lot of courage, Lauren. You know that, right?"

"I guess, but at the time, I was just mad at myself for not leaving sooner. Then Kat wouldn't have had to go through it at all."

"Sometimes something major has to happen to push a person into taking such a monumental step," Sarah said. "People just kind of get used to the rut they're in."

Easy for you to say. What's it going to take to break you out of your rut, hmm? You've got the social life of a hermit.

Sarah tucked that thought away for later, then brought her attention back to Lauren.

"It took me about three weeks to make my preparations," Lauren was saying. "Kat had to finish up her final exams, but as soon as she did, we were ready. The next day when Trent went to work, Kat and I packed up the car and left. I wrote a note and told him we needed to get away for at least the summer, and I'd contact him soon. That was it."

"Holy cow. He must've blown a gasket when he got home."

"Probably, and I am extremely glad we weren't there to see it. So now you know our sordid tale," Lauren said, meeting Sarah's eyes with a sigh. She looked lighter, like a huge weight had been lifted from her shoulders. Sarah could see the strength behind those incredible blue eyes, and she was impressed.

"And quite a tale it was." She reached across the table and touched Lauren's arm. "You and Kat are pretty remarkable, I hope you know." She noted the blush that crept across Lauren's cheeks and reluctantly withdrew her hand. "I have a much better understanding of Kat now. Thank you for sharing your story with me."

"And thanks for listening. It felt good to talk about it with someone other than Kat." She held Sarah's gaze for several long moments.

Sarah, suddenly feeling warm, broke the eye contact and glanced at her phone. "Holy crap," she exclaimed. "It's past ten thirty, and we've got an hour's drive ahead of us to get home."

"Wow," Lauren said, jumping to attention and gathering her things. "Time sure went by fast. I'm sorry I kept you so late."

"No worries at all. Time flies when you're with good company."

Lauren just smiled, but Sarah groaned inwardly at her corny line, embarrassed. She busied herself with throwing out her coffee cup and grabbing her keys.

"Mind if I follow you back to the Thruway?" Lauren asked. "I got kind of turned around coming over here."

"Not at all. Let's go."

Making sure not to get too far ahead of the headlights following her, Sarah drove home, smiling all the way. It had been ages since she'd made this kind of connection with someone, and it felt good. Lauren was an incredible person, and who couldn't use another friend, right? Replaying the night in her mind, Sarah tried not to analyze too deeply why she'd felt all tingly every time Lauren smiled.

CHAPTER NINE

I'll be down in a minute," Kat hollered. Bridget had come to pick her up for the Halloween party at Natasha's and was waiting in the living room. Kat's mom had almost burst out laughing at the sight of Bridget when she let her in the door, which was excellent proof the costumes would be a hit, as far as Bridget was concerned.

"Come on already, Kat. I've been down here for twenty minutes, and you know I can't really sit in this thing," Bridget hollered back.

"All right," Kat said from the top of the stairs. "Promise you won't laugh." She slowly descended, and Bridget couldn't keep the grin off her face.

"Oh my God, you are the most adorable crayon I have ever seen."

"Shut up," Kat said, but she was smiling. "You look pretty colorful yourself."

"Yes, I rock in green, it's true, but you, my dear, are smashing in blue," Bridget said, putting on her best dramatic expression.

Kat laughed. "And you are a goof."

Bridget noticed Mrs. Emerson watching them from the kitchen doorway with an amused smile. "What time is this party supposed to wrap up?" she asked.

"Um...two a.m.?" Kat said, hopefully.

"Yeah, not gonna happen. I'll see your blue behind back here by midnight. That is the witching hour, you know. Bad things could happen if you're late."

"Mom, seriously?" Kat groaned.

"I'll have her home right on time," Bridget declared, holding up two fingers. "Crayon's honor."

Mrs. Emerson laughed. "Get out of here, you two. Have fun."

The girls awkwardly walked to Bridget's car and squeezed themselves in.

"Your mom's great," Bridget said, as they drove the few blocks to Natasha's house. They were heading there early to help set up for the party.

"Yeah, she is. I'm lucky to have her."

"I can tell. You two are really close, huh?"

"Yep, we always have been, but things are even better since we moved up here. She isn't as stressed as she used to be, and she's more fun to hang out with."

"I wish I had that with my mom," Bridget replied wistfully. "She's so busy with the triplets, we almost never have time together, just us."

"It *is* pretty chaotic at your house," Kat said. "Your mom never stops moving."

"That's because the boys never stop getting into stuff. I like it at your house. It's so peaceful."

"It is." As they pulled up to Natasha's, Kat pointed. "Oh. My. God." Natasha's family had gone all out decorating the yard and house. It looked like a haunted graveyard, complete with zombies, ghouls, and a hapless bloody victim or two.

"Wait till you see it when it gets really dark. They have these creepy strobe lights that make the zombies look like they're coming right at you."

"Fabulous," Kat said, none too convincingly.

"You're not scared of that stuff, are you?" Bridget teased.

"Hey, I'm a poor defenseless crayon. What chance would I have against a zombie attack?"

"I'll protect you," Bridget said, grabbing Kat's hand gallantly.

Kat met Bridget's eyes, and something warm passed between them. "I really think you would," she said softly. The moment was broken by Natasha hollering from her porch.

"A little help here, you two?"

Bridget smiled as Kat blushed and got out of the car.

Natasha was dancing around in her red crayon suit, which she had accessorized with rainbow pride and smiley face pins. "You two look great," she said, and practically squealed with excitement. "We are so going to put everyone else's costumes to shame."

"Without a doubt," Bridget agreed. "Somebody'd better take a picture of all six of us lined up in rainbow order. So, what can we do to help?"

"I'm putting you two to work stringing white skull lights across the ceiling."

Um, are ladders involved?" Kat asked. "I kinda don't do ladders."

"First zombies, now ladders." Bridget fussed with fake exasperation. "Must I handle everything?"

"Yes," Kat said with a wink, and walked into the house. Natasha laughed and followed Kat, leaving Bridget to stare after the adorable blue crayon who was creating a stir inside her little green heart.

❖

"I can't remember the last time I did something fun like this for Halloween," Kat said, as she snagged a handful of candy corn from a bowl on the coffee table.

"What, they don't do Halloween in Alabama?" Bridget teased.

"Yes, they do Halloween, goofball, but the people I hung out with would never dream of dressing up like this, unless there were massive amounts of alcohol present."

Bridget shook her head. "I just can't see you hanging out with people like that. It seems so...not you."

"The longer I'm away from them, the more I agree with you. I guess it's just, they were the people I'd known forever. It didn't occur to me to not be friends with them, even though some of them had changed so much, and not in a good way."

Bridget sensed Kat's mood taking a turn toward melancholy, so she changed the subject quickly. "Check out these costumes. Do these people seriously think they can compete with the Crayola Six?"

Kat brightened. "Clearly they are lacking. What is the guy over there supposed to be?" She pointed to a boy who had his back to them and seemed to be wrapped head to toe in plastic wrap. At that moment, he turned around, and they could read the sign he had hanging around his neck.

"*No glove, no love.*" Kat laughed. "Oh my God, he's a condom."

Bridget rolled her eyes. "True class right there, that's what that is." She watched Kat as she giggled, her gorgeous eyes shining. Bridget couldn't get enough of their sparkle and vowed to make Kat laugh any chance she could. "C'mon, let's go round up our crayon friends. I think we should start a conga line or something, get this party hoppin'."

She took Kat's hand, and Kat threaded her fingers through Bridget's, as natural as anything.

Kat looked at Bridget and blushed, but didn't take her hand away. "Lead on," she said with a quiet smile.

Bridget grinned as her heart did backflips. She gave Kat's fingers a squeeze, then led her off to find their friends.

❖

By ten p.m., more than twenty-five people had come to Natasha's party. It seemed like everyone was having fun just being silly and enjoying all things Halloween-y. A motley assortment of people were dancing in the living room, including three witches, a convict, a cheerleader, two nuns, and President Obama. Several guys were having a vicious bob-for-apples contest, and in the kitchen, blindfolded partygoers were playing Pin the Arm on the Zombie.

Kat watched the whole scene with wonder; she had never been to a party like this in her life. Back home, all the parties seemed to be about drinking and hooking up, and she never really felt comfortable at any of them. She certainly never relaxed enough to actually have fun, but it had been too much trouble to keep deflecting her friends' demands to join them, so she'd gone along.

Against her will, Kat's mind went to the last party she attended, the one where everything went to shit in her life. She could almost feel the suffocating heat, smell the cheap beer and pot smoke. Something else tickled at her memory, and she suddenly felt cold. Her heart began to thud painfully in her chest, and she felt like she couldn't breathe. She broke out into a clammy sweat. *Oh no. I have to get out of there, I have to...*

A warm hand touched her arm, then someone gently grasped her shoulders. Shaken back to the moment, Kat tried to push away, then looked up into very worried brown eyes.

"Kat...Kat, are you okay?" Bridget asked. "You look like—I don't mean to be funny, but you look like you've seen a ghost."

Kat tried to shake off her panic and took a deep breath. "I'm fine, I just...I need to get out of here." She pulled away from Bridget and headed for the front door, awkwardly pushing her bulky costume through the crowded living room. Once she had moved to the lawn, outside the halo of the porch light, Kat took several deep lungfuls of the cold night air and tried to get her bearings. *What the hell just happened?* Kat knew she had just had a panic attack, as her therapist called episodes like this. What she didn't get was why. She'd been having such a great time, and—

"Kat?" Bridget stood on the porch step, looking tentative and very concerned. "Do you need anything?"

Kat didn't answer, couldn't begin to explain.

"Okay, you're kinda scaring me here. What's wrong?" Bridget came to stand beside Kat, and the genuine compassion on her face helped Kat to calm slightly.

"I'm okay. I just had a panic attack. Happens sometimes." Kat tried to shrug it off, but she was still shaking.

"I saw you standing there, smiling, and then all of a sudden, you went white as a sheet," Bridget said, stepping closer. "Did something happen?"

Kat sighed and wrapped her arms around her middle. "I was remembering something from back home, and it just hit me."

"Do you need to talk about it?" Bridget asked gently.

Kat was touched at Bridget's concern. "No, I...do you think maybe we could just take off? I kinda don't want to go back in there."

"Okay, sure. Wait here while I tell the girls, okay?" Bridget stepped back up to the porch and disappeared inside. She returned in five minutes, keys in hand.

"Was Natasha upset?" Kat asked.

"Nah, I just told her you weren't feeling well. Too much candy corn." Bridget winked. "Come on, I'll take you home."

"I don't want to go home yet. Could we just drive?"

Bridget took her hand and nodded. "Whatever you need, Blue."

❖

They drove down to the elementary school and parked by the playground. Bridget had a jacket and a hoodie in her backseat, so the girls both took off their costumes and put on the warmer clothes to ward off the chill.

"Wanna swing?" Bridget asked.

Kat nodded, and they made their way to the swings in the hazy glow from a spotlight on the corner of the school. Kat was silent for a while, just twirling herself on the swing, then letting go and spinning. Finally, she spoke.

"I'm sorry I freaked out back there. I was having such a good time, but then I just thought of something out of the blue, and..." She shrugged.

"You don't have to apologize, Kat. I was just worried because you looked scared to death. I know you don't like to talk much about your life before you moved here, but I'll listen if you need me to."

"I know," Kat said. She quietly stared at the ground for a few moments, then looked up at Bridget. "I've only known you for two months, and I think you're the best friend I've ever had." Bridget quirked up an eyebrow but didn't speak. Kat continued, "I thought

I had a best friend, back in Alabama. Her name's Amber, and we've known each other since kindergarten. We were really close when we were little, but she was always the outgoing one, and I was shy. So by junior high, she was super popular, and I was sort of her sidekick, you know? Good old Kat, always there when she needed me." Kat snorted bitterly. "I would've done anything for her, and she knew it. But then she got all crazy into boys. She started going out with this kid Joe, who's, like, this major jock, and I got really jealous. It took me a while to figure it out, but I finally realized the reason I got so upset about him was because *I* wanted to be the one she liked. And it scared the shit out of me."

Bridget nodded with understanding. "Must've sucked for you."

"You have no idea. So I spent the next two years pining after my best friend in secret, and grabbing every minute I could get with her. Pathetic, right?"

"No, not pathetic, Kat. You can't help who you love."

"Well, I was stupid to love her. It sure backfired on me."

"Did she know how you felt?" Bridget asked.

"She knew I loved her like a best friend, I guess, but I blew it one day and gave away too much. I was consoling her because she'd had a fight with Joe, of course. Supposedly he was pressuring her to have sex, and she wasn't ready. Her parents are crazy conservative, and she was scared to go there. So he was guilt-tripping her, saying she must not love him and all that crap."

Bridget shook her head in disapproval. "Why can't guys just respect a girl enough to wait?"

"Right? That's pretty much what I told her, but then I said I didn't think he was good enough for her, and *I* would never treat her that way."

"Whoa," Bridget said, wide-eyed. "What did she do?"

"Well, we were hugging at the time. She pulled away and looked at me kinda funny. I remember realizing what I had said and my face getting hot. She didn't say anything, though, not then."

"So I'm guessing she got suspicious?"

"Seems so, because the next weekend, she made a point of telling me she'd slept with Joe, and how it was so great. I thought

I was gonna throw up. Then she and Joe kept trying to hook me up with his buddies."

"Eww, so not cool," Bridget said in disgust.

"You have no idea. One guy in particular, Eddie, wouldn't take no for an answer. Every time he saw me, he hit on me, and he was just...ugh, gross," Kat said, shuddering. "One night at a party, I'd had enough, and I told him I wanted nothing to do with him or any of his friends, and to just leave me alone. I remember he got pissed, but later on, he pretended to be all nice again. He even apologized." She didn't tell Bridget she had no memory of the rest of that night. How could she explain something that didn't make any sense?

"Okay, good. And?" Bridget pressed.

"And not good at all. My life went to hell in a handbasket, as my mother would say. Obviously Eddie's apology meant nothing. Things started popping up on Facebook, like *Kat's a tease* or *Kat's a bitch*, but it got way worse real fast. They started calling me a dyke, saying I wouldn't know what to do with a guy's, um, appendage, and shit like that. It was humiliating."

"Man, they're lucky I wasn't there," Bridget fumed. "I'd have shown 'em all about what a dyke could do with a guy's appendage, and it wouldn't be pretty."

Kat laughed out loud. "What?" Bridget said innocently. "When someone gets my Irish up, I cannot be held responsible for my actions."

"I'll keep that in mind," Kat said with a grin, but then sobered as her thoughts turned back to her story. "See? You're all ready to defend me, and my so-called best friend didn't do a damn thing to support me through it all. When it came down to it, our friendship meant nothing."

"I'm sorry." Bridget reached over from her swing to take Kat's hand.

Kat sighed. "It got worse."

"Are you freaking kidding me? How much worse could it get?"

"A couple of people actually told me to go kill myself. That's when I cut," Kat said, her voice low.

"What, you mean you cut yourself?" Bridget asked, fingers tightening in Kat's.

"Yeah. I just couldn't stand it anymore. I never told my mom what was going on, but she found me bleeding in the bathroom. I had to go to the ER and get evaluated and stuff. Then she made me tell the principal."

"Oh God," Bridget groaned.

"I had to show him the messages, and he could see they were from Eddie, Joe, and a few of their friends. So they got suspended for a week, and they missed two baseball playoff games. Of course Joe was team captain, and he and Eddie were star players, so everyone had a fit. My dad was away at a work thing when this all happened, and I didn't want him to know, because he's kind of a hothead. But he found out before he got home from his friend, who happens to be Eddie's father. My dad blamed me for the whole thing." Kat's voice hitched as the tears came. "He said I was just stirring up drama to get attention, and I had no right to ruin the boys' chances of being scouted for college ball."

"Oh, my achin' ass," Bridget said angrily. "I can't even believe this. But your mom had your back, right?"

"Yeah, thank God. If she hadn't, I'm not sure I'd be here talking to you right now." Kat paused and took a deep breath. "My mom was *so* pissed at my dad, she just packed us up and left as soon as school ended. And here I am."

"Wow, that's just craziness. I can't stand that you had to go through so much shit," Bridget said, getting to her feet and pulling Kat into a hug. "I'm glad you aren't there anymore."

Kat allowed herself to sink into the hug, feeling safe with a friend for the first time in a long while. "So am I." They held each other quietly for several moments, emotionally spent. The silence was broken by an insistent chirping sound. Bridget let go of Kat and checked her phone.

"Ruh-roh, eleven forty-five, better get going. We promised your mom we'd be back before the witching hour, remember?"

"Gotta keep our promises. Lucky I only live three blocks from here," Kat said with a laugh. Then she leaned in close to Bridget. "Thank you," she whispered, then placed a soft kiss on her friend's cheek.

She started walking to the car, leaving Bridget grinning while her heart did the increasingly more frequent flip-flop thing.

CHAPTER TEN

"Okay, let's review committees," Bridget said, running the True Colors meeting like a corporate CEO. They were planning the Sweetheart Dance, and Bridget was all business. "Justin and Matt, you are in charge of door prize donations. Steph and Kylie, you've got refreshments. Jordan and Natasha, you're booking the DJ and getting chaperones, with Ms. O's help. Fabulous freshmen, you four are in charge of advertising, and Kat and I will handle decorations. Sound good, everyone?"

The club members nodded their agreement, then split off into their respective groups to strategize. Sarah smiled at Bridget's leadership ability. She made it very easy for Sarah to be the club advisor. In years past, it had been like pulling teeth to get the kids to accomplish anything, and for Sarah it had been lots of work for which she frankly didn't have time. But Bridget excelled in the role of club president, a fact Sarah would be including in her college recommendation letter.

"Ms. O," Natasha and Jordan said, approaching her, "which teachers do you think we should ask to be chaperones?"

"Well, we should probably start with an email to staff, asking for volunteers, and see how many responses we get. You can write the email, and I'll forward it for you. If we need more, we can ask parents, too." She knew she could probably rope Jamie into helping, but they needed at least twelve adults.

"Okay, we're on it," Natasha said, and the girls went off.

"Before you beg, yes, I'll chaperone," Jamie said from her desk.

"Oh, good," Sarah replied. "I hate begging. It's embarrassing."

"Bridget certainly has the troops in line, doesn't she?"

"Mark my words, in twenty years, she'll be running a Fortune 500 company, or maybe the country," Sarah boasted with pride. "She's one of a kind."

"Looks like she's really helped Kat settle in," Jamie remarked, watching the two girls across the room with their heads close together.

"I'd say so. Bridget is as loyal as the day is long, and she's exactly the kind of friend Kat needed. I'm glad they hit it off so well."

"So," Jamie said slowly, changing the subject, "I've got news."

Sarah perked up with interest. "Is this news I'm gonna like, or should I brace myself?"

"It's not bad news, exactly. Jay's company offered a huge sales incentive a couple of months ago, and he won."

"That's great! What did he win?"

"A four-day cruise to the Bahamas," Jamie said flatly.

"Explain to me why you are not jumping for joy right now," Sarah demanded.

"It's a Thanksgiving cruise." Jamie hung her head meekly.

"Oh, I get it. You're actually worried about me, aren't you?"

"We always do Thanksgiving together. I'd feel terrible leaving you alone." Jamie sighed dramatically.

"Look at me, Jamie Gibson. You will go on this cruise, you will have a fantastic time, and you will not think of anything but relaxing with Jay. Am I clear?"

"But what will you do for Thanksgiving?" Jamie said, looking slightly less guilty.

"I will cook myself a lovely dinner, relax with a good book, and spoil my kitties with leftovers. Then over the weekend, I will volunteer at the SPCA like I always do, catch up on all my Netflix shows, and do absolutely nothing else I don't want to do. And I will enjoy every minute."

"You're the best, you know that?" Jamie said, letting the excitement of her impending trip take over.

"Yes, I am well aware of how fabulous I am," Sarah teased.

The students were gathering their things to leave. Sarah waved good-bye to everyone as they left, then let her gaze rest on Kat for a moment. *Hmm*, she said to herself, an idea taking root.

❖

A week later, Sarah was leaving work when she saw Lauren's SUV idling at the curb. She'd been debating whether or not to share her idea with Lauren, but now the opportunity to speak with her was presenting itself. "Here goes nothing," Sarah mumbled under her breath.

Waving as she approached the car, she saw Lauren's face light up in recognition.

"Hey there," Lauren said, smiling. "How've you been?"

"Good, but very busy. College application season is in full swing."

"Oh, I know," Lauren replied. "I nag Kat every other day about the to-do list you gave her. She had trouble logging in to the Common Application website and hasn't tried again since."

"Have her stop by. I'll help her with it. The Common App seems kind of daunting at first, but once you get going, it isn't bad at all."

"Thanks. I'll let her know."

"So," Sarah began. Lauren looked at her expectantly. "I was wondering, are you staying around here for Thanksgiving?"

Lauren's smile didn't quite reach her eyes. "Actually, we are."

"I hope this isn't presumptuous of me, but I thought maybe that was the case, and I wondered if you'd like to have Thanksgiving dinner with me?"

"Wow," Lauren said, surprised. "That's quite an offer. But don't you spend Thanksgiving with your family?"

"No," Sarah replied, "not since my parents passed. My brothers are spread all over the country, so we try to get together at Christmas and maybe in the summer. I usually spend Thanksgiving with my friend Jamie, but she and her husband won the trip of a lifetime and will be away. So I thought—"

"So you thought of us," Lauren finished. "Well, if you're absolutely sure, it would be wonderful to share Thanksgiving with you."

"Do you think Kat would mind?" Sarah worried.

"Not at all. Kat really likes you. Besides, she will probably head over to Bridget's at some point, because I think she was invited for dessert."

"Well then, I guess we have a plan," Sarah said, smiling warmly. She felt like a little kid who just learned she was going to Disney World.

"I guess we do." Lauren smiled back, and their gazes lingered on each other for several beats.

"Hey, Ms. O."

Sarah hadn't noticed Kat approaching until she opened the car door.

Kat tossed her backpack in the back seat. "What's up?"

"Ms. O'Shaughnessy invited us to have Thanksgiving dinner with her. Isn't that sweet?"

"Cool." Kat shrugged with the kind of nonchalance only a teenager could muster. "I can still go to Bridget's after, though, right?"

"Fine with me."

"Cool," Kat said again, plugging her earbuds into her iPod.

"And you thought she'd mind," Lauren said, rolling her eyes.

Sarah laughed. "We'll talk soon, then. Bye."

As Lauren and Kat drove away, Sarah couldn't hide her grin of pleasure. She had just invited a beautiful woman to her home for dinner. Whoa. Although she'd been around the block a time or two, she felt like she'd just arranged her very first date. *Hey*, she chastised herself, *this is not a date. Lauren is just a friend.* Mm-hmm. Why was she feeling so giddy, then? It's not like she'd never been in this position before, although admittedly, it'd been years. Sarah felt a twinge of pain, recalling the reason why, but she shook it off. Then another thought occurred to her. Thanksgiving was only a week away. She had some serious cleaning to do.

CHAPTER ELEVEN

Thanksgiving Day dawned misty and gray, but Sarah was feeling all sunshine and rainbows at the thought of spending the day with Lauren, despite the fact she kept reminding herself Lauren was just a friend, and a straight one at that.

Sarah set about putting the fifteen-pound bird in the oven and mixing the stuffing, seasoned with summer savory, just like her mom used to make. She had done a major cleaning, the likes of which she hadn't had the time or energy to do since school started. Every inch of her house shone; hell, even Martha Stewart couldn't find fault. She'd even broken out her fancy tablecloth, ironed it, and put it on her rarely used dining room table. Sarah was determined to be the consummate hostess for her guests.

After she'd prepared all she could do ahead of time, Sarah took a shower and then stood in front of her closet, trying to find something decent to wear. She'd put on weight in recent years, and getting dressed was no longer an activity she enjoyed. Looking in her full-length mirror, Sarah was not at all happy with the body reflected back at her.

Watching Forensic Files *marathons on the couch with Ben and Jerry will do that to a person.*

Sarah growled at the unbidden thought, then let out a resigned sigh. She finally chose a pair of tan slacks and a hunter green V-neck sweater, which brought out her eyes and complemented the shades of red in her hair. She gave herself a last once-over, then went downstairs.

At precisely noon, the doorbell rang. Sarah opened the door to find a smiling Lauren, bearing a foil-covered dish. Kat was right behind, holding a bottle of wine.

"Come on in, you two," Sarah said, motioning them into her living room. "Welcome to my humble abode."

Lauren held out the dish. "Here is my contribution to our feast. Sweet potato casserole, complete with marshmallows."

"Ooh, sounds positively decadent," Sarah enthused, taking the dish from her guest and bringing it into the kitchen. "We won't be eating for another half hour or so. Should I put it in the oven to warm?"

"Sure," Lauren said, removing her coat and looking around. "Kat, honey, why don't you hang up our coats there in the closet?"

Lauren moved into the room, taking in the simple but cozy décor. Her eyes were drawn to the inviting deep red sofa which faced the dancing flames of the fireplace. She moved closer to the fire to warm her still-cold hands and began looking at the pictures on the mantel. On one end was a photo showing Sarah with five men, all with varying shades of red hair. They were decked out in St. Patrick's Day attire and raising a toast, all smiles and laughter. At the other end was a gorgeous heart-shaped frame of inlaid wood. The photo inside showed a younger Sarah on a beach, her arm around a laughing blond woman. She was gazing at the woman with undisguised adoration, and Lauren felt a twinge of embarrassment, as if she'd interrupted a private moment. She couldn't help herself from looking more closely at the photo. Sarah, with her lovely skin and sun-kissed hair, looked absolutely radiant.

"Uh, Mom?" Startled, Lauren turned around to see Kat holding up the bottle of wine.

"Oh, sorry. Let me take that." She brought the wine into the kitchen.

Sarah was arranging pickles and olives on a relish tray.

"Where would you like this?" Lauren asked, indicating the bottle.

"Well, I guess it should go in the fridge to stay chilled, right? I will confess right now, I'm not much of a drinker, and I know very little about wine."

Lauren feigned a look of horror. "You live in the Finger Lakes, and you don't drink wine?"

"Tell me about it. I am an embarrassment to my entire family. My brothers say I must've been left on the doorstep as a baby, because I don't even like beer. Well, except root beer. I am a root beer connoisseur."

Lauren laughed. "Well, you can try this wine and see what you think. If you don't like it, no worries."

"Fair enough."

"I absolutely love this kitchen. It's so bright and cheerful." Lauren looked around in appreciation at the butter-yellow walls, honey oak cabinets, and colorful touches of reds and oranges. The wide window looked out upon a tidy backyard, where several bird feeders in various shapes and sizes were arranged. A few late-fall birds were pecking away at their lunch.

"I love to watch birds, hence my feeder colony out there."

"I do, too," Lauren said. "There's something about waking up to the birds singing that starts a day off right. Of course, it's getting too cold up here now to keep the windows open."

"Do you miss the South?"

"You know, I do sometimes," Lauren answered with a sigh. "We were only a couple of hours away from the Gulf, and we lived in a very pretty area. But when I was there, I missed the seasons, and snow, and the lakes up here. Can't have it both ways, I suppose."

"Well, you can always visit, right?"

"I'm thinking that's not a good idea, at least not yet. Trent's still pissed at me for leaving, but I told him it was up to him to make things right with Kat."

"Has he tried to?" Sarah asked.

"He texts or calls me about once a week, and he *has* asked about her. But she doesn't want anything to do with him right now. She is still so hurt. I asked her if she was upset about not doing our usual holiday thing, because her cousins always have a Christmas Eve party she enjoys, but she said she was fine with it. Not sure I believe her, but I'm not going to push."

"You know, I can hear you talking about me in there," an annoyed voice said from the living room.

"Maybe you should come in here and be sociable then," Lauren called back. Kat shuffled into the kitchen, thumbs flying away on her phone. "Ahem," Lauren said, leveling her daughter with the mommy glare. Kat sighed and reluctantly put her phone in her pocket.

Sarah jumped in and immediately engaged her. "So, Kat, I know it's weird to be hanging out at your counselor's house, but I just wanted to thank you." Kat looked at her questioningly. "You and your mom are saving me from a totally boring and lonely Thanksgiving. Without you, I'd probably be eating Chinese food and crying all night at sappy movies."

Kat smiled. "That would be bad, Ms. O." She glanced at her mom. "And thank you, too, for inviting us."

Lauren smiled, and the tension was gone. Gazing at Sarah, Lauren marveled at how effortlessly she had put Kat at ease. Something about Sarah just made people feel good.

Suddenly, a streak of gray went flying through the kitchen.

"Whoa," Kat said, eyes wide. "You have cats?"

"Oh, is it a problem? I never thought to ask if you two had allergies or anything," Sarah said in alarm as Kira and Fiona raced back the other way in a full-on kitty chase.

"No way," Kat said with a grin. "I love cats, but we could never have pets because my dad is allergic."

Fiona had stopped racing and was rubbing her cheek on Kat's offered hand. The kid looked like she had died and gone to heaven.

Sarah smiled. "Well, then, you have officially been named cat entertainer for the rest of the day. The one loving on you is Fiona, and her sister is Kira."

"They're so cute."

"There's a basket of toys out there in the living room. They especially like the laser light and the fishing pole. Go play," Sarah said, shooing them out of the kitchen. She looked up and met Lauren's misty eyes. "What?"

Lauren shook her head with a sad smile. "Seeing her so excited makes me feel awful that she missed out on having a pet all these years."

"It's tough if someone has allergies, though."

"Yeah, well, Trent *said* he had allergies, but I think mostly he just didn't want to be bothered dealing with animals in the house."

"Did you want pets?" Sarah asked.

"I wouldn't have minded. I had pets growing up, like guinea pigs and hamsters, but one Christmas my parents got me a calico kitten. Her name was Gracie, and we were inseparable." Lauren wiped away a tear. "She died eight months before my parents were killed."

"Oh, honey." Sarah gave Lauren a quick hug.

"You must think I'm a basket case." Lauren sniffed. "Every time I see you, I end up crying." Normally she'd be uncomfortable crying in front of others, but with Sarah, Lauren felt like she could just be.

"I do tend to bring out the best in people."

Lauren laughed. "Luckily, you make me laugh more than you make me cry."

"Well, I certainly hope so." Sarah peeked into the oven. "Hey, looks like the thermometer popped up. Turkey's done," she announced.

The three sat down to a lovely dinner of turkey, stuffing, sweet potato casserole, veggies, fresh rolls, and cranberry sauce.

"This is so good," Kat moaned around a mouthful of stuffing.

"Slow down, kid. You know the rule," Lauren chided.

Sarah quirked an eyebrow. "What rule is that?"

"Since it takes hours to prepare a Thanksgiving meal, we have a rule that we must try to take at least thirty minutes to eat it. Sometimes we're even successful," Lauren explained.

"Most of the time, we're not," Kat added, shoveling in a spoonful of cranberry sauce.

"Good Lord, child. Ms. O is going to think I don't feed you."

Sarah laughed. "I don't think anything of the sort. Now, Kat, tell me what's going on with the dance preparations."

The next hour passed with easy conversation, laughter, and lots of eating. Lauren felt completely comfortable, as if she and Kat had known Sarah for years instead of months. She finally sat back in her chair and groaned. "I may not be able to move for a week, but it was worth it. You're a great cook, Sarah."

"Thank you. I don't make much for myself, but I enjoy cooking meals for others. You learn how to do that in a big family."

"How many siblings do you have?" Kat asked.

"I'm the youngest of six. I have five brothers."

"Wow. I can't even imagine."

"Yep, my childhood was pretty chaotic. My mother was a saint for putting up with all of our shenanigans."

Kat's phone chimed. "That'll be Bridget. Speaking of chaotic families, Bridget invited me to join hers for dessert. Is it okay if I go, Mom?"

"Yes, sweet pea, as soon as you thank our gracious host."

"Absolutely. Thanks, Ms. O. Dinner was fantastic." Kat jumped up to grab her coat from the closet.

"You're welcome, kiddo. Say hi to Bridget and her mom for me," Sarah said, walking to the door with Lauren.

"Come give your mother a hug." Lauren embraced her daughter. "And be careful walking over there."

"I will, Mom—it's not far. Love you." Kat practically skipped out the door.

"Somebody seems pretty happy," Sarah observed with a smile.

"Yes, she does. It sure is nice to see."

"So," Lauren said, surveying the remains of their dinner, "would you like me to wash or dry?"

"Oh, you don't have to do that. You're my guest." Sarah waved off the offer.

Speaking slowly and sternly, Lauren repeated, "Would you like me to wash, or dry?"

"Ooh, don't use that mommy voice on me. It's intimidating," Sarah said, feigning fear.

"That's kind of the point," Lauren replied with a grin, loving their playful banter.

"Fine, you can dry. There won't be too much once I load the dishwasher."

Sarah put three CDs in her changer, and they worked together companionably to a mish-mash of The Cranberries, KT Tunstall, and Amy Macdonald.

"I love all these Celtic female singers," Lauren said.

"Me, too. Great voices."

Lauren reached for the serving bowl that Sarah was rinsing, accidentally grabbing her finger. "Oops, sorry," she said, very conscious of their close proximity as they touched. She felt so comfortable, so easy with Sarah, and that awareness made her feel a rush of warmth.

Lauren suddenly had the urge to learn more about her. "So, tell me, Ms. O, what do you do with your free time when you're not at work?"

"Well, I volunteer at the animal shelter every week, and in the warm weather I grow vegetables out back and sell them at the farmers' market. Nothing else particularly exciting, I'm afraid."

"But what's your favorite rainy day hobby?"

Sarah tilted her head and smiled. "I don't think anyone has ever asked me that before. Hmm, I'd love to say that I do something super creative, like quilting or painting, but I guess for me, it'd be word games."

Lauren just stared. "Shut up. Did you just say word games?"

"Yeah. Why?"

"Because I just happen to be a word game master. I dare you to challenge me to a game of Scrabble."

"Oh, you're on, girl. I challenge your so-called mastery," Sarah said with a cocky grin. "Loser scrubs the roasting pan." She went to a cupboard to retrieve her Scrabble board.

Lauren tossed her dish towel on the counter. "Bring it."

❖

Forty-five minutes and several dictionary verifications later, Lauren was five points ahead. Sarah thought she'd had it in the bag until Lauren played *zephyr* on a triple word score.

"I can't do anything with this stupid *C*, so I reluctantly concede defeat," Sarah said dramatically.

"Well, since you were a very worthy opponent, I'll give you a chance to redeem yourself. Best out of three?"

"Absolutely. I was just getting warmed up," Sarah replied as she flipped over the letter tiles.

"Speaking of warm, I'm getting a bit overheated in this sweater." Lauren removed her baby blue cashmere cardigan to reveal a sleeveless cream silk shell and gorgeously defined arms.

Sarah bit her lip. *Lord have mercy.*

Trying not to stare, Sarah made light of her jolt of arousal by joking. "I have to ask—how does one get Greek goddess arms like yours? Good genes, or hard work?"

Lauren flushed and self-consciously glanced down at her arms. "Um, neither, really. And I'm certainly not in the Greek goddess category. I guess I've gotten kind of strong over the years by lugging my camera equipment."

"Camera equipment?"

"Wow, we've never discussed what I do for a living, have we? I'm a photographer. Freelance and portraits, at your service."

"That's so cool. I had wondered if you were just independently wealthy or something."

"I wish." Lauren snorted. "I took a leave of absence from my portrait studio job, but I have been looking for freelance work online lately."

A thought suddenly occurred to Sarah. "Hey, we were planning to hire someone to take photos at the Sweetheart Dance. Would you be interested?"

"Sure, sounds like fun."

"Good. So now that we've taken care of that, there's a game here I need to get back to winning."

"Shall I pour the wine? This may take a while," Lauren said with a smile.

By nine p.m., the two women had played several more games, consumed round two of Thanksgiving dinner, finished the bottle of cranberry wine and some pumpkin pie, and were now sprawled on opposite ends of Sarah's couch.

"I don't wanna move," Lauren said sleepily. Fiona had curled up on her lap and was sound asleep. Sarah watched the two, deciding that she very much liked the looks of Lauren all comfy on her couch.

Lauren was gazing at the fireplace. "Tell me about your pictures up there."

"Well, that's my brothers and me on St. Paddy's Day a couple of years ago," Sarah said, pointing at the group photo. "We were at a pub after the parade in Syracuse."

"And you're toasting with a glass of…?"

"Yes, root beer," Sarah said, sticking her tongue out at Lauren. "And those are my nieces and nephews when they were younger." She looked down then, not really wanting to continue.

After a moment, Lauren said, "That wooden frame is so beautiful. It caught my eye the moment I walked in. The craftsmanship is exquisite."

Sarah looked at Lauren, who was smiling warmly. "The woman in the photo made it."

Lauren said softly, "Looks like she's pretty special to you."

Sarah took a deep breath, then looked Lauren in the eye. "That's Kris. She was…my wife." She watched as Lauren looked away, digesting this new information.

Finally, Lauren again met her eyes. "You must have loved her very much."

At that moment, Sarah's heart swelled with gratitude. Lauren had not passed judgment or changed the subject. Rather, she had taken the news in stride and focused on the truth that the photo conveyed.

"Yes, I did. She died nearly four years ago now. Aneurism. We were together for nine years, and just like that, she was gone."

Lauren reached over and patted Sarah's leg. "I'm so sorry. That must've been awful for you."

"Yeah, it was pretty rough. For months it was all I could do to get out of bed."

"I remember that feeling. When my parents were killed, I just wanted to curl up in a corner and stay there," Lauren said.

"I know. It's never easy to lose a loved one, but when it happens suddenly, I think it's worse. Not having a chance to say goodbye really sucks."

"Agreed," Lauren said with a nod, then went back to gazing at the fire. After several more minutes, she shook herself. "I'd better get going before I can't move. Wine always makes me sleepy."

Sarah nodded. "Ditto. I told you I was a lightweight in the drinking department. That wine was surprisingly good, but the third glass did me in."

"Well, luckily, you only have to travel down the hall. I have to find the energy to get up and drive home. I told Kat I wanted her back by ten," Lauren said, yawning.

Sarah stood, gently removed the sleeping Fiona from Lauren's lap, and reached down to pull Lauren up. Lauren clasped her hand, and Sarah felt a jolt. She held Lauren's hand a tad longer than necessary, but Lauren didn't seem to notice.

"Here, let me get your coat," Sarah said, feeling suddenly nervous. Lauren followed her, and as she turned from the closet, Sarah found herself quickly wrapped in a warm hug.

"Thank you, Sarah, for opening your home to Kat and me and giving us a lovely Thanksgiving. I can't remember when I've had such a good time."

Sarah gave Lauren a quick squeeze and pulled back, not trusting herself, because if she was being honest, she wanted to hold Lauren and not let go. "It was my pleasure, and thank you for not letting me spend the day alone, either. This was really fun. Perhaps we can do it again and, you know, break out the Boggle."

"That's a deal," Lauren replied. "But be forewarned. I cut my word-game teeth on Boggle."

"So noted." Sarah held the door as Lauren stepped out into the night. "Be careful going home."

"Will do. Thanks again," Lauren said with a wave, and then she was in her car and gone.

Sarah stood in the doorway for several moments, until the chilly night air drove her back inside. She looked around the room, listening to the silence and feeling very much alone.

As Lauren drove home, she pondered the new revelation about Sarah, which made her feel inexplicably intrigued. No, that was the wrong word. Maybe she was just interested in getting to know more about a new friend. She already knew Sarah was warm, kind, and funny, but now that they'd spent such an enjoyable time together, she found Sarah even more interesting. Lauren was feeling kind of tingly, low in her belly. Must be the wine. The fact that Sarah was a lesbian had absolutely nothing to do with it.

Chapter Twelve

Sarah sat back in her chair with a sigh, pinching the bridge of her nose in an attempt to ward off her building migraine. It had been a hell of a day. In addition to being the busiest month for college applications, December had had its share of kids in crisis. Sarah didn't know if it was a version of Murphy's Law or what, but something serious always seemed to come in the door about an hour before work ended on Friday afternoon.

As Sarah gathered her things to leave, over an hour later than she had intended, her cell phone chimed. *Pizza, wings, and root beer—you up for it?* the text read. Lauren. Sarah smiled, feeling her stress slide away at just that simple communication.

Since Thanksgiving, Sarah's friendship with Lauren had solidified and grown. They talked and texted frequently, but they hadn't really hung out since the holiday. Although she was tired, Sarah felt her spirits lift significantly at the thought of spending time with her. Lauren's company always had a way of making everything better.

She replied, *I'm there. What time?*

My place at 6. 134 Timber Lane.

Things were looking up.

Snow had begun to fall as Sarah pulled into Lauren's driveway. A penetrating cold wind made her shiver as she walked up to the front door and knocked. Despite the chill, Sarah felt a flush of warmth when Lauren greeted her with a radiant smile.

"Get in here. It's freezing," Lauren said, ushering Sarah in the door.

"Yeah, that wind is brutal tonight," Sarah agreed, shrugging out of her coat. This was her first time in Lauren's home, and she looked around at the simply furnished living room. There was a dove-gray sofa and matching chair, a TV on a dark wood stand, and built-in bookcases on either side of a gray stone gas fireplace. A few books and framed photos sat on the otherwise empty shelves. A couple of afghans and a plush throw rug in jewel tones of blue, purple, and green lent color to the décor.

"This room is fantastic. I love the hardwoods and the fireplace, and the colors really suit you." Sarah looked at Lauren, who was wearing that gorgeous blue cashmere sweater that matched her eyes. Her dark hair was down and fell to her shoulders in soft waves. She was beautiful.

"Thanks. It's pretty sparse, I know. We didn't bring much with us from Alabama, but I wanted to make it as homey as I could for Kat."

"Well, you succeeded," Sarah responded, bringing a smile to Lauren's face with her praise. *God, that smile*, Sarah thought, feeling warm. "Speaking of Kat, where is she tonight? No, wait, let me guess—Bridget's?"

Lauren laughed. "Bingo. Those two are inseparable, which still amazes me. Kat was so scared to trust anybody. I never thought she'd let someone in like she did Bridget."

"Well, Bridget is a very special young woman. Kat's lucky to have her as a friend."

"She has you to thank for that. I don't think she ever would have acclimated so easily if you hadn't introduced them."

"I'm glad. So, how was your week?" Sarah asked, taking a seat on the sofa.

"Good. I landed a freelance job."

"Great—what kind of job?"

"It's for a local magazine called *Finger Lakes Living*, and they're looking for photos of winter around the lakes."

"Fantastic. You should be able to get a lot of terrific shots."

"I was going to ask if you had any ideas of locations I could check out. I haven't lived around here in so long, and I don't want to miss anything good," Lauren said.

"There are tons of things we could do," Sarah mused.

We're a we *now, are we?* Ignoring the intrusive thought, Sarah rattled off her ideas as they came to her. "Sunset at the pier on Seneca Lake, the vineyards, maybe the pavilion in Skaneateles, oh, and Belhurst Castle. And of course pretty nature shots, like snow on pine trees. And we can't forget birds. You could probably get great pictures of cardinals and chickadees right in my backyard."

Lauren laughed. "Such enthusiasm. I'm going to have to hire you for your creative input."

"We could just drive around on the weekends looking for the money shots," Sarah offered, laughing, too.

"Great. Wanna start tomorrow? Looks like we won't have to go far," Lauren said, looking out the window. The snow was coming down more heavily, and there were already a couple of inches on the ground. A car was making its way down the street, then suddenly pulled into her driveway. "I think the food's here."

"What can I contribute?" Sarah asked, reaching for her purse.

"Nothing. My treat. It's the least I can do for your future photographic assistance." Lauren met the delivery guy at the door, paid him, and brought their dinner to a two-person bistro table in the kitchen. "Come eat. I didn't think to ask what you like on your pizza, so I got the basics. Half cheese, half pepperoni. And the wings are mild charbroiled."

"You might as well have asked, because this is *exactly* what I would have ordered," Sarah said, meeting Lauren's eyes with a smile. "And you got it from my favorite place, too. Best wings in New York."

"Well then, dig in," Lauren replied, holding Sarah's gaze for an extra beat. "I'll get the root beer."

They attacked their meal with gusto and the occasional moan. They were so at ease in each other's company, like they'd been friends for years. This development was not lost on Sarah. She hadn't spent this much time with anyone outside of work, other than

Jamie, since…well, since Kris had died. Something about Lauren reached into a place she hadn't paid attention to in a long time. She felt like she was waking up from a long, boring, monochromatic dream to a world full of excitement and color. But what if it was all just her imagination?

Lauren broke Sarah's silence. "Everything okay?"

"Yes, sorry," Sarah said, giving her head a shake and instantly regretting it. "I've been fighting off a migraine all day, but it seems to be winning."

Lauren immediately jumped into action. "Come on, let's get you out into the living room. I can dim the lights." She led Sarah to the couch. "Here, lie down. I'll be right back."

Sarah wanted to protest, but she was suddenly so very tired. And honestly, it felt really good to be fussed over. She lay back with her head on the plush arm of the couch and closed her eyes. She opened them a moment later, just as Lauren returned with a towel-wrapped ice pack, which she placed at the back of Sarah's head.

"Thanks. These headaches kick my butt sometimes," Sarah said, grateful for the help.

"I've had migraines before. They're the worst. Do you get them a lot?"

"Probably two or three times a month. Today was a pretty stressful day, though." Sarah recounted all that had transpired at work. While she talked, Lauren knelt beside the couch and began gently rubbing Sarah's forehead, eliciting a soft groan.

"This is where they get me," Lauren said quietly. "Right above my eyes. Same with you?"

Sarah nodded slightly. "Mm, yeah…that feels good." A blessed lassitude replaced the tension.

With Sarah's eyes closed, Lauren took the opportunity to study her face. Her features were relaxed, full lips slightly parted. A light smattering of freckles dusted her nose and cheeks, and her soft hair shone like burnished copper in the light from the fire. Lauren had never looked at another woman so closely before, and she was acutely aware of all the finest details of Sarah's lovely face. She felt a surge of tenderness for the woman before her and then, inexplicably, a stronger wave, desire. As she stared at Sarah's lips, she wondered what it would be like to kiss them. Startled at this line of thought, Lauren looked up to find Sarah's green eyes gazing back at her. Caught, Lauren felt her heart jump but didn't break eye contact. A look of understanding passed between them, an awareness that something had shifted. And just as quickly, Sarah sat up.

"Thanks, Lauren. That really did the trick."

Lauren sat back on her heels. "Do you feel better?"

"Definitely. I've never tried using an ice pack before. It really took the edge off," Sarah replied, looking everywhere but at Lauren.

Feeling suddenly awkward, Lauren stood up. *What the hell just happened?*

"The roads are probably a bit messy," Sarah continued. "I'd better get home. Thanks so much for dinner. This was a very good way to end such a crazy week."

Disappointed that Sarah wanted to leave, Lauren asked, "Do you still want to go photo-hunting with me tomorrow?"

"Sure. I've got early dog-walking duty at the shelter in the morning, but I'll be done by nine thirty. How about I pick you up at, say, ten o'clock? Snow's supposed to let up by dawn, so the plows should have the roads cleared by then."

"Sounds great. Be careful driving home," Lauren said, as Sarah put on her coat.

"Will do, and thanks again." Sarah reached out and gave Lauren a quick hug, then headed out into the cold. Lauren watched her brush off her car, then drive off. She stood looking out at the snow for a long time, trying to make sense of her jumbled emotions. The pull she had felt toward Sarah stunned her with its strength. *I wanted to kiss her. What does that even mean? Okay, so she was hurting and I wanted to help. And she has been so kind and supportive, so of course I feel affection for her.* Even as her mind ticked through these rationalizations, Lauren's body, humming with arousal, told a different story.

❖

Sarah drove home slowly, but her thoughts raced. She knew she was attracted to Lauren, but that was something she would never act on. Lauren was the parent of one of her students, for God's sake, and a very vulnerable student at that. Because Kat had enough to deal with, Sarah couldn't go complicating things, and she had been pretty confident in her ability to keep her attraction hidden. What she had never seen coming, however, was that flash of desire in Lauren's eyes.

You've really stepped in it now, she thought.

Sarah thumped her gloved palms on the steering wheel. "Damn."

CHAPTER THIRTEEN

The next morning dawned clear and cold. Sarah stopped to pick up coffee on her way to Lauren's, as much to wake up as to warm up, since she had slept fitfully the night before. She was kind of hoping she had imagined the electricity between them; if she hadn't, things were going to get complicated. Sarah was bound and determined to focus on the friendship she had developed with Lauren, which had come to mean so much to her.

When she pulled up to the house, Kat was outside shoveling the last of the snow from the driveway.

"Hey there, kiddo," she greeted the young woman. "Hope you haven't frozen anything vital out here."

"You and me both. My feet are numb," Kat grumbled. "Mom says you guys are going to go take pictures of snow. I don't know why you have to go anywhere. There's plenty right here." With a sarcastic grin, she pointed to the snow pile she'd made.

"You've got it all wrong," Sarah teased. "The idea is to take pictures of pretty things that just happen to be covered with snow."

"Well, in that case, we'd better go hunting for those winning shots," Lauren said as she stepped out the front door. She was lugging a bulky camera bag and another equipment case.

"Here, let me help you with that," Sarah offered, reaching for the case.

"Thanks." Lauren flashed that smile that made Sarah's heart skip a beat.

Oh my good God, Sarah said to herself, watching Lauren walk ahead of her to the car. *This is not going to be easy.*

❖

As they headed down the Thruway to Geneva and Seneca Lake, Lauren asked Sarah about where they should spend their time and the types of photographic subjects they could try to find. Sarah had a wealth of great ideas, and Lauren was having as much fun watching Sarah's enthusiasm as she was taking pictures. By early afternoon, they'd been to several different locations, and Lauren's stomach was growling.

"Are you hungry?" she asked.

"I am." Sarah nodded as she drove. "I brought some lunch along—wasn't sure if you'd want to take the time to eat at a restaurant. It's in that cooler in the backseat."

"You're so good to me," Lauren said as she reached back for the cooler. Looking at Sarah, she noticed that her cheeks were pink and dimpled with a smile. Sarah glanced over then and caught her eye. As Sarah's blush deepened, Lauren felt heat rise in her own cheeks. She quickly looked away and busied herself with the cooler's contents.

"Cheese, crackers, fruit, turkey sandwiches…you packed us quite a feast. Thank you," Lauren said, popping a grape into her mouth.

"No problem. I'm going to pull over here so we can eat," Sarah replied, turning into the driveway of a public library. "We can go in and use their restroom afterward before we do more sightseeing."

"Sounds like a plan." Lauren unwrapped a sandwich and handed it to Sarah. "This has been so much fun. You're a great photography assistant."

"Thanks. I've had a wonderful time with you, too."

As Sarah took her sandwich, she met Lauren's eyes for a long moment. It was as if someone had turned the heater on full blast in the car. Lauren felt the intensity of that look *everywhere*. Sarah cleared her throat and looked away, leaving Lauren both baffled and aroused.

"I'm going to check what we've gotten so far," she said, needing to focus on something other than the woman sitting mere inches away. Lauren flipped through the pictures on her digital camera. They had gotten several good shots of Belhurst Castle and its surrounding grounds, as well as cardinals in a tree and a lucky view of a fox stepping gingerly through the snow in an open field. After they finished their lunch and took a bathroom break, she showed Sarah.

"You've got a talented eye there, Lauren," Sarah said, oohing and aahing over the different scenes. "Let's go find more."

Lauren laughed. "Drive on." They headed around the lake to the state park, where they were able to capture dozens of examples of nature in all its snow-covered beauty.

As the December sky shifted from blue to rose, they watched the sunset, happy with how productive the day had been. The afternoon had warmed up to nearly forty degrees, but as evening approached, it was getting colder. As Sarah looked out on the water, Lauren couldn't resist taking a few photographs of her. She looked adorable in her wool peacoat and bright multicolored scarf, with her cheeks all rosy from the cold and her hair peeking out from beneath her knit cap.

Sarah turned and caught her, flushing red. "There had better not be pictures of me on there," she scolded, pointing a gloved finger at the camera.

"Hey, I'm a photographer. I have to shoot anything and everything that catches my eye," Lauren said with a grin.

Whether the meaning Sarah took from those words was intended or not, she suddenly felt warm all over. "We'd better go. It's a bit of a walk back to the parking area."

As they walked, Lauren said, "Thanks so much for coming with me today. It was such a gorgeous day, and I think I've gotten several really nice shots for the photo series."

"It was fun," Sarah replied. "Looking for photo-worthy subjects made me pay a lot more attention to the details of everything. Winter really is beautiful." *All the more so when I can share it with such a stunning woman*, Sarah thought.

"Yes, it is. I missed this when I was down South." Her voice had taken on a melancholy tone, and Sarah glanced at her face, noting the sadness etched there. She said nothing, but wrapped an arm around Lauren's shoulders and gave her an affectionate squeeze. Lauren offered a tiny smile, remaining quiet as they walked the final distance to the car.

Sarah warmed up the car and got them on their way. Once they were back on the Thruway, she broke the silence. "Are you okay?"

Lauren sighed and looked at her booted feet. "Trent called last night."

"Ah," Sarah replied, now understanding Lauren's sudden change in mood.

"He told me that my little vacation had lasted long enough, and that it was time to get my ass back home. I think he was well on his way to drunk, because the more I tried to talk, the angrier he got."

"I'm sorry, honey." Sarah wished she could knock that man out for how he made Lauren feel. "What did you do?"

"I told him that clearly nothing had changed on his end, and that Kat and I are doing fine right where we are. He started f-bombing me, so I hung up on him."

"Good for you," Sarah said, internally applauding.

"Then why do I feel like shit?" Lauren was obviously torn up by the exchange she had had with her husband.

"Oh, Lauren, who ever expects to be in this position, to have to deal with what you're going through? You are a kind, caring person. If you didn't feel like shit, I'd be worried."

Lauren sighed. "Thank you for saying that. It's just that I'm so disappointed in Trent, you know? Why doesn't he see what he's doing to Kat? And to me?"

Sarah reached over and squeezed Lauren's hand. "From what you've told me, it sounds like he's got his own issues to work through, and that won't happen until he's ready." She reluctantly put her hand back on the steering wheel. "Are you happy here?" she asked quietly.

"You know, I really am, and that makes me feel guilty somehow. But when I see how well Kat is doing, I know I did the right thing."

"Then that's what you hold on to," Sarah said. "I'm a firm believer that everything happens for a reason. It'll all sort itself out in time."

"You're really good at keeping me grounded," Lauren said with a laugh, "but I don't know how you deal with listening to people's problems all the time."

"If I'm honest, it can be draining at times, but I figure if I can help even one person find their way, I'm doing my job." Sarah smiled ruefully. "There are definitely times, though, when I want to curl up with my cats and go off grid for a week."

"But that's because you're such a kind, caring person yourself," Lauren said, returning the compliment. "You're invested in your students, and you're a very good friend. I honestly don't know if I'd still be in New York if I hadn't had you to support me."

Sarah felt her face flush, becoming very aware of feelings she never thought she'd be having. She played it off with humor. "I think we can conclude this first meeting of the mutual admiration society, since we're home." She pulled into Lauren's driveway, grinning at her peal of laughter.

CHAPTER FOURTEEN

Sarah's next two weeks flew by as everyone seemed to be gearing up for the Christmas holiday. She was swamped at work, dealing with a flurry of college applications that would be due while school was on break. A significant portion of her days were spent sending transcripts and writing recommendation letters. One of those letters was for Kat Emerson.

Kat had decided to apply to several colleges in New York and wanted to major in art or graphic design. She had been putting in a lot of extra time with her art teacher to create a portfolio of her work, since she didn't have any of the pieces she had done while in Alabama. Sarah was impressed with Kat's motivation.

Recommendation letters were usually pretty easy for Sarah to write, but she was taking much longer than usual with Kat's. Although the young woman was smart and talented, there was still the issue of her junior year grades that had negatively affected her GPA. The discrepancy, while not severe, would be noticeable to colleges. Sarah wanted to make sure she adequately conveyed that the drop in grades was due to traumatic events, and that Kat was mature, resilient, and of excellent character.

As she reread what she had written, she heard a knock. Sarah turned in her chair to see Kat standing in the doorway. "Well, that's freaky. I was just thinking about you." Sarah motioned to her computer. "Working on your letter."

Kat nodded, looking uncomfortable. "Can I talk to you for a minute?"

"Of course," Sarah said, concerned at the look on Kat's face. "Have a seat, kiddo. What's up?"

Kat dropped into the chair, letting her backpack fall to the floor with a thud. She was silent for several long moments, and Sarah could see that she was trying not to cry. Finally, Kat looked up, took a deep breath, and began to speak.

"I know my mom told you about what happened last year."

Sarah nodded, hoping Kat wasn't upset.

"I'm glad, because now you'll understand. Last night at home, I was doing homework and Mom was putting laundry away. Her phone rang and she asked me to grab it. Like a dumbass, I just answered it without checking to see who it was. It was my dad."

"That was awkward for you?"

"Yeah, way awkward. I haven't talked to him in months." Kat fell silent.

Sarah watched the emotions flash across Kat's face, and noted her protective body language as she wrapped her arms tightly around herself. Sarah waited another few moments, then gently asked, "How did it go?"

Kat sighed and looked down at her shoes. "He was all nice at first, asking me how I was doing, what school was like. I answered his questions without saying too much. I guess it kind of pissed him off that I wasn't into the conversation, because then he started in on me." Kat's knee started bouncing up and down. "He said I needed to come back home and graduate with my class, and that everything had blown over and I needed to quit being a baby about it."

Kat looked at Sarah, her blue eyes shimmering with tears. "How can someone who's supposed to be my father, who I've lived with my entire life, know absolutely nothing about me? It's like he doesn't care about who I am or how I feel at all."

Sarah once again had the urge to throttle the man for being so clueless. "I don't know, hon. Sometimes parents don't live up to the way their kids need them to be."

Kat snorted. "No, it's because I'm not who he thinks *I* should be. Before we left Alabama, he was so horrible to me." A few tears escaped and slid down Kat's cheek. She wiped them away angrily. "Kids were harassing me, spreading rumors, and he sided with them. He said people wouldn't be calling me a dyke and a bitch unless I was acting like one!"

"Kat, you weren't the problem. Those kids and your father acted that way because of their own issues."

"Yeah, well, their issues hurt me, and I'm the one who had to run away to escape it all." Kat's tears had stopped, replaced by a flush of anger in her pale cheeks. "Not that I'm complaining. Even if my dad hadn't been such a jerk, I don't think I could have stayed there."

Sarah was relieved Kat was willing to talk about and process the trauma she'd experienced. Her therapist must have been helping, because Kat had a very mature level of insight about the whole ordeal. "Kat, can I ask you a question?"

"Sure," Kat replied, seeming calmer.

"Are you happy here?"

Kat looked at Sarah, and a smile tugged at her lips. "I didn't think I'd be, but I really am. I like it here." Then the smile disappeared. "Why do I feel guilty?"

"Well, that's a tough question. Why do you think you feel guilty?"

Kat thought about it. "I don't know. Maybe I feel like it's weird that I left everything behind and it was easy. I don't miss things, or people, like I should."

"I don't think it's weird at all," Sarah replied. "You had a bad experience there, with those people, and you needed a fresh start." Kat nodded. "You know what I've found over the years? Sometimes our worst experiences open doors for us we never would have found otherwise."

And what open doors have you *walked through lately?* Sarah shook off the thought.

Kat seemed to be contemplating Sarah's comment, and her smile returned, along with a slight blush. Sarah would've bet money she was thinking of Bridget.

"Yeah, I think you may be right, Ms. O," she said. "And my mom seems happier, too. I think this move was good for both of us."

Sarah was glad to hear it. "So, what about school? Everything going okay?"

"Yep. Trig class is kicking my behind, but I'm getting through it. I love my art classes, and Mr. Baker is helping me do extra pieces for my college portfolio."

"Speaking of college, have you finished your activity sheet and questionnaire? I need those to finish your recommendation letter," Sarah said.

"Almost done. Can I give them to you tomorrow at True Colors?"

"Absolutely."

"Oh," Kat said, as she stood to leave, "that's another thing I love about being here. True Colors is awesome." She flashed a smile. "Thanks for talking with me, Ms. O. Bye."

"Anytime, kiddo," Sarah called after her. She was smiling to herself when Mrs. Hayden popped her head in the door.

"It sure is nice to see that lovely girl smiling. Quite a change from the first day, hmm?"

"Yes," Sarah agreed, "quite a change."

❖

"All right, woman," Jamie said, plopping down on a chair in Sarah's office. "I've got fifteen minutes before my prep period ends. Let's talk Christmas break."

Sarah smirked. "What about Christmas break?"

"Well, since I bailed on you and cruised the high seas at Thanksgiving, I have to make it up to you. I'm thinking epic shopping trip to hit the day-after sales, followed by a massage at the spa. Then you have to reserve a night for us so we can have you over for dinner."

"Ooh, you had me at massage," Sarah said with a grin. "I'm trying to make arrangements for getting together with my family, but otherwise, I'm pretty much available. My brother John invited all of us to spend Christmas with his family in Philly, so I'll probably drive down right after we get out of school. Hope the weather is decent, because it's a lousy drive in snow."

"Need me to check in on the cats for you?"

"Actually, someone else is going to do it for me," Sarah said, feeling a little flustered. Anyone else might never have noticed, but she feared Jamie knew her too well.

"Someone else, eh? And who is this someone else that's getting you all pink in the cheeks?"

"Oh, stop. It's not like that," Sarah said. At Jamie's raised eyebrow, Sarah explained, "You know Kat, right? Well, when she and her mom came over for Thanksgiving, she fell in love with my cats. When I mentioned to her mom that I was going away for a couple of days, she offered Kat's pet sitting services."

Jamie just stared. "Hold it right there, sister. Kat and her mom spent Thanksgiving with you? And you neglected to mention this to me?"

"We mostly talked about your cruise when you got back, remember?"

"Well, if I had known you had such exciting news…"

"It was no big deal. They were new in town and alone, so I offered," Sarah said, trying to play it off with a shrug. It didn't work. Jamie was like a bloodhound on a scent.

"I beg to differ, honey. This is a very big deal, huge even. You have done very little in the way of socializing since Kris died. I am surprised, but absolutely thrilled you took that step."

No one had been more surprised than Sarah. She had invited a virtual stranger to her home, but it hadn't been a difficult decision. She just felt at ease with Lauren, more than she had with anyone else in a long, long time.

"I've gotta say, though," Jamie continued, "giving your house key to someone you've only known for four months is definitely not like you."

Sarah sighed. "I can't explain it, Jamie. You know how you can just get a feeling about someone? I know Lauren and Kat are good people." She shrugged.

"Well, you're generally a good judge of character, so I'm sure it'll be fine. Just hide your valuables," Jamie teased.

"What valuables?" Sarah scoffed, but she was smiling now.

"So anyway, do you want me to book a spa day?"

She was thankful Jamie had changed the subject. "Absolutely. I'll be home from my brother's by the twenty-eighth, so let's shoot for then."

"Will do," Jamie said, jumping up just as the bell rang. She walked out, then turned and poked her head back in the door. "Later, you can tell me all about that blush." She winked, chuckling as she left.

Sarah tried to feel indignant, but all she could do was smile.

On the last day of school before break, Sarah left work as soon as she could. Thanks to the good weather and clear roads, she made it to her brother's house in record time. As she popped the trunk of her car to retrieve her bags, her brother's loud voice boomed from the front door.

"Boo!" John came over and enveloped his sister in a huge bear hug, lifting her off the ground.

Sarah grunted. "Thanks, Johnny. Now I don't have to see my chiropractor for another month," she said with a grin. "But you can put me down now. Am I ever going to outgrow that nickname?" Sarah's brothers had dubbed her *Boo* when she was a toddler and had always tried to sneak up and scare everyone.

"Not a chance. How you been, Sis?" John grabbed Sarah's bags for her and headed for the house.

"Good. Same old, same old. How about you?"

"Can't complain, and who would listen if I did?"

"Right?" Sarah laughed in agreement. As they entered the front door, Sarah was tackled by three warm pajama-clad bodies.

"Aunt Boo!" her nephews yelled in unison.

Sarah squatted down and hugged the boys. "My goodness, are you sure I'm in the right house? These boys are way too grown up to be my nephews."

The boys giggled. "'Course you're in the right house, silly," said Hunter, the oldest. "I'm not so big. I'm only eight."

"And I'm five," hollered Toby, jumping in a circle around Sarah. She felt a tug on her sleeve and looked down into the solemn brown eyes of little Connor. He held up three fingers.

"You're three?" she said to him, feigning disbelief. He nodded, then snuggled in for another hug. Sarah's heart melted, and she mentally chastised herself for not visiting more often.

"Boys, give Aunt Boo a chance to get in the door," said Sarah's sister-in-law, Linda, shooing them away with a dish towel. Sarah straightened and gave Linda a hug. "How was your drive?"

"Actually pretty easy. The traffic wasn't bad at all. I'm sure it'll be worse tomorrow, so I guess it was good I came down tonight."

"Well, the boys insisted on staying up until you got here. Connor's practically asleep on his feet."

"I've got this," Sarah said, handing her coat to Linda. "Okay, boys, front and center." The boys ran over and lined up, grinning. "Now, who's got his jammies on?" Three hands went up. "Who has brushed his teeth?" Again, three hands. "And gone potty?" Two hands went up; Toby's hand flew to his mouth and he scampered off to the bathroom. He returned quickly, and Sarah continued. "Now, have Mommy and Daddy gotten their hugs and kisses?" The boys ran over to their parents to bestow their affection, then ran back to stand at attention. "All right then. I think we're ready. Let's march."

"God, I wish you were here every night," Linda said in playful exasperation.

Sarah marched down the hall to the boys' bedrooms, and they followed dutifully behind. After two bedtime stories and a dozen more hugs, Sarah finally emerged. "They're down. Connor and Hunter are already asleep, and Toby's close behind." She flopped down on the couch, exhausted.

"So, Sarah," Linda said, handing her a cold bottle of root beer, "how are you?" It was a simple enough question, but Sarah knew there were a dozen layers to it. Linda was like the older sister she'd never had, and she was protective as hell.

"I'm fine. Work's busy, of course. I'm still volunteering at the animal shelter every weekend, too." She smiled to herself, thinking of a secret she'd been keeping. "But otherwise, there's nothing earth-shattering going on. What about you guys?"

"Remember the promotion I told you about a couple of weeks ago?" John asked. "Well, you're looking at the new production manager of the medical supplies division."

"Oh, Johnny, that's great. Congratulations." Her brother had been busting his butt at the same manufacturing company for years. A management position was long overdue and well deserved.

"Couldn't have come at a better time," Linda said quietly, smiling at John and rubbing her belly. He just looked back at her with a silly grin on his face, then pulled her into a none-too-chaste kiss.

Sarah stared at them for a moment, her heart aching in the face of such obvious adoration. Then the realization hit her. "No way— you're pregnant?"

Linda nodded, and Sarah let out a whoop.

"Quiet. You'll wake the boys." Linda shushed her, giggling softly.

"When did you find out?"

"Just a few days ago. You're the first one we've told."

"Wow, I'm so excited for you. Maybe this time, you'll get the baby girl you've been hoping for," Sarah said, giving them both a hug.

"I don't care as long as the baby's healthy," Linda said aloud, but behind John's back, she held up crossed fingers and winked at Sarah.

The three stayed up late, catching up on each other's lives. It was after midnight when Sarah finally retired to the guest bedroom. After getting ready for bed, she plugged her phone in to charge and noticed a text from Lauren. She opened the message eagerly. *The kitties are fed and watered for the night, and all is well at the house. Hope you had a safe trip. Have a Merry Christmas.*

Even though Sarah was exhausted, she sent back a response. *Thanks. Arrived safely around 8:30, heading to bed now. A Merry Christmas to you, too.*

Her phone chimed almost immediately with a reply. It was a kitty emoji wearing a Santa hat. Sarah fell asleep with a smile on her face.

❖

The next two days flew by. Sarah's other siblings showed up on Christmas Eve morning, and it was controlled chaos from then on. They resurrected a couple of childhood traditions, like making gingerbread houses and driving around after dark to check out other people's lights and decorations. The kids all had a blast with their cousins, and the grownups soaked up as much togetherness as they could, knowing it would be quite a while before they'd all see each other again.

Although Christmas Eve and Christmas morning had been full of laughter, food, and fun, Sarah felt a niggling sense of melancholy she couldn't shake. She loved her brothers and their wives dearly, and they were very loving in return, but the fact remained she was solo. The holidays were still hard without Kris, and when she found herself tearing up, she escaped outside to the back deck for a few moments of fresh air and solitude.

"There you are," Linda said, coming to stand beside her at the deck rail.

"Sorry. I needed a minute. It was like a gift tornado went through in there."

"You got that right. The kids have been given the job of cleaning up every scrap of wrapping paper, and your brothers are trying to free all the toys from their packaging."

"Well, I'm usually on battery insertion detail, so I'd better go back in," Sarah said, turning toward the house.

"Wait a minute." Linda put a hand on Sarah's arm. "Are you all right, honey?"

Sarah waved off the question. "I'm fine. It's just, you know, everybody all together is a bit overwhelming."

"True, but am I wrong to think there's something else bothering you?" Linda asked gently.

Sarah turned away as tears threatened again. She was silent for several moments, then felt Linda's arms encircling her from behind. Sarah leaned her head back on her sister-in-law's shoulder. "When will it get easier, Lin? Just when I think I'm doing okay, something happens and the grief just punches me in the gut again."

"Oh, honey. Grief is an unpredictable beast, isn't it?" Linda said. Sarah nodded. "Of course, the holidays are always rough when you've lost someone. My mom died twelve years ago, and I still miss her terribly."

"I know I'll always miss Kris, but that's not the problem. It's like I feel stuck. I can't seem to find the same motivation to do all the things I used to do."

"Well, are you doing *anything* besides work?" Linda asked.

Sarah sighed. "I advise a club after school, and I volunteer at the SPCA, but that's about it. Kris and I did so much together, but I don't feel like doing those same things alone."

"What about friends?" Linda asked.

"People have invited me out, or to join a book club and things like that, but I haven't really hung out with anyone but my friend Jamie."

Hey, now, that's not completely true. Sarah thought of Lauren.

Linda turned Sarah around to face her. "If Kris were here right now, what would she say?"

Sarah snorted. "She'd tell me to put on my big girl panties and move on. She was always really good at getting me to do things I didn't think I could do."

"Maybe," Linda suggested, "she is still trying."

Sarah was silent, thinking about Linda's words. Then she reached out and gave the other woman a hug. "Thanks for coming out here to check on me, Lin. It does help to talk about things."

Linda laughed. "Well, I would hope you'd feel that way, Miss Counselor Lady!"

Sarah slapped Linda's arm playfully. "Go on inside where it's warm. I'll be along in a minute."

After Linda left, Sarah leaned again on the deck rail and gazed out over the backyard. Kris's face flashed through her mind. "I miss you, Krissy," she whispered, as she began to softly weep, "but I know I've got to get back to living. Maybe you could put in a good word for me on your side, because I'm gonna need help." Sarah was startled by the next image that entered her mind: Lauren's smiling blue eyes.

CHAPTER FIFTEEN

The school break was half over by the time Sarah got back home. After the spa day with Jamie, she had taken a day for herself, to just relax in her jammies and read or putter around the house. Today, however, she had invited Lauren and Kat over once again, to thank them for cat sitting but also to give them a gift for Christmas. She was a nervous wreck about the gift, as she didn't know how it would be received, but something had told her to go for it anyway.

A knock sounded on the door, and Sarah jumped up from the couch to answer it. She grinned broadly when she laid eyes on Lauren, who looked stunning in her deep blue winter coat, hair spilling over her shoulders.

"Hey there." She hugged Lauren before inquiring, "Where's Kat?"

"She dropped me off because she has a job interview. She got a call yesterday, and they asked her to come in," Lauren replied, shedding her coat. "It's at the frozen yogurt place in the mall."

"Fantastic. Go on in and sit down. Can I get you anything to drink? Water, juice, hot chocolate?"

"Ooh, hot chocolate sounds fabulous," Lauren replied. "With marshmallows?"

Sarah laughed. "Is there any other way?"

With hot mugs in hand, they settled on the couch.

"Thanks again for taking care of my girls," Sarah said, pointing to the two mounds of gray fur curled up by the fireplace.

"It was no trouble at all. Kat absolutely loved doing it. Oh, and before I forget, here's your key."

"Thanks," Sarah said, accidently brushing Lauren's fingers as she took the item. She shivered a little at the contact.

Lauren seemed not to notice. "So, how was Christmas at your brother's?"

"Wonderful. I had a lot of fun hanging out with everyone. It was the first time we'd all been together in quite a long time. All the kids have grown so much. I couldn't believe it. How about you?"

"Different, but good. Kat and I got a tree and some new ornaments to decorate our place. And we made our favorite cookies. Did you find the tin of them I left on your counter?"

Sarah nodded. "Yes, thank you. I've sampled several already."

"Kat is the main cookie maker. I was worried she wouldn't be into it this year, but she seemed fine. I cooked a ham, and we had a nice dinner. Then Bridget came over, and we all watched Hallmark movies until midnight."

"Oh my God, I think I've seen every Hallmark Christmas movie ever made," Sarah said. "I even watch them when they re-air in July."

"Wow, you are hardcore." Lauren laughed. She set her mug down near a magazine on the coffee table, then seemed to remember something. She took her phone from her pocket, pressed it a few times, and handed it to Sarah. "Take a look."

Lauren had brought up the online version of the magazine for which she'd done the photo spread. Sarah looked at the photos, reliving the day they had spent together. Beautiful pictures of Belhurst Castle, cardinals in a pine tree, and the red fox in the snow had made the cut, as well as others Lauren must have taken on a different day. The last photo was captioned *Sunset On Seneca Lake*. It was a lovely shot of Sarah in profile, gazing out on the rose-hued water.

"That one's my favorite," Lauren said at Sarah's shoulder.

Sarah smiled. "You're quite talented with a camera. You even managed to make me look good, which is no easy feat."

"Oh, stop. I happen to think you're very pretty," Lauren said, making Sarah's belly flutter. Lauren had stayed close beside her, and Sarah had a sudden urge to turn and kiss her. *Whoa.*

"Well, thanks," Sarah replied, standing abruptly. "I hope the magazine gives you more assignments. This one is terrific."

After they'd chatted and enjoyed each other's company for a while longer, Sarah decided it was time to present Lauren with her gift.

"So, I got you and Kat something for Christmas," Sarah said, nervousness returning.

"Oh, you didn't have to…What is it?" Lauren rubbed her hands together with childlike excitement.

Sarah laughed. "Hold on a sec," she said, retreating to her bedroom. "Close your eyes." She brought out the gift and placed it in Lauren's lap. Lauren's eyes flew open when she made contact with fur.

"Oh my goodness, look at you," she exclaimed, cuddling the tortoiseshell kitten. Her eyes filled with tears as she looked up at Sarah. "I can't believe you did this for us." The kitten had nuzzled up to Lauren's neck and was purring like a motorboat.

"I hope you're okay with me being so bold, but I had to do it. Her name is Gracie."

Lauren's eyes widened as she let out a sob, then stood to pull Sarah into a long hug, Gracie rumbling contentedly between them. "You remembered," she whispered, then planted a kiss on Sarah's cheek. "You are the sweetest person I've ever met."

Sarah's heart soared. "I'm so glad you're not upset with me. But look at her—I couldn't resist. She was just spayed last week, and she's had all her shots. I've got all the supplies you'll need to start out, too."

"Wow, wait until Kat finds out," Lauren said happily.

"Well, her interview ought to be over by now. Give her a call."

Lauren handed Gracie over to Sarah and texted her daughter. "I just said if she was finished at the mall, she needed to get over here."

That only gave Sarah a little while longer to soak up the beautiful sight of Lauren cuddling the kitten and smiling with joy. Her heart twinged a little as she thought of how much she missed Lauren when they weren't together. She couldn't resist putting her arm around Lauren's shoulder and petting Gracie.

"Isn't she beautiful?" Lauren asked, eyes shining.

"Yes, she is," Sarah replied, not at all referring to the kitten.

Twenty minutes later, Sarah answered the knock at her door. "Hi, Kat. Come on in."

"Hi. What's going on?" Kat said, looking around but not seeing her mother.

"Your mom's in the kitchen. She has something to show you."

"Um…okay," Kat said, clearly suspicious. She disappeared into the kitchen, and a few moments later, Sarah heard a shriek. She laughed as Kat ran back into the room to give her a hug.

"Ms. O, you are the best." Lauren had followed her daughter into the living room, holding Gracie. Kat took the kitten from her and proceeded to shower the little beastie with kisses and endearments. Sarah smiled at Kat's antics, then looked up to meet Lauren's bright, tear-filled eyes.

Thank you, Lauren mouthed to her, and the warmth passing between them very nearly weakened Sarah's knees.

You're welcome, she mouthed back. Then they joined Kat and Gracie in their cuddle fest on the floor. Kira and Fiona had stirred and were now sniffing the kitten with interest. Sarah observed the scene, conflicting emotions bombarding her.

Be careful. Dangerous waters ahead.

Sarah knew she should heed her mind's warning, but she was finally feeling engaged in life again. And it felt really, really good.

CHAPTER SIXTEEN

With the holidays over, Bridget felt herself speeding head-long toward midterm exams and the semester's end. She and Kat were feeling the stress and frequently commiserated over their workload.

"I swear these teachers get together and plan to hit us with ten papers or projects all at once," Bridget whined during one of their after-school study sessions. She ran her hands through her now blue-tipped blond hair and groaned.

"Right? It's a conspiracy," Kat agreed. "They tell us it's to prepare for college, but enough already."

"I've got three finals and three midterms in four days. My brain may explode," Bridget said dramatically.

Kat laughed. "You're the smartest person I know. I don't think you need to worry. I, however, am faced with a bunch of stupid Regents exams I have to pass to graduate. No pressure there." She pulled her long dark hair out of its ponytail, shook it out, then pulled it back again and refastened the hair tie. Bridget always got turned on when Kat did that, and she tried not to stare. Oblivious, Kat looked over at Gracie, who was sound asleep on the bed. "Why couldn't I have just been a cat?"

Bridget suddenly jumped up. "You'll be fine, but I think we need a break from all this. Wanna go get coffee?"

"With all of my heart and soul," Kat replied, and the girls headed off to the Tim Hortons around the corner from Kat's house.

When they entered the coffee shop, they encountered a group of kids from school. Bridget groaned inwardly, as the group included a couple of girls who were not particularly nice.

True to form, they took the opportunity to start shit.

"Hey, Bridget," one of the girls said with a sneer, "when are you going to introduce us to your girlfriend?"

Bridget felt Kat stiffen beside her.

"Just ignore them," Bridget said under her breath, and she placed herself between Kat and the group.

"Oh, look. The dyke is protecting her little bitch," the girl said, while her cronies laughed.

"You're a senior in high school, Marissa," Bridget said calmly. "Could we please not engage in this junior high nonsense?" While she spoke, she slowly inched past the group, keeping Kat behind her. "You might want to move along, especially since you just got off suspension and all."

Marissa's face broke into a nasty grin. "I don't see anybody here who's gonna make me, unless you think you wanna try. Go ahead, try." Her friends gathered closer, clearly hoping for a fight.

Bridget stood up straighter. "Perhaps you don't remember what happened the last time we went down this road. You might want to watch what you say."

The bully reddened. "Fuck that. I can say whatever I want." Despite the verbal posturing, Bridget could tell the girl was re-thinking her choice to engage with her. "Whatever. You dykes can go fuck yourselves." She turned and pushed past a couple of the others, then slammed open the door and left. Marissa's friends glared at Bridget, then followed suit.

Bridget watched to make sure they were really gone, then let out a huge breath. "Idiots," she muttered, then turned to Kat behind her, only she was no longer there. Bridget spun around, frantically looking for Kat. She was not inside the coffee shop. Bridget went outside and checked the parking lot, then all around the building. Nothing. Then it occurred to her Kat might have gone to the bathroom. She rushed inside, and sure enough, Kat's shoes were visible under one of the stall doors.

"Kat, are you okay?"

Kat didn't answer, but Bridget could hear what sounded like a sob.

"Kat, please…"

The stall door opened, and Kat looked out. Her ghostly pale face was mottled with red. She motioned for Bridget to come into the stall, then closed the door again. Without a word, she flung her arms around Bridget's neck and hung on for dear life.

Bridget held her as she trembled, stroking her hair to try and calm her. "It's okay. I'm right here," she whispered.

After several long moments, Kat looked up at Bridget, eyes wide and wet with tears. "Panic attack," she said softly. "I'm sorry. I had to get away from people."

"No need to be sorry. I was just scared when I couldn't find you."

"I didn't think—but you *did* find me," Kat said. "You're always there. I don't know what I would have done if they had found me alone."

"They wanted to mess with me, not you. Marissa thinks she's badass and she has a loud mouth, but she won't do anything. Are you okay?"

"I will be, as long as I'm with you," Kat replied, then abruptly pulled Bridget's mouth down to meet her own.

Bridget's head spun; she'd imagined this moment for so long, but never in a million years did she think Kat would initiate their first kiss. She pulled away, eyebrows raised in question, searching Kat's eyes for clues to how she was feeling.

Kat smiled in answer. "Yes, Bridget, I'm okay. Yes, I wanted to kiss you. And I really, really want to kiss you again."

Bridget didn't need to think twice. She placed her lips very gently on Kat's, savoring the softness, the taste. Kat's arms tightened around her neck, and her mouth opened in invitation. Bridget deepened the kiss, and with tongues dueling, the girls unleashed all the feelings that had been building for months.

"Mommy, I gotta *go!*" a tiny voice said. Then, "Mommy, why are there four feet in that potty?"

Mortified, Kat and Bridget froze, and Bridget suddenly remembered the *Out of Order* sign on the other stall. Then she composed herself and opened the door, looking properly concerned.

"Are you sure you're okay, Kat?" she asked loudly, then turned to the mother. "I'm so sorry. My friend wasn't feeling well. We'll get right out of your way."

Kat, in her thoroughly kissed and disheveled state, definitely passed for one who might be under the weather. She walked out of the stall, mumbled an apology to the mother, and went to wash her hands. The woman, probably imagining all the germs Kat might have left behind, looked like she wanted to bolt, but her toddler's bladder won out.

"Mommy!"

Kat and Bridget fumbled out the door, trying desperately to hold it together. Once outside, they burst into laughter.

"Oh my God," Kat said. "Awkward. I completely forgot where we were."

"Lucky for you, I think fast on my feet," Bridget said, still giggling.

"Yes, you do. Hey, what did you mean before when you warned that girl that you'd been down this road before?"

Bridget smirked. "Marissa has been obnoxious possibly since birth, and she's just never grown up. In eighth grade, after putting up with her for years, she finally got on my last nerve when she targeted Jordan's younger sister Dani, who has Down syndrome. For the first and only time, I felt it necessary to kick her wannabe punk ass. She's never gotten over it."

Kat laughed out loud. "Holy crap. Didn't you get in trouble?"

"Nope. She was too embarrassed to say anything, and nearly everybody else figured she had it coming. I'm not proud of what I did, but it got her to stop messing with the poor kid."

"Always a hero," Kat said with admiration.

"Hey," Bridget said, a little defensively, "I'm no hero, Kat. It just pisses me off when people are mean."

"I'm sorry. I didn't mean to offend you. It's just, I love how compassionate you are. And you certainly have come to my rescue more than once."

"That's what friends are supposed to do," Bridget replied with a shrug.

Kat touched Bridget's hand. "Those girls did get one thing right. They think I'm your girlfriend." She looked intently into Bridget's eyes. "I mean, if that's all right with you, because I'd really like to be."

Bridget nodded, her heart pounding. "I think that can be arranged."

"Do you think maybe we could find a more private place, so we can pick up where we left off?" Kat asked shyly. Bridget just grinned and led the way back home.

CHAPTER SEVENTEEN

"All right, everybody, let's do a status check," Bridget said to the True Colors members. "The dance is in two weeks, and we've got more to do."

"Yes, General," Kat teased, saluting. Everybody laughed, and Bridget stuck her tongue out at Kat. Sarah watched, noting how happy Kat was. It had been fun telling her earlier that she'd passed all of her Regents exams, and her excitement hadn't waned a bit.

"Anyway," Bridget continued, "Jordan and Natasha were able to get all of the chaperones, and Ms. O even got Kat's mom to agree to be our photographer." The kids clapped. "Justin, how did you guys do with door prizes?"

"We went to every place in town we could think of."

"He's not kidding," Matt interjected. "We must've walked twenty miles last weekend. My feet were killing me."

"Poor baby," Justin replied sarcastically. "We won't talk about why your mom took your car away."

"That was so not fair," Matt grumbled under his breath, while the group laughed.

"Anyway, we got lots of donations, like restaurant gift cards, movie passes, car wash coupons, and free games of bowling. But the grand prize for the raffle is…"

"Drum roll, please," Matt said, pounding on the table.

"An iPhone 7! My uncle owns the electronics store in the mall, and he donated it." Justin grinned triumphantly.

"Woo-hoo," Bridget exclaimed. "Well done, guys." The others cheered in agreement.

Sarah chimed in, "You did a great job. Please thank your uncle for us, Justin. So for tickets, then, I think we agreed students would need to buy a one-dollar raffle ticket along with their dance tickets to be entered into the door prize drawing. Maybe, since the iPhone is such a big item, we could have a separate drawing. What do you think of having a more expensive raffle ticket for it? Maybe three dollars, or five?"

"Sounds reasonable," Natasha said. "Since we're giving more than half of our proceeds to charity, I think most kids would be willing to pay extra."

"I agree," Bridget said. "What do you think, everybody?" The other students all nodded their support. "Great idea, Ms. O. And I think we already have raffle ticket rolls in two different colors." She looked at the freshmen who were in charge of making posters. "Can you guys add this on?"

A girl named Bethany answered, "Yes, we haven't finished the posters for ticket sales yet, so we can still fit it on them."

"Great. And refreshments?"

"Most people will probably have dinner beforehand, so we're getting snacks, veggie trays, and lots of cold water," Natasha answered.

"Sounds like you have everything under control," Sarah said with a smile.

"Yep," Bridget said. "The custodians said they'd set up the tables and chairs in the gym for us as soon as the basketball practices are over that morning, and then we can decorate. Kat and I found a bunch of those red, heart-shaped paper doilies, and we're going to cut them to look like snowflake hearts. We have red and white tablecloths, plates, napkins, and drink cups. When we're done, it'll look like Cupid and a hundred of his closest friends did the decorating."

"Guess we're in good shape, then. We'll start ticket sales right after next week's meeting. Remember, I need at least two of you to sell tickets in each lunch period. We'll figure out the schedule next time. Thanks, everyone. True Colors is the best it's ever been because you all are so dedicated. Makes my job easy." Sarah smiled and said good-bye as the teens left.

"You've got a great group this year," Jamie said from her desk, where she was correcting papers. "The dance ought to raise a lot of money. Which charity did you choose again?"

"They decided to give to the Wounded Warriors Project this time. The dance is our most important fundraiser, so I hope we do well."

"Hell, if I was a teenager, I'd be putting all my money into the iPhone raffle," Jamie laughed.

"I'm counting on it. I can't believe the boys got all those donations."

"So," Jamie said, changing the subject, "Kat's mom is helping out with photography, huh?"

"Yeah, isn't that great?" Sarah warmed at the mention of Lauren.

"Tell me about this woman," Jamie demanded.

"What do you mean? She's very nice."

"And?"

"And we've hung out a couple of times," Sarah said vaguely.

"Uh-huh, and you think she's hot," Jamie stated matter-of-factly.

"Jamie, I don't know what you're talking about." Sarah's face felt like it was going to burst into flames.

"Bullshit. Remember who you're talking to here, girlfriend. The last time I saw you like this was when you were with Kris."

"Fine," Sarah said testily. "I like her, but it's not like anything is going to happen. She's straight, married, and the parent of one of my students. I'm obviously not going there. Not to mention when I even think about dating again, all that comes to mind is Kris. I still miss her."

"Honey, Kris has been gone a long time. You know she wouldn't want you pining away. You've got to move on sometime," Jamie said gently.

"That's exactly what my sister-in-law said," Sarah mumbled.

"Smart woman. I know how hard it's been for you. I've watched you go through it all, haven't I?"

"Yeah," Sarah said. "I'm just scared, I guess."

"Of what?"

"Pain," Sarah replied with a sigh. "I don't ever want to hurt like that again."

"Life has no guarantees, my friend." Jamie came around her desk to wrap an arm around Sarah's shoulder. "But there is one thing you can be sure of. If you don't open yourself up, any future opportunities to be happy again will pass you by."

"Fine, I get it," Sarah said. "But Lauren can't be that person, for all of the aforementioned reasons."

"Maybe not, but if she can be your friend and help you knock down those walls you've built, wouldn't it be a good thing?"

"I worked very hard on those walls. They won't come down easily," Sarah said, almost in a whisper.

"Then Lauren must be a very special person. As far as I can tell, she's the only one who's even come close."

❖

The day of the Sweetheart Dance finally arrived, and Kat was excited as she got ready. She and Bridget, with Jordan's and Natasha's help, had spent all afternoon decorating the gym. Kat surprised everyone with the photo props she'd made. They were heavy cardboard pieces with holes cut out for people's faces, like the kind found at tourist attractions, except these were themed for the dance. One was shaped like a huge heart, for couples. Another sported the title *BFFs* in sparkly letters. Kids could even pose with their own heads atop life-size cutouts of swimsuit-clad male or female supermodel bodies, which Kat had found online. She hoped they would be a hit, in addition to the more traditional photos her mom would take.

On her bed was the dress Kat had found at an amazing vintage clothing shop in Syracuse. The fabric was a deep blue jacquard with a fitted lace-up bodice, lace-accented shoulder straps, and a flared skirt with a tulle underlay that fell just above her knees. With her dark hair and blue eyes, the dress suited her perfectly.

Bridget would be picking her up in less than an hour. Bridget. Her girlfriend. Kat still couldn't believe the turn their relationship had taken, and she had never felt happier. It was the perfect example of how, just when you think things can't be worse, life can put something amazing in your path to turn things around.

Kat had decided to leave her hair down, and it cascaded around her shoulders. She was just finishing her makeup when her mom called up the stairs.

"Kat, Bridget's here."

"She's early," Kat yelled back, then heard both of them laughing downstairs. It was a joke between them that Bridget could get ready, run a marathon, then get ready again, all before Kat was done with her own regimen. Whatever. She wanted to look good, and that took time.

As Kat listened to the chitchat between her two favorite people, she was struck once again by how awesome her mom was. When she and Bridget told her they were officially dating, her mom had responded, "It's about time you two figured it out." Then she had given them both a huge hug. Although her mom had already known Kat was coming to terms with her sexuality, it was at PFLAG that Kat really saw how accepting she was. They had been driving to Rochester nearly every week for the last three months, and that, coupled with her therapy appointments, had Kat feeling pretty good about herself these days.

Except for the stupid panic attacks. She hadn't had one since the coffee shop incident, and she knew it had been triggered by the aggressive behavior of those girls. But what she didn't know and couldn't explain was why she always felt like there was a blank space in her mind, a missing piece that teased her from the edges of her memory but never made itself known. Her therapist said it was likely just a symptom of her PTSD and not to worry too much about it, and she really hadn't given it much thought lately. Probably because whenever she was with Bridget, she felt safe, and she'd been with her as often as possible. Kat smiled at herself in the mirror, then realized ten more minutes had gone by and she was expected downstairs.

As she descended the staircase, Bridget looked up at her and her mouth fell open. Kat flushed and smiled. Bridget always made her feel like she was the only one in the room.

"Hey, Bridg," Kat said softly.

"Hey, Blue. Wow." Bridget cleared her throat. "That dress looks so much better on you than it did on the hanger."

"Well, I should hope so," Kat's mom chimed in. "You look gorgeous, honey. You two make a great-looking pair."

Kat gave Bridget a long, appraising look. Her girlfriend looked fantastic, in black tailored pants, a patterned white-on-white dress shirt, and an adorably quirky blue bowtie. Bridget had said she wouldn't be caught dead in a dress, but her boyish outfit hugged all her feminine curves just the same. She was beautiful.

"If you two could quit staring at each other, I'd like to get a few pictures before we leave."

"*Mom*," Kat fussed.

"I'm just saying. Here, stand in front of the fireplace."

Bridget held out her arm to Kat, and they gave in to the obligatory parental picture taking. Kat's modest heels brought her equal to Bridget's height, and Bridget's arm fit perfectly around her waist.

"You look absolutely stunning, you know," Bridget whispered in her ear.

"Thanks. So do you," Kat whispered back, giving Bridget a kiss on the cheek.

"Come on, girls. We have to be at the high school by six thirty so I can set up my equipment."

Bridget tucked Kat's hand beneath her arm, and Kat's heart flipped with the excitement of new love.

❖

Sarah was standing at the raffle table when Lauren, Kat, and Bridget arrived at the school, lugging camera equipment.

"Can I help with anything?" Sarah asked, hurrying over to the door.

"We've got it, but can you point out the spot where I should set up?" Lauren replied.

"Absolutely. We've got a great area over here, away from the gym, so it won't be too noisy. See, we even set up a queue for the kids to wait in line."

"You guys thought of everything," Lauren said, pleased.

"The kids have done an outstanding job getting ready for this dance. Wait until you see the decorations in the gym."

"The girls told me it took hours. Let me get set up here—then I'll go check it out," Lauren replied.

Kat and Bridget went off to find their friends and make sure all was set before they opened the doors to the students. Sarah went back to the raffle table, but she couldn't help watching Lauren as she worked. Even in plain black jeans and a red V-neck sweater, she was stunning.

Sarah tore her gaze away and turned to see several chaperones and True Colors members milling around the doors. Showtime.

"Okay, Jordan," she called, "let 'em in!"

Several dozen students flooded through the doors and lined up to show their tickets and IDs. Sarah and Jamie kept the line organized, and within an hour, over five hundred students had entered the dance. The principal and resource officers kept a sharp eye out for misbehavior, Breathalyzer kits at the ready, and the chaperones fanned out across the gym, hoping to keep the PDAs and twerking to a minimum.

Sarah spent the next hour selling extra raffle tickets. After another chaperone relieved her, she checked the snack table, restocked the veggie trays, and then went to see how Lauren was faring. There had been a steady line for photos all night, and Lauren hadn't had a minute to breathe.

"Everything going well?" Sarah asked.

Lauren held up a finger while she finished completing an order form. Students she photographed tonight would be given a complimentary print, but she was also taking orders if students wanted to purchase additional copies or poses. When she was done, she straightened and stretched her back.

"Wow. I haven't given my camera this much of a workout in months."

"Can I get you a drink or something to eat?" Sarah offered.

"God, yes, if you don't mind. I'd love some water."

Sarah returned shortly with the drink and a plateful of crackers, cheese, and veggies.

"Thanks. You're a lifesaver." Lauren took a long drink of water and snagged a cracker. She looked at the remaining line of students, then at her watch. "It's nine twenty. Can you announce a last call for pictures in a few minutes?"

"Yep, sure can," Sarah replied, then stepped back to watch as Lauren chatted with the teens while expertly posing them for their keepsake photos. She smiled and laughed with them, putting them at ease, and Sarah felt an intense surge of emotion. Lauren was so damn gorgeous, and kind, and…When a couple of her students said hello, diverting her attention, Sarah felt her face grow hot with embarrassment, as if she was a teenager busted for staring at her crush. Sarah caught Lauren's eye and gave a wave, then went into the gym.

After getting the DJ to announce Lauren's last call, Sarah slowly walked the perimeter of the gym, watching the kids dancing and having a good time. Kat's cardboard stand-ins were at various places along the walls, and they'd been a huge hit. Flashes from phone cameras constantly illuminated the dimly lit space, and the disco ball and black lights her kids had set up had effectively transformed the basketball court into a dance club.

Sarah caught sight of Bridget, Kat, Justin, and Matt dancing at the edge of the dance floor. She smiled, so happy they were able to attend the dance as couples without any backlash. As recently as seven or eight years ago, that would not have been the case. Certainly a changing society had a lot to do with it, but Sarah also credited her amazing kids for living bravely and openly, and advocating for themselves and others. She was very proud to be a part of their journey.

As Sarah headed out of the gym to prepare for the raffle giveaways, she saw Lauren heading toward her, carrying her equipment.

"All done?" Sarah asked, reaching for one of the cases.

"All done and ready to get off my feet. I just want to get this stuff back in my car first."

"Come on, then. I'll help." The two women grabbed all the equipment in two trips and stowed it safely away in Lauren's SUV.

"Why don't you just go home?" Sarah suggested. "Your much-appreciated work here is done."

"Nah. I'll hang out awhile with you. Need help with the raffles?"

"Sure. You can pull the tickets, and I'll announce the winners. We need to go get the mic from the DJ. It's almost ten o'clock."

The DJ played the last two songs he had queued up, and then Sarah took over.

"Hey, Easton High. Are you having a good time?" Whoops and cheers erupted from the crowd of students. "Thanks so much for coming tonight. We need to interrupt your dance party for just a few minutes. First, let's give a round of applause to the student group that organized and sponsored this year's Sweetheart Dance—True Colors."

Thankfully, the student body applauded and no hecklers booed or yelled derogatory words, as had happened in the past. Sarah moved on quickly.

"Now it's time to find out the winners of our door prizes. Before we choose the tickets, I'd like to thank you for your generosity. This year's dance raised over two thousand dollars for the Wounded Warriors Project. Great job."

Lauren and Bridget joined Sarah at the mic, and they proceeded to award the door prizes, culminating with the coveted iPhone.

Sarah drew out the suspense. "And the winner of the iPhone is…"

After about ten seconds, the kids started shouting. Sarah grinned, teasingly holding up the winning ticket.

"Elizabeth Johnston." A ninth grade girl screamed, and the whole gym erupted in laughter and disappointed groans.

"Okay, everyone. You've got more dancing to do." Sarah stepped away from the mic as the DJ began his final sequence of high-energy songs. She walked quickly out of the gym, and Lauren followed.

"You're a great emcee," Lauren said.

Sarah laughed. "Then I guess it wasn't obvious my head is about to explode."

"Oh no…another migraine?"

"I don't think so, just several hours of stress and loud music. Let's move over here." They went to the farthest corner of the lobby, away from the booming bass vibrating the floor.

"I haven't been to a dance like this in twenty years," Lauren said. "Our senior prom was held here."

"Wow, you're old," Sarah teased, earning herself a smack on the arm. "The kids did a great job getting it all together, though, didn't they?"

"Yeah, they really did. I'm impressed. I'm glad Kat doesn't mind her *old* mom being here, because I've really enjoyed seeing her have so much fun."

"She and Bridget make quite a striking pair, don't they?" Sarah commented. She knew Lauren was accepting of the girls' relationship, but they hadn't really talked about it much.

"Yes, they do. But it's kind of freaking me out to see my little girl looking so grown up. She'll be off to college soon, and I won't know what to do with myself."

Bet I could help you with that. Sarah felt her face flush yet again at the flirtatious thought, and she shook her head.

"I never thought she'd come this far," Lauren mused, apparently unaware of Sarah's embarrassment. "Bridget and PFLAG have made a huge difference, and so have you." Lauren looked at Sarah, warmth and gratitude showing in her eyes. "Kat thinks the world of you. We're very lucky to have you in our lives."

Sarah was deeply touched by Lauren's words. "Thank you," she said, putting her hand on Lauren's arm. "You both are really important to me, too."

Lauren smiled, then abruptly asked, "When did you know you were gay?"

Sarah looked at her in surprise, then glanced around to make sure no one was close enough to listen in on their conversation.

"Well, I guess my first clue was in junior high, but I wasn't really sure until around tenth grade. Why?"

"I don't know. I guess I've been looking back, trying to remember if I saw any signs. I mean, about Kat." Lauren seemed flustered. "How did you know?"

"Probably the way a lot of women figure it out. You know, I wasn't into boys like my friends. I had a massive crush on my best girlfriend, and was brokenhearted when she starting dating guys. When I watched romantic movies, I was checking out the female leads. Stuff like that."

"Huh," Lauren said, suddenly pensive. "But you were young. Is it possible for people to be adults before they get those clues?"

"Well, yes, I suppose—"

Sarah was interrupted by a frantic Natasha. "Mrs. Emerson, Ms. O, come quick!"

CHAPTER EIGHTEEN

Bridget was on cloud nine. The dance was a huge success, and she and Kat were having an awesome time. Even though there were a ton of people in the gym, Kat seemed to be fine, as long as they danced on the outer edge of the crowd. Kat was happy, beautiful, and hers. Bridget couldn't believe how lucky she was.

The time flew by, and soon it was already ten o'clock and time to do the raffles. The winners seemed happy with their prizes, especially the screaming freshman and her iPhone. Now the dance was beginning to wind down, and Bridget didn't want it to end.

She and Kat had just danced their butts off to five songs in a row, and they were taking a break.

"I am *so* sweaty, ugh," Kat said, dropping into a chair near the dance floor.

Bridget wiped her brow with her sleeve. "I'm gonna go get us water, okay?"

"Fabulous. I won't move a muscle, mostly because I can't."

Bridget made her way to the refreshment table and snagged a couple of waters. She turned when she heard voices chanting loudly, and saw a handful of rowdy boys trying to start a mosh pit. The next thirty seconds seemed to move in slow motion. Bridget saw two chaperones moving toward the boys, and then one boy, shoved by his buddy, went flying. Bridget watched in horror as the boy hurtled headlong toward Kat, who had her back to him. He smashed into her chair, and she was thrown to the floor. Bridget dropped the water and ran.

❖

Kat was exhausted and her feet hurt, but she was having a blast just the same. The dance was so much fun, and Bridget had barely left her side, knowing crowds made her anxious. They and the other True Colors members hung out most of the night, laughing and dancing. Kat was still nervous when the slow songs played and a handful of same-sex couples danced together. She half expected people to freak out or start a fight. But when Bridget took her hand, inviting her to slow dance, the rest of the room seemed to fade away.

Now Bridget was off getting them water, and Kat bent over in her chair to fix a loose strap on her shoe. Suddenly, a huge pain erupted in her back, and she was facedown on the floor, with someone on top of her.

Lights flashed and voices became distorted. Kat was in a dense fog, struggling toward clarity. She heard distant laughter, and the pungent odor of marijuana smoke and booze invaded her nostrils. A hot, heavy weight pinned her down, and she smelled the overpowering scent of sweat and cheap cologne. She remembered that smell. Suddenly, brutally, it all came back to her. And she began to scream.

❖

Bridget heard Kat scream as she pushed through the crowd, then saw her flailing and kicking at the boy who was desperately trying to disentangle himself and get up.

"I'm sorry, I'm sorry," the boy cried, clearly upset at the reaction of the hysterical girl he had fallen on.

Several chaperones and one of the resource officers rushed over to tend to Kat and clear the crowd away. Bridget tried to get to Kat's side, but Mrs. Gibson held her back. Kat was still kicking and hitting at anyone who came near.

"What's wrong with her?" Bridget practically wailed, pulling against Mrs. Gibson's grasp.

"I don't know, honey, but we have to give them the space to help her."

Ms. O and Kat's mom suddenly appeared at their side. Mrs. Emerson ran to her daughter, and Ms. O turned to them.

"Jamie, Bridget—what happened?"

Bridget, voice shaking, replied first. "A few boys were dancing crazy, and one of them fell right onto Kat. Then she just started screaming and hitting. It was just a stupid accident, but it's like she can't see or hear anybody. Why won't she stop screaming?"

Bridget was frustrated and scared. She'd seen Kat have a panic attack before, but this was way worse. All she wanted to do was hold her girlfriend, but the adults were keeping her away, which made her want to scream, too. She turned to watch the mass exodus of students leaving the gym and caught sight of Jordan, hanging back and waving at her.

"Mrs. Gibson, I'm going to go with Jordan, okay?"

She ran over to Jordan just as Natasha arrived to join them.

"They called for an ambulance, Bridget. Kat's going to be taken to the hospital."

Jordan put a hand on Bridget's shoulder. "I can call my mom and see if she'll let me take you there."

Bridget nodded, then stared numbly over at the commotion surrounding Kat while Jordan made the call.

"My mom said yes. Let's go."

Sarah had her guesses as to why Kat was in crisis mode, but instead of responding to Bridget's question, she went after Lauren. She was kneeling on the floor at Kat's head, with her daughter's face in her hands.

"Kat, Kat, it's okay," Lauren was saying. "I'm here, and you're safe. Kat, come on, baby. Look at me."

Kat looked at her mother, wild-eyed. "Mom? Oh my God..." She tried to sit up, and promptly passed out cold.

The adults had all sprung into action, quickly moving students to the lobby and away from the commotion. The last thing they needed was somebody filming the incident on their cell phone. Luckily, it was close to eleven o'clock, and students were supposed to be leaving anyway.

Sarah flagged down the EMTs when they arrived and led them to where Kat sat, leaning against her mom. The distraught girl had come to, but she wouldn't speak or look at anyone. Lauren seemed beside herself with worry.

As they loaded Kat onto the stretcher, Jamie pulled Sarah aside. "Listen, the kids are leaving, and a couple of the chaperones and I will stick around and make sure everything else is taken care of. Go to the hospital with Lauren. She'll need you."

Sarah hugged her gratefully. "Thank you. Are you sure you don't mind?"

"Go, hon. Don't worry about a thing."

Sarah caught up to Lauren, who was walking beside the stretcher and holding Kat's hand as the EMTs pushed her to the ambulance. She gently drew Lauren away from the stretcher. "You ride with Kat, and I'll drive your car up to the hospital, okay? Can you give me the keys?"

Lauren numbly fished around in her purse until she found them. She was shaking, and tears had begun to run down her face. Sarah pulled her into a hug. "It'll be okay, Lauren." Sarah pulled back and put her hands on Lauren's cheeks, making their eyes meet. "She's going to be okay." Lauren nodded once, then got into the ambulance. Sarah slid into the driver's seat of Lauren's SUV and followed.

When they arrived at the emergency department's entrance, the ambulance crew unloaded Kat's stretcher. As Sarah approached, Lauren was pulled aside by one of the EMTs.

"Ma'am, you'll want to sign in at the desk. Once they get your daughter situated, they'll call you in to see her."

"Is she all right?" Lauren asked him.

"Her vitals are stable. The docs will be able to tell you more."

"Thank you," Lauren said, as she watched Kat disappear through a set of double doors.

Sarah touched her arm. "Lauren, let's go take care of the paperwork. It'll help to focus on something else for a few minutes." As they walked to the desk, Sarah heard the sliding doors open again and glanced back toward the entrance. Bridget, Jordan, and Natasha rushed in, looking very worried. When Bridget caught sight of Sarah, she made a beeline toward her.

"Is Kat okay? What's going on?" Bridget was as white as a sheet.

Sarah led Bridget and the other girls into the waiting room so Lauren could have privacy while talking to the admitting nurse. "I think she'll be fine, girls. It seems like she might have just had a bad scare. Do your parents know you're here?"

"Yeah, we called them," Jordan replied. "They said we can wait as long as we check in with them."

"Was it one of those panic attacks?" Bridget asked.

"Well, I can't say for sure," Sarah responded, "but we've got her in the right place to find out. Let's just sit and wait. And please make sure you're not texting about it to anyone. It's very important to protect Kat's privacy."

"Okay, Ms. O," the girls replied. They all sat for a few minutes in silence, but then Bridget's nervous energy got the best of her. She jumped up and started to pace. Lauren had already been taken back to be with Kat, and Sarah was just as anxious to know what was going on as Bridget was.

"Hey, why don't you girls walk down to the café and see if you can grab a drink or a snack?" Sarah suggested. She knew they'd be better off having something to do. Realizing the girls hadn't brought anything in with them, she took out her wallet. "Here," she said, pulling out a twenty-dollar bill, "see if you can find me a Diet Pepsi and something for yourselves."

Jordan, the calmest of the three girls, took charge of the money and her friends. "Thanks, Ms. O. Come on, you guys. I'm sure it'll be a while before they give us any news."

Bridget hesitated, eyes welling with tears. Sarah stood and gave the frightened girl a hug. "Go," she whispered. "I'll be right here."

❖

The interminable wait was fraying Sarah's nerves. She couldn't help but remember the last time she'd been in an emergency room, waiting for news. Kris had died that day, turning Sarah's world upside down. Thankfully Kat wasn't in physical danger, but Sarah still knew how helpless and scared Lauren must be feeling.

The girls had returned from their snack run a while ago, and were now intermittently staring at the floor or the TV, which was set to a twenty-four-hour news channel. It had been nearly three hours since they'd arrived, and they were all exhausted. Despite their fatigue, everyone's head popped up when a voice said, "Sarah?"

Sarah rose to meet Sharon Keller, one of the therapists she knew from the county mental health center. "Sharon. How come you're here at this hour?" The two women shook hands.

"It seems to be due to a providential stroke of luck," Sharon replied with a smile. "This just happens to be my on-call weekend. Several of our clinical social workers do after-hours rotations here for emergencies. I'm so glad I was here for Kat. It saved the poor thing from having to rehash her life story to a stranger."

"Thank goodness," Sarah replied, grateful that Kat was in good hands. "How is she?"

"She's much calmer and is responding to us. Mrs. Emerson asked me to come get you. She'd like you to be there to hear what's going on."

Sarah glanced over at the girls, who were hanging on Sharon's every word. Bridget looked like she might explode out of her skin. Sarah called the girls over.

"Girls, this is Ms. Keller. She came out to let us know Kat is doing fine. Mrs. Emerson asked me to go on back there, so I think it's time you headed home."

"But can't I see her?" Bridget protested.

"Not just yet, sweetheart. She needs time and space right now." Sarah knew it was killing Bridget to be so helpless. She loved Kat; that much was obvious. "Try not to worry, okay? I'll tell her you all were here. I'm sure she'll contact you as soon as she can."

Bridget's eyes were moist. "Please tell her…"

Sarah nodded. "I know, honey. I'll tell her." To the others she said, "Why don't you call your parents and let them know you're on your way? Who drove here?"

"I did." Jordan raised her hand. "I'll drop them off at home. We can go back to school tomorrow to get Bridget's car."

"Sounds like a good plan," Sarah agreed. "Here, let me have your phone for a sec." Sarah took Jordan's phone and typed in her cell number. "Please text me when everyone is home safe, okay?"

"I will," Jordan replied.

Natasha, who had been very quiet, finally spoke up. "Tell Kat we're thinking of her, okay?"

"Count on it. Be careful going home, and try to get some sleep. I'll see you on Monday."

The girls left, and Sarah had to restrain herself from running to Lauren and Kat. She and Sharon walked through the emergency room to the last bay on the left. It was relatively quiet for a Saturday night, and Sarah was thankful. When Sharon pulled open the curtain to the bay, Lauren jumped out of her chair. Wordlessly, Sarah wrapped her arms around the now sobbing woman and held her tightly.

Kat was in the hospital bed, looking pale and disheveled. She appeared to have fallen asleep.

After a few moments, Sharon spoke quietly. "There's a consultation room across the hall. How about we go in there and talk?"

Lauren let go of Sarah, grabbed a couple of tissues from a box on the counter, and nodded. They all went to the other room and sat at a round table. Sharon had left the door slightly ajar so they could see across to where Kat lay.

"So," Sharon began, filling Sarah in, "physically, Kat is much better now. When she arrived, her blood pressure was elevated and she appeared to be in shock, but her vitals are back to normal. They gave her a mild sedative, so she should rest for a few hours. She has bruises on her back, knees, and chin, and a stiff neck, but no other injuries were found."

Sharon looked at Lauren. "Would you like to tell Sarah what happened? I can if you need me to." Lauren shook her head and pointed at Sharon to continue.

"Okay. Sarah, I know you're aware Kat has been seeing me for therapy for quite a while now." Sarah nodded. "Our staff psychiatrist diagnosed her with post-traumatic stress disorder, related—we thought—to the bullying Kat had endured at her previous school. Kat was having panic attacks, usually when she was around large groups of people, but those had been getting less frequent."

"Yes," Sarah said, "Kat has been doing very well lately. She's seemed much more at ease."

"Exactly. She appeared to have gotten past the awful experience she had last year, so much so that I was going to suggest we meet less often. But I was still concerned about a recurring dream Kat reported, as she got very upset whenever it happened."

Lauren spoke then. "Kat has had nightmares ever since we left Alabama. Sometimes she wakes up crying, but she can never remember why. She said she feels like there's something just out of reach in her mind. But now…" Lauren choked back a sob. Sarah immediately took her hand and held it.

"Sarah, the incident at the dance tonight has triggered what appears to be a repressed memory of a past trauma. There has been no indication Kat was aware of the trauma until now."

Sarah could feel Lauren trembling beside her, and she tightened her grip. "What trauma?" Sarah asked, afraid she already knew the answer.

Sharon took a deep breath and let it out slowly. "Kat has remembered being raped."

CHAPTER NINETEEN

Lauren felt like she'd been hit by a truck. She was stiff and sore from sitting so long in the uncomfortable plastic hospital chair, yet numb from the emotional shock she'd endured. Rape. The vile word ran through her head on an endless loop she couldn't seem to stop.

Sarah was still sitting beside her and had dozed off, her head resting against the wall behind them. Even though she was asleep, her arm lay protectively along the back of Lauren's chair. Sarah had held her while she cried and ranted, not once leaving her side. Lauren was beyond grateful to this woman who gave so much.

Hearing the sheets rustle, Lauren quickly looked to where her daughter lay, pale and vulnerable, in the hospital bed. Kat's eyes were open, and she looked confused.

"Mom?"

"I'm right here, baby," Lauren soothed, going to Kat and taking her hand. With her other hand, she brushed wayward strands of hair from Kat's forehead. Kat looked at her with wounded eyes and silently began to cry. Lauren sat on the edge of the bed and drew her daughter into her arms, her own tears falling unchecked.

She felt a gentle hand on her shoulder. "I'm going to step out," Sarah whispered. "I'll be right outside if you need anything."

Lauren nodded, then turned back to her daughter, wondering how on earth she was going to get Kat through this.

❖

It was after seven a.m. by the time Kat was discharged from the ER, and all she wanted was to get the hell out of there. Her mom had insisted Ms. O go home a couple of hours ago, promising she'd call her later. Kat had texted Bridget that she was okay, but she was far from ready to talk about anything more. She had an appointment with Sharon Keller on Monday, but she couldn't help feeling like all the progress she'd already made with her had been erased.

Kat felt like her heart was being squeezed every time she thought about *it*, which was pretty much constantly. For months she'd been wishing she could understand her confusing, frightening dreams and the reason behind her panic attacks. Now that she had the answer, she would give anything to go back to blissful ignorance.

It seemed to take forever for the nurse to bring her discharge papers, but finally she showed up.

"Be sure to keep your appointment on Monday," she said briskly, and was gone.

"Come on, sweet pea," her mom said tiredly. "Let's get you home."

❖

Sarah was dozing on her couch Wednesday evening when her phone rang, startling her awake. The caller ID let her know it was Lauren, and she answered immediately.

"Hey there, how are you doing?"

"Better than I thought I'd be," Lauren replied with a sigh, "considering how hellish the last couple of days have been."

"How's our girl feeling?"

"She's doing okay. In some ways, I think she's relieved to have an explanation for the panic attacks and nightmares, but the reality has shaken her badly. I want so much to take it all away." Lauren sniffled and cleared her throat.

"She's had quite a shock. You both have, but she's strong, and she's got good people helping her."

"Speaking of which, I wanted to thank you again for being there for me, and for Kat. You have no idea how much it means to have your support," Lauren said, voice cracking.

"No need to thank me, hon. You'd have done the same for me. That's what people who care about each other do, right?"

"Right. I know you care about us and I'm so very glad," Lauren said, trying to express her gratitude adequately over the phone.

Sarah was deeply moved. "Lauren, all that matters to me is that you and Kat are okay."

"We will be. I called, though, to ask if we could get together. Have you eaten supper yet?"

"No, actually. When I got home from work, I sort of fell asleep," Sarah replied. "It's so easy to do with a warm afghan and a couple of kitties."

"Tell me about it. Gracie is quite the lap cat. Do you mind if I come over? I want to fill you in on things. I could pick up Chinese on the way."

"Okay," Sarah replied, glad to have the chance to see Lauren.

Forty minutes later, they were sitting in Sarah's kitchen, sharing pork lo mein, rice, and sesame chicken. Sarah noted how tired Lauren looked, and that the worry lines on her forehead had deepened.

"So, I wanted to talk to you about Trent. You knew I called him Sunday morning from the hospital, right?" Lauren asked.

"Yes. I was wondering how that went."

"Well, the first time I called, I just told him Kat was in the hospital because of a major panic attack. She's still on his insurance, and of course he needed to know, but I didn't tell him the rest of it, at least not then."

"Well, the hospital's not the most private place in the world to have that kind of conversation," Sarah said.

"This is true. But it was mostly because I needed time to think about how to tell him. Kat's been working through this with Sharon, who said since the repressed memories have resurfaced, the clarity of her recall is remarkable. Kat thinks she knows who may have assaulted her."

"Holy shit—so it was someone she knew, then?"

"She thinks so. And she thinks she knows when it happened. Remember I told you about Kat's best friend Amber, her boyfriend, and the boyfriend's buddy who kept bothering Kat to hook up with him?"

"Yes. You said those boys started the bullying."

"Right. Well, Kat said right before all the bullying got really bad, Amber had asked her to go to a house party with them. She said the boys were acting much nicer than usual, and they even got her a cup of soda because they knew she didn't like to drink alcohol. She remembers feeling really tired and someone bringing her to a bed to lie down. Amber told her she had just fallen asleep."

"My God," Sarah murmured. "They drugged her?"

"Can't prove it, but it seems to be the best explanation. She's had flashes of awareness, but she thought it was just a dream. Like the feeling of a weight on top of her, and the smell of cologne. Sharon thinks it was those two things that triggered everything at the dance."

"Poor girl," Sarah said, feeling horror and anger in equal measures.

"Kat says she always remembered having blood in her underwear and feeling crampy the morning after the party, but she got her period later in the day and didn't think anything more about it," Lauren continued. "Amber had insisted she was asleep, and that they woke her up before they left the party. Kat couldn't really remember getting home, but she knows she didn't feel well the next day."

"I'm sorry to play devil's advocate, but how can she be sure who the perpetrator was now?" Sarah asked.

"She says it was the cologne. She remembers Amber's boyfriend used to tease his friend about marinating in it, and she remembers smelling it when the same boy kept hitting on her and she told him off. That was right before everything hit the fan with the cyberbullying," Lauren replied. "Apparently the kid that fell on her at the dance was wearing the same cologne."

"Wow," Sarah breathed, incredulous. "So what are you going to do?"

"I have no fucking idea," Lauren answered, clearly frustrated. "I called Trent again and told him what happened. I so didn't want to do that, but he *is* her father."

"Well, of course you had to call," Sarah agreed. "Every parent should know when something serious happens to their child."

"I know, but I was afraid of his reaction. And then I realized I've been afraid of his reaction to a lot of things over a lot of years. Why the hell didn't I see it sooner?"

"I don't know, honey. Sometimes you get so used to things, you don't have a clear perspective anymore. So when you told him, what did he say?"

Lauren's eyes flashed at the memory. "I explained to him what happened as best I could. He didn't say a word. It was like freaking radio silence on the other end. Then he used that voice that tells me he's getting mad. He said I was making a very serious allegation, and it sounded to him like Kat was just overreacting again. Of course he's good friends with the kid's father, so the boy must be innocent, right? Not once," Lauren said, punctuating her words with fist blows to the table, "not once did he ask if Kat was okay or show any concern for her well-being." Angry tears welled up and spilled down her cheeks. "I think that was it, Sarah."

"What?" Sarah reached across the table to take Lauren's hand.

"The final nail in the coffin of my marriage. How could I ever go back to that?" Lauren shook her head, then ran her free hand through her hair, her sadness palpable.

Sarah was silent, still holding Lauren's hand. She wanted to respect Lauren's sense of loss, but she couldn't help but be relieved. Lauren had finally realized her relationship was toxic.

"You know," Lauren said, looking up at Sarah, "I feel sad, but not because of Trent. I think I'm grieving all the wasted years I spent with him, when I could have been with someone who makes me happy." Her eyes searched Sarah's, until Sarah had to look away from the intensity.

She got up from the table and walked to the kitchen sink, keeping her back to Lauren. She was trembling inside from the barely veiled message in Lauren's words, and she was both excited and scared to death.

"Sarah," Lauren said softly from behind her. Sarah took a deep breath and held it, then let it out with a whoosh, but she didn't turn around.

"Sarah," Lauren repeated, putting a gentle hand on Sarah's shoulder. Sarah reluctantly turned to face the cause of her unease. She looked at the woman who had come to mean so much to her. Every fiber of her being was focused on the warmth of Lauren's touch, and the need that was building inside.

"Why did you turn away?" Lauren asked, looking troubled. "This thing between us. You feel it, don't you?"

Sarah shook her head. "It doesn't matter what I feel. You don't understand—"

"What don't I understand?" Lauren demanded, putting an arm on either side of Sarah and trapping her against the counter's edge. "I understand I care deeply about you. You make me feel things I've never felt before—it's like my body has come alive after years of being numb. I understand that I'm happiest when I'm with you, and for the first time in years, I feel safe being me. You know, Kat and I have been going out to the PFLAG meetings. I thought I was going along to support her, but I ended up realizing some things about myself. Things that never made sense until I met you."

Sarah felt herself drowning in Lauren's eyes. "You don't know what you're doing, Lauren. Yes, I feel this thing between us. And I've been fighting it, because I can't let my feelings run away with my judgment."

"What do you mean?" Lauren said, not budging an inch.

"I can't. You're vulnerable, and I won't take advantage of you." Sarah dragged her gaze away from the beautiful face in front of her. "And Kat's been through so much. I don't want to risk making things more difficult for her."

"Damn your impeccable ethics, Sarah. You're not taking advantage of me. You don't even have it in you." Lauren brought her hands up to cup Sarah's cheeks, forcing their eyes to meet again. Sarah's pulse quickened, and her gaze dropped to the full lips that were slowly closing the gap between them. "Please don't push me away," Lauren whispered, and Sarah's resistance shattered.

Time stood still as lips crashed together, hands became entangled in soft hair, and moans echoed in the heat of the moment. Then Sarah pulled back to more gently explore Lauren's soft lips, her fingertips tracing the line of Lauren's jaw and trailing down her throat, causing Lauren's body to thrum with need. She parted her lips in invitation, and Sarah responded with a low moan. They deepened the kiss, tongues reaching, tasting. Lauren was stunned at her arousal, and she never wanted their kiss to end. After what seemed like forever, Lauren reluctantly moved her mouth away to catch her breath, and she rested her forehead on Sarah's.

"That was the most incredible kiss I've ever had," Lauren said, awestruck at what Sarah awakened in her. "My God, my body is on fire."

There was no response, and Lauren looked up to see tears coursing down Sarah's cheeks. She reached up and slowly wiped the droplets away with her thumbs. "Sarah, honey, what's wrong?"

A sob escaped as Sarah tried to speak. "I'm so sorry," she whispered. "I shouldn't have done that. Forgive me."

"Forgive what? The best kiss of my life? You have nothing to apologize for," Lauren said, confused about the stricken look on Sarah's face.

"The kiss was amazing, but…you don't understand," Sarah said, looking away.

"Then help me to understand, Sarah. I need to know what you're feeling."

"Scared. I'm feeling scared and guilty somehow," Sarah said, fresh tears spilling down.

Lauren laced her fingers through Sarah's and waited for her to say more.

"I'm trying to get my head around the fact that you're the first person I've kissed since my wife died," Sarah said quietly. "I know it doesn't make any sense to feel guilty, but I do."

Lauren sighed. "I get that. I'm still married, at least legally. But Sarah, we're both allowed to move on with our lives, aren't we?"

"I suppose, but that's not why I'm scared." Sarah looked Lauren in the eye. "You are very important to me, and I want you in my life. But you've never been with a woman before. What if you decide being with me isn't what you want? I can't be your experiment, Lauren. It would hurt too much."

Lauren felt like she'd been stung. She paused for a long time, measuring her words carefully. As she watched Sarah wiping away her tears, she finally spoke.

"I understand it may be hard for you to trust what just happened, and you've been grieving your wife for a long time. But I'm not some kid looking for an ill-advised teenage fling. I know how I feel, and my feelings for you are very real."

"Oh, Lauren," Sarah said, pushing away from the counter's edge, "my feelings for you are real, too. That's why I'm freaking out. Can you honestly say you're prepared for what could happen? Many people know I'm gay, but not everyone. This is a pretty conservative town in a lot of ways, and it's also a hotbed of gossip, especially when it involves the school district staff. I'm sure there are people who would have a field day if they found out I was romantically involved with a parent."

"You tell the kids to be proud of who they are, to advocate for themselves, but you can't?"

"Whoa, now. That's not fair," Sarah replied. "Of course I want the kids to be proud of who they are, and I am perfectly happy in my own skin. But I also tell the kids to be careful if they choose to out themselves, because the world is full of homophobes and judgmental people. You haven't lived this life, Lauren. It's not easy, always having to watch your pronouns and censor what you tell people about yourself. But there it is. For myself and for the kids, I have to be careful." Sarah sighed. "I know I'm making this difficult, and I understand if you want to walk away."

Sarah went back to the table and sat, bracing herself for Lauren's response. The possibility that Lauren might turn tail and leave made her stomach hurt.

Lauren sighed. "I can see in your eyes how much this bothers you. I know that even if you're conflicted in your feelings, you won't compromise your convictions. It's one of the things I admire most about you." She paused and ran a hand through her hair, and Sarah watched her, feeling a glimmer of hope.

"And I'm sorry," Lauren continued. "I know you're right, but my newly acknowledged feelings for you don't like it." She managed a smile. "So let me get this straight...no pun intended."

Sarah groaned, but at least the bad joke had brought a smile to Lauren's face. "Go on."

"You feel the same way I do, right?" Lauren waited until Sarah nodded. "But you can't explore this thing between us while Kat is still your student." Again, Sarah nodded. "So I have a solution. Why don't we tentatively schedule our first official date for the day after graduation?"

Sarah laughed aloud at Lauren's youthful enthusiasm.

"What? I'm serious. It will give us both the next four months to make sure our feelings aren't just a passing fancy, and once Kat graduates, poof—no more ethical dilemma." Lauren crossed her arms, leaned back on the counter, and grinned, clearly pleased with her plan.

Sarah sighed, unable to stop smiling at the adorably determined woman in front of her. "Sounds like a plan," she said.

"But we still get to be best friends and hang out, right? Play word games and such?" Lauren asked teasingly.

"I suppose I can manage."

"Okay, then, it's a deal. Shake on it."

Sarah took her hand and pulled her into a warm hug. "Thanks for understanding," she whispered into Lauren's ear.

"I'll be understanding for four months, my dear. Then all bets are off," Lauren replied, giving Sarah a sassy peck on the cheek. "Now I'm going to head home to check on my daughter." She gathered up her coat and purse.

"Thanks for dinner," Sarah said, walking Lauren to the door.

"It was my pleasure," Lauren replied with a wink, and then she was gone.

Sarah watched after her, shaking her head at all that had just transpired.

Now that you know how she kisses, four months will feel like an eternity. Sarah brought her fingers to her lips as she remembered.

CHAPTER TWENTY

Lauren was sure about her next move, but she needed to run her intentions by a very important person—Kat. She watched from the kitchen doorway as Kat made herself a peanut butter and banana sandwich. She was humming along to a tune on her ever-present iPod, oblivious to her mom's presence. This gave Lauren a private moment to observe her daughter, and what she saw brought tears of pride to her eyes. The last few weeks had given Kat time to come to terms with the rape, and she had handled everything remarkably well. Seemingly overnight, Kat had grown into a beautiful, strong, and mature young woman, and Lauren was beyond grateful.

Reluctantly, Lauren ended the moment by entering the kitchen and taking a seat at the table. Kat didn't see her, and when she turned toward the table, she jumped and nearly dropped her plate.

"Jeez, Mom, don't sneak up on me like that."

"What choice do I have?" Lauren countered. "It's not like I can give you fair warning when you've got whatever that is blaring through those earbuds."

"It's Twenty One Pilots, and it's not blaring. I have it at a perfectly reasonable volume," Kat replied, but she turned the music down anyway. They both grinned at the familiar banter, and then Lauren gestured for Kat to join her at the table.

"Listen, Kit Kat. I've got something I want to talk about with you."

"Sure, Mom. What's up?" Kat said, taking a bite of her sandwich.

Lauren hesitated, not sure how to begin now that the moment was here. "Tell me what you think about being up here in New York."

Kat smiled as well as one can around a mouthful of peanut butter. Taking a moment to swallow, she replied, "I really like it here. School's good, I have a way better art teacher than I used to, and I can actually make a snowman here in the winter." Kat gestured out the window to the slightly misshapen snowy creation she'd made in the backyard the day before. "And there's Bridget," she added with a slight blush. "Plus, you know I need to be here to... get past everything." A cloud passed over her features fleetingly. "Sharon's awesome, though, and I'm really comfortable with her. And of course, there's the acceptance letter I just got from Ithaca College. So all in all, I am glad to be in New York. How's that for an answer?" Kat grinned and took another bite.

"All excellent reasons. Well, I really like it here, too, and I'm thinking I'd like to stay permanently."

Kat stopped chewing and looked at her, wide-eyed.

"Tell me what you're thinking," Lauren gently demanded.

"I always thought you were planning to move back to Alabama when I graduated."

"I guess that was the plan, initially. But being here has given me the chance to take a long look at my life, and to think about what makes me happy."

"And you're happy here?" Kat asked.

"Yes. You're a smart cookie, kiddo. I'm sure you knew things weren't great between your dad and me back home."

"Well, yeah," Kat acknowledged with a frown, "but I thought it was mostly because of me."

"Oh, honey, no. Please don't ever think that. Having you just shone a spotlight on how different, and incompatible, your dad and I became over the years." Lauren shook her head, thinking back. "We were so young. He was my first boyfriend. What the hell did we know about anything back then?"

"If you're about to tell me how young and stupid you were at seventeen, please remember who you're talking to, okay?" Kat said with a sarcastic smirk.

"Got it. Sorry," Lauren said, grateful for her daughter's attempt at levity. "It's just that circumstances kept us together. If my parents hadn't died when they did, I'm pretty sure your father and I would've gone our separate ways eventually."

"Mom," Kat interjected impatiently, "are you trying to tell me you don't want to be with Dad anymore?"

Startled at her daughter's directness, Lauren quickly looked up to meet Kat's eyes. She saw no turmoil, no concern there, just frank interest. "Well, yeah, I guess that's what I'm saying."

"Well, hallelujah and pass the cornbread," Kat hollered in her best exaggerated Alabama twang.

Lauren just stared at Kat for several beats, then burst out laughing. When she could catch her breath, she smacked Kat in the arm. "I've been agonizing for weeks over telling you this, and that's all you've got?"

"Mom, I'm not an idiot. I can see how much happier you've been here, and I remember how you and Dad barely even talked to each other before. You always tried to keep stuff from me, but I heard you two fighting at night. Why was he always such a fucking asshole?"

"Katherine Emerson, language," Lauren scolded. "And you shouldn't talk about your father like that."

Kat just rolled her eyes. "Why not, Mom? Am I wrong?"

Lauren's shoulders slumped as she let out a huge sigh. "Unfortunately, no, you're not wrong. But it wasn't just him. I share the blame for our failed marriage. I wasn't who he needed me to be."

"Correct me if I'm wrong here, Mom, but isn't loving someone all about accepting them for who they actually are?"

Out of the mouths of babes, Lauren thought with chagrin. Had she loved Trent for who he was? Had she tried to be a good partner to him? *Yes*, she thought, *I did try, for years.*

"Yes, Kat, ideally that's how it works. But there's a lot more to relationships than love, and without things like trust, respect, common interests, and compatibility, love won't be enough to keep the ship afloat. I think with your father and me, we were still just kids when we got married, and we ended up growing in very different directions. The problem is, I recognize this, but he won't admit it."

"So what are you going to do?" Kat asked.

"Well, I think it's time for me to file for a divorce," Lauren replied. Distance from Trent made her braver, but saying the D-word still caused her to shake inside with anxiety.

"He'll flip out, you know," Kat said matter-of-factly.

"I know, baby. I know."

CHAPTER TWENTY-ONE

Kat stared out the window at billions of rapidly swirling snowflakes. When Bridget had come over earlier to work on their project for English class, there was barely a snowflake in the sky. By the time they took a break for lunch, however, there were six inches of snow on the ground, and the flakes were falling so thickly they couldn't even see across the street. Her mom had gone out earlier, and Kat was starting to worry.

"I'm gonna call my mom," she said to Bridget. "She was supposed to be back by now."

Her mom picked up her cell on the third ring. "Hi, honey. I was just about to call you. The roads are horrible, so you girls stay put, okay?"

"Yeah, but what about you, Mom? We were just watching the Weather Channel, and they said the lake effect band has stalled out and is dumping over an inch an hour. Where are you?"

"I'm still on the other side of town," her mom replied. "I thought I'd have time to get my errands done. This snow wasn't supposed to hit until later this afternoon. I'll probably need to hunker down somewhere until the plows get the roads under control. You guys okay?"

"Yeah, we're fine. Bridget's mom called and told her to stay here, too. Be careful, Mom, okay?"

"I will, sweetheart. I'll get home as soon as I can. Love you."

"Love you, too. Bye." Kat ended the call and turned to Bridget. "My mom's kind of stuck across town," she said, feeling her anxiety ratchet up a notch.

"Is she okay?" Bridget asked, rubbing Kat's arm to calm her.

"Yeah. She said she'll stay there until the roads are better."

"The plows will be out all over the place. Once the snow stops, she'll be able to get home. You're really worried, aren't you?" Bridget gave Kat a hug.

"I have never seen this much snow in my entire life, at least not in person. Shit, if two inches fall in Alabama, the whole state shuts down."

Bridget laughed. "We Northerners are much hardier folk," she boasted. "Two feet of snow ain't nothing."

Kat rolled her eyes, but she grinned, relaxing a bit. Affecting an exaggerated accent, she said, "Well, we're almost done with our project, and your mom *did* tell you to stay over tonight, you know, because of the dreadful weather and all. My goodness, however will we pass the time?" She batted her eyelashes at Bridget in her best Southern belle impression.

Bridget wrapped her arms around Kat's waist and planted a kiss on her lips. "I do believe we'll be able to think of some excellent ideas."

❖

Lauren sat in her car, cursing herself for not checking the weather report again before she'd headed out this morning. If she had, she would've seen that the winter storm warning had been moved up by about two hours, and she wouldn't be sitting out here in a blizzard. She was ten miles from home in whiteout conditions, and the roads were treacherous. As she watched the huge wet flakes coat her windshield, her phone rang.

"I hope you're wrapped up in a blanket with a cup of hot chocolate," Sarah's voice greeted cheerfully.

"I wish." Lauren groaned, switching on her wipers to keep the snow from freezing to the glass. "I'm actually sitting in my car in a parking lot out near the mall." The thought of snuggling under a blanket with Sarah entered her mind, and she felt a little shiver that had nothing to do with the cold.

"Ooh, not good," Sarah replied. "Are the roads bad?"

"Awful. I'm sitting here watching people fishtailing all over the place," Lauren said.

"I'm less than two miles away from you. Do you think you could make it here?"

The warmth and concern in Sarah's voice made Lauren wish those two miles could just melt away. She wanted nothing more than to be with Sarah right now, safe and warm. Brightening at the idea, Lauren considered her best options for getting there. "If I stick to the main road, I could head over toward the hospital and backtrack to your place from there, right?"

"Yep, that would probably be the safest bet. I'll head outside and clear the driveway. Thank God I got my snowblower fixed."

"And thank God I splurged for snow tires. I'm on my way," Lauren said.

❖

After warning Lauren to be careful, Sarah disconnected, excited that she'd be seeing her. Every time she thought of Lauren, the memory of their kiss made her pulse speed up. Now she also felt a rush of protectiveness, needing her to be safe. She bundled up and headed outside.

Half an hour later, Sarah's driveway was free of most of the snow, but Lauren hadn't shown up yet. Sarah went inside to thaw and wait by the window. Ten more minutes went by, and she was about to call Lauren when she saw headlights inching down her street. She made out Lauren's SUV through the blowing snow, and breathed a sigh of relief. She quickly went to turn up the flame in her gas fireplace.

A few moments later, a snow-covered nervous wreck of a woman stumbled in the front door. "That was the drive from hell," Lauren said shakily, stomping the snow off her boots in the entryway.

"Are you okay? Why are you all snowy?" Sarah inquired, taking Lauren's wet coat and draping it over a chair.

"It's coming down so thick, my wipers kept icing up. I drove with one arm out the window so I could grab the wiper blade and smack it against the windshield every quarter mile or so. I'm freezing."

"Here, sit by the fire," Sarah said, taking Lauren's ice-cold hand and leading her to the sofa.

"You're so warm," Lauren said, clutching Sarah's hands. Sarah smiled and warmed Lauren's fingers with her own for a few moments, wanting to gather her into her arms in the worst way. Instead, she disappeared into the kitchen to get their cocoa.

❖

Lauren sipped her steaming drink with a grateful sigh. "Have I told you lately you're a lifesaver? God, I'm still shaking. I couldn't see five feet in front of me the whole way."

"Well, I'm glad you made it. There's no way you would've gotten all the way to your house in this mess," Sarah said, throwing a blanket over Lauren's legs.

"Thanks. Oh, I'd better call Kat. She and Bridget are at our house, and I told them to stay put." She dialed the number, and Kat picked up immediately.

"Mom, where are you?"

"I'm okay, honey. I couldn't get all the way home, but I made it to Ms. O's house. This snow is insane."

Kat breathed out a sigh of relief. "Are you gonna be stuck there all night?"

"Well, now that you mention it, probably. There's a travel advisory, and it'll be dark in a couple of hours anyway. Are you girls okay there by yourselves?"

"Yes, Mom, we're fine. I'll call you later, okay?" Kat said.

"All right, hon. Bye." Lauren set her phone down and looked over at Sarah, who was curled up on the other end of the sofa. "Kat asked if I was going to be stuck here all night. That's looking like a distinct possibility if the snow doesn't stop soon. Would you be okay with me staying?"

"Of course, silly. You'd be crazy to go back out in this storm," Sarah replied.

Hmm, stuck in all night with the Great Kisser. Lauren was embarrassed her head had gone there so quickly.

Sarah also seemed a bit uneasy at the thought of her spending the night, if her bouncing knee was any indication. Lauren met Sarah's eyes, and the gaze smoldering between them left no doubt they were of the same mind.

They both looked away quickly and studied the fire in silence, sipping their cocoa for several minutes. Abruptly Sarah stood up and brought her mug out to the kitchen sink.

When she returned, Lauren smiled up at her. "I know what you're thinking," Lauren said, "but we are grown women, perfectly capable of keeping to our agreement. I promise I won't attack you." She winked, and Sarah grinned.

"Likewise," Sarah replied. "I mean, it's not like we're Kat and Bridget."

Lauren's mouth dropped open as the realization hit, and Sarah laughed out loud.

"Oh my God—do you think…? Why did you make me think about that?" Lauren asked.

"Oh, relax," Sarah said, still giggling. "They're both nearly eighteen, and at least nobody will get pregnant."

"True," Lauren conceded. "And Bridget has been extremely supportive and gentle with Kat." Her voice fell away as her daughter's trauma, which was never far from her mind, came to the forefront.

"I'd bet my next paycheck Bridget lets Kat lead if there's anything physical, so I don't think you have to worry about Kat being uncomfortable," Sarah said, sobering as well.

"I just don't want to see her get hurt. But you're right, Kat trusts Bridget and so do I." Lauren chuckled as a thought occurred to her. "Can you imagine how much trouble I'd be in if Kat knew we were talking about her love life? I'd get the silent treatment for a year."

"Oh, is that all? I'd have guessed extreme bodily harm," Sarah teased.

"Perhaps. That's why she'll never find out, right?" She shook a finger at Sarah in mock warning.

Sarah crossed her heart and then held up three fingers. "My lips are sealed. Scout's honor."

"Were you a Scout?" Lauren inquired dubiously.

"Well, I was a Brownie for a couple of months. Does that count?"

"It'll have to do," Lauren replied, then stretched and stood. "Excuse me. Gotta use the ladies' room."

"Okay. Want a refill on your hot chocolate?" Sarah asked, reaching for Lauren's mug.

"Most definitely."

Sarah flashed her a dimpled smile that shot like an arrow to her heart. Lauren was astounded at the reaction she was having. She smiled back, and as she left the room, she felt Sarah's eyes on her.

"This is going to be a long night," she mumbled with a sigh.

They were the picture of cozy contentment: two girls, one soft warm blanket, and a kitty, all snuggled together on the couch. Kat lay on her side with her head on Bridget's thigh, and Gracie was curled up at her feet, snoring softly. Bridget stroked Kat's dark hair as they watched the tail end of *Loving Annabelle* on Netflix.

As the final credits rolled, Kat turned over and looked up at Bridget. "Well, that was a sucky ending," she said. "What happened to happily ever after?"

"Actually, I saw this on video once, and there is an alternate ending," Bridget replied, "where they show Annabelle going out to Simone's beach house."

"Oh, good. They ought to at least have a chance, although it's kinda trippy how Annabelle falls for a teacher."

"Right?" Bridget agreed. "You've got to admit, though, their love scene is pretty hot."

Kat looked away, then back at the beautiful deep brown eyes she loved. "Don't laugh, but until now, I'd never seen two women... together."

"Ah," Bridget said. "And?"

"And I'm incredibly turned on right now."

Bridget leaned forward and lifted her into an embrace. Kat shifted to straddle her lap, and they kissed, slowly at first, then with increasing urgency. The intensity of what Kat was feeling was incredible, and she unconsciously began to move her hips against the thighs below her. Bridget responded with a moan, gripping Kat's hips and pulling her closer. They began to move together, kisses sliding from lips to throats and back again, their desire building until Kat thought she might explode. She let out a strangled whimper, and Bridget pulled back quickly.

"My God, baby, we have to stop. Are you okay?"

Kat pressed her forehead to Bridget's, breathing heavily. "Yes, I'm okay. Holy shit." She brought a hand to Bridget's cheek.

"We don't have to..." Bridget began, her forehead furrowed with concern.

"Holy shit," Kat repeated. She had never in her life felt her body respond like this. She had touched herself before, but her explorations hadn't come close.

"I'm sorry, Kat. I should've stopped sooner." The pained voice broke through Kat's fog of desire, and she realized that Bridget had misread her reaction.

"Oh, Bridg, it's fine. I'm fine." She ran her hands through her girlfriend's hair, mussing up the short strands until they stood adorably on end.

"I don't want you to feel like I expect...like we have to have sex, okay?" Bridget frowned. "I get so mad when I think about...I just don't want to hurt you."

Kat sat back on Bridget's knees and sighed. "I know what you're thinking. What happened to me before has nothing to do with you. I've been working through it with Sharon. The rape." She could finally say the word, but Bridget flinched and looked away.

"You don't have to talk about it, Kat," Bridget said quietly.

"Girl, look at me." Kat put her finger under Bridget's chin and sought her eyes again. "I need to talk about it so you'll know. Nothing about that experience comes to mind when I'm with you. Everything about you makes me feel safe, and happy, and loved. How I feel, what we just did—it's what I want."

"I do love you," Bridget said, eyes moist. "That's why I'm so angry the asshole hurt you."

Kat's eyes welled up as she watched her sweet, wonderful girlfriend struggle with her feelings, and she remembered what Sharon had said—rape hurts more than just the victim, and the fact that rapists are out there steals a piece of every female's sense of security.

"Bridget, I love you, too. You help me so much. Together we have to let it go, you know?" Kat hugged Bridget's head to her chest, then placed a kiss on top.

"How do you do that?" Bridget asked, rubbing Kat's back as they hugged.

"Do what?"

"Every time I think I'm taking care of you, you end up taking care of me."

Kat smiled. "Isn't love supposed to be taking care of each other?"

"Yeah, it is." Bridget gave Kat a squeeze.

"Hey," Kat said, gently pushing Bridget away by her shoulders, "I have a question."

"What?"

"Have you ever had sex with a girl before?"

Bridget's mouth dropped open, and she blushed scarlet. "Do I have to answer?"

"Yes, you do," Kat replied, swatting Bridget on the arm.

"Okay, then—yes, twice."

"Tell me," Kat demanded, eliciting a groan of protest from Bridget.

"It was in tenth grade. I went out with a girl for a couple of months. It was all just raging hormones and fumbling hands—kind of awkward, to be honest."

"Did you love her?" Kat asked.

"I guess I thought so at first. I mean, she was the first person I ever dated. She was a junior, and when she asked me out, I thought I was pretty badass."

Kat laughed. "I bet."

"But she was pushy, you know? She was always trying to get me to do stuff, like smoke weed and go to drinking parties in the woods. When I wouldn't follow her around like a puppy, she dumped me for a senior guy."

"Jeez," Kat said. "But I'm glad."

"You're glad I got dumped?"

"No, you goof," Kat said, wrapping her arms around Bridget's neck. "I'm glad you didn't let her turn you into someone you're not."

"Me, too. Later, she got busted in school for possession of marijuana and was suspended. She moved away that summer."

"Wow. You dodged a bullet there, huh?" Kat whistled.

"Yep." Bridget shifted uncomfortably. "Babe, my legs are numb."

"Whoops, sorry." Kat laughed. When she tried to get up, Bridget flipped her back onto the couch, causing Gracie to jump down with a disgruntled squawk.

"Are you done with all your questions about my sordid past?" Bridget asked, tickling Kat in the ribs.

Kat giggled, squirming. "Yes, yes! No more questions."

Bridget's fingers stilled, then moved up to stroke Kat's face. "I love you, Blue," she whispered.

"I love you back," Kat replied, pulling Bridget down for a kiss. "Let me show you." She ran her hands slowly across Bridget's back as they kissed, then down to cup her bottom. As things began to heat up again, Kat realized the narrow sofa was too confining. "Let's put the blanket on the floor. More room," she said, panting softly.

"Good plan."

The girls giggled as they struggled to get up quickly and retrieve the blanket. They spread it on top of the rug, making a cozy spot near the fireplace. Kneeling, they embraced, caressing each other and reveling in the feel of their bodies pressed together. Kat leaned forward, pushing Bridget backward slightly as she kissed her neck.

"Lie down," she demanded, her voice husky.

Bridget complied, and Kat straddled her hips. Leaning down, she delivered a scorching kiss that left them both breathless, then sat up slowly, brushing her hands over Bridget's chest. Looking into Bridget's eyes, which were heavy-lidded and nearly black with desire, Kat grasped the bottom of her own shirt and slowly pulled it over her head. Tossing it aside, she captured Bridget's hands and placed them on her breasts, eliciting deep moans from both of them. Bridget began to caress Kat's breasts through her bra, and realizing it had a front closure, she quickly flicked open the clasp.

Kat gasped as Bridget began circling her nipples with her thumbs. They hardened instantly, and she moaned as the sensation shot straight to her groin. She caressed Bridget's stomach, then ran her hands under her T-shirt to feel her hot skin. Moving her hands higher, she pushed the shirt up until she reached Bridget's ample breasts, the nipples straining at their confining sports bra.

"These need to come off," she whispered, and she moved back to sit on the floor between Bridget's legs, allowing her to sit up. Together they hastily removed Bridget's tee and bra, then embraced, savoring the exquisite feeling of soft skin on soft skin.

Bridget kissed Kat's neck, then nibbled a trail back to her waiting lips. Their kisses alone were nearly enough to send Kat into orbit, but she wanted, *needed* more. Kat sat with her legs over Bridget's thighs, their centers close. She could feel Bridget's heat even through her own jeans, and she reached between them to touch the origin of that heat. Bridget's breath hitched, and she began to move against Kat's hand. Kat stroked her through her pants, feeling Bridget's arousal dampen the fabric.

Not to be outdone, Bridget returned the favor, rubbing Kat along the moist seam of her jeans. They moved together, faster now, the delicious friction sending them hurtling toward orgasm. Kat came first, crying out in shocked delight, and Bridget followed quickly, shuddering as the wave of sensations overtook her.

"Oh my God," Kat said, as soon as she could breathe.

"You can say that again," Bridget replied, chuckling in wonder.

"Oh my God," Kat repeated with a grin. "That was—"

"Incredible?" Bridget finished.

"Most definitely." Kat tenderly kissed Bridget's forehead. "Imagine how it'll feel with our pants off."

Filling her hands with Kat's breasts, Bridget captured her lips in a kiss meant to fan the flames. "Let's find out."

CHAPTER TWENTY-TWO

"All right, tiebreaker," Sarah said, shaking the Boggle cubes for a fifth game.

"I will crush you," Lauren taunted.

Sarah laughed. "We'll see." As she flipped over the timer, Lauren's cell phone rang.

"Hang on a sec," Lauren said, looking at the screen. Her stomach clenched. "It's Trent."

"Do you want me to leave the room?" Sarah asked, moving to get up.

"No, stay," Lauren replied, grasping Sarah's hand. She took a deep breath and answered the call. "Hello?"

"What the fuck, Lauren."

"Hello to you, too, Trent," Lauren said calmly.

"I don't know what you think you're doing. When I was checking in at work yesterday, some fucking douchebag showed up to serve me with papers, right in front of everybody. I had to work my whole fucking double shift, all upset. Why would you embarrass me like that, or don't you give a shit?"

"I had no control over where or when they'd serve you," Lauren replied.

"Well, you had fucking control over filing for divorce in the first place," Trent raged.

Lauren struggled to keep her voice low, but her hands were shaking. "We can discuss this when you calm down."

"Calm down, my ass," Trent bellowed. "How am I supposed to feel when my goddamn wife blindsides me with divorce papers?"

"If you'd been paying attention over the last few months, you would've seen this coming, Trent. I told you how I felt several times." Lauren's shoulders slumped, and she removed her hand from Sarah's to rub her forehead. "Our marriage has been in trouble for quite a while now. You can't possibly tell me you haven't realized this."

Sarah moved to stand behind Lauren's chair, pulling her hair back and lightly rubbing her shoulders. Lauren reached back and touched her hand in thanks.

"You know I have a stressful job, Lauren. I don't know why you think it's such a big fucking deal if I need to let off steam after work by having a couple beers with the guys. None of the other COs' wives make an issue of it." Lauren could tell Trent was trying to rein in his anger.

"The problem is you don't stop at a couple of beers," Lauren answered, "and when you're drunk, you're mean. The whole point of blowing off steam after work is so you don't bring your work stress home. But you do bring it home, and you take it out on Kat and me. Even your lieutenant said you needed to work on your anger."

"So what, then—if I stop drinking, you'll come home?" Trent's voice was starting to take on the plaintive whine that always made Lauren cringe.

"It's not just the drinking, Trent. I've been after you for years to work on your relationship with our daughter."

"Oh, come on, L, she's a mama's girl. It's not my fault," Trent said dismissively.

Lauren could feel her blood starting to boil. Clearly this man would never take responsibility for his part in their problems.

"We were nineteen years old when I got pregnant, Trent. Don't you remember telling me I should consider having an abortion? What I think is you've always resented me, and Kat, because I wouldn't. You got tied down and had to grow up when you weren't ready."

Trent didn't deny her words, but he still tried to defend himself. "Hey, I went out and got a good fucking job to support you both. Do you think this is what I planned on doing with my life? I was gonna be a sports announcer, remember? I've made sacrifices."

"I never asked you to make those sacrifices, Trent, and Kat certainly isn't responsible for your choices. Last year, when all that crap went down, she really needed your support, and you turned on her."

"I didn't turn on her," he argued. "I just thought she was making a big deal out of nothing."

"Really," Lauren countered, "and what about now? Is rape nothing? Should she just forget it happened, too? I didn't tell her how you reacted to *that* news." Lauren was clenching the phone so tightly, her hand hurt.

Trent was silent for several moments, breathing harshly into the phone, before he responded. "Okay, okay, I hear you. So I made mistakes. I'm sorry. How am I supposed to fix them if you two won't come home? Come on, Lauren, just come back and we'll work on things together. I still love you."

Trent had predictably moved on to his say-anything-to-appease phase of the argument, but Lauren didn't bite. Time and distance had finally given her the clarity to see through his bullshit, as well as the strength to stand up to it.

Taking a deep breath, Lauren put an end to his futile attempts to sway her. "Trent, I'm done. I'm sorry this upsets you, but I no longer want to be in this marriage. You have the papers. Have your attorney call mine, and hopefully we can settle things peacefully. Good-bye."

As Lauren brought the phone away from her ear to disconnect, she could hear Trent's voice raging. "Fuck—wait." Then with a growl, he screamed, "You fucking bitch!" Silence. Lauren had ended the call. With a trembling hand, she put down the phone, then burst into tears.

"Oh, honey," Sarah said, and she walked around the chair to Lauren's side. Wordlessly, Lauren stood and sought the comfort of Sarah's arms. Sarah held her close, rubbing her back and hair with soothing strokes until Lauren was spent from crying.

"Come here," Sarah said, leading the way to the sofa. Lauren dropped heavily onto the cushion, and Sarah sat beside her. "Are you all right?"

It took Lauren several moments and a couple of shuddering breaths before she could answer. "Yes. No. Damn, that was hard."

"I heard a lot of it. Has he always been so abusive?" Sarah asked, rubbing the back of Lauren's hand with her thumb.

"No, not always. I mean, he always had a temper, but he didn't start getting so nasty until about five or six years ago. When Kat was in middle school, he was passed up for promotion twice. That's when I really noticed he was drinking more."

Sarah's eyes widened. "You've been putting up with that for six years?"

"Yeah, I know. I'm an idiot," Lauren said, a bitter edge to her voice.

"Hey, I didn't mean—" Sarah began.

Lauren put a hand up to stop her. "I know you meant it out of concern, not judgment. But you're right—six years is a long time. I beat myself up plenty, mostly because I kept Kat in a house full of tension for so long. At least he was never physically violent to us, although lots of household objects took a beating over the years." Lauren laughed mirthlessly. "Still, Kat was afraid of his temper."

"Well, at any rate, I think you handled the conversation beautifully," Sarah said. "I'm not sure I could've made it through without raising my voice."

"Really? Oh my God, I was a wreck. But I've learned yelling at him just makes things worse. Having you here helped me, though. It was much easier for me to stay calm. Thank you." Lauren covered Sarah's hand with her own, feeling immense gratitude for her.

"I'm glad, but you are a very strong woman, Lauren. It was all you, putting Trent in his place," Sarah replied.

"I'm going to need to be strong. Don't think for a minute this is over. I basically just poked a wounded bear."

"Well, no matter what happens, I've got your back," Sarah said. "There's something to be said for growing up with five bullheaded Irish brothers. I've learned not to take shit from anyone."

"Maybe we could send your brothers on a road trip to Alabama to talk sense into my husband," Lauren said with a laugh. A thought occurred to her, and she sobered. "You know, that word sounds strange to me. I haven't thought of him as a husband in a long time. But that seems so wrong."

"I don't think it's wrong. Most people would like to think *husband* describes a supportive, loving man. I'm sure it's what women hope for in one. Since you haven't felt much love or support from him lately, it makes sense the word has lost its meaning." Sarah grinned. "How's that for deep psychoanalysis?"

Lauren smiled. "Well done, Doc. Hope you don't charge three hundred bucks an hour, or I'll be broke by the end of the night."

"Seriously, though, Lauren—are you okay?"

Lauren stared thoughtfully at the crackling fire, her emotions in a jumble. "I will be. Moving up here, watching Kat blossom, meeting you...all of it has shown me how my life can be, how I want it to be. And I won't go back."

Feeling the intensity of Sarah's gaze, she turned. Sarah's green eyes were dark in the low light, and her lovely face was full of such tenderness and compassion, it took Lauren's breath away. She swallowed hard.

"If you keep looking at me like that, my self-control will be seriously tested," she said softly, "and I don't think I've got the energy to fight it." The burnished reds and golds of Sarah's hair shone in the firelight, and Lauren reached out to brush a strand from her forehead. Sarah caught Lauren's hand and held it.

"You don't make this easy, either, you know," she said. "We'd better find a safe distraction. How about I whip us up something to eat and we watch a movie? You choose," she said, pointing to her DVD collection, "but stay away from the romances. Deal?"

"Yes, ma'am." Lauren saluted and got up to check out the titles.

"Do Southwest omelets sound good to you?" Sarah called from the kitchen.

"Mmm, sounds great."

"I make 'em spicy, with peppers, onions, and salsa. Will that be okay?"

"Fine with me. Spicy onion breath is a great deterrent," Lauren teased, feeling lighthearted again.

"I'm not going there, you little troublemaker," Sarah responded, chuckling.

Lauren perused the rather impressive collection of DVDs, learning a bit more about Sarah through her taste in movies. "Ooh, let's watch *The Heat*," she suggested, a few minutes later. "Melissa McCarthy cracks me up."

"Good choice," Sarah agreed, carrying two plates from the kitchen.

Lauren cued up the movie, and they settled in, on opposite ends of the couch. They were joined by the cats, who curled up between them on their shared blanket, tail to tail, like furry chaperones creating a barrier. Sarah and Lauren exchanged glances and smiled, then dutifully turned their attention to the TV.

By eleven o'clock, they had watched two movies, and Sarah was now checking the news to get a weather update while Lauren called Kat.

"Are the girls all safe and sound?" she asked, as Lauren hung up her phone.

"Yep. Kat knows how neurotic I am, so before I even asked, she assured me the doors are locked, the stove is off, and the cat is fed."

"At least you know she's responsible, right?" She gestured toward the TV. "The lake effect band is shifting back up north. Looks like the worst is over. The plow crews will be working all night, so we should be able to dig you out in the morning and get you on your way."

Sarah called Lauren over to the window to look at the substantial amount of snow the storm had deposited. Illuminated by the streetlights, it sparkled like millions of tiny diamonds.

"It's so beautiful, but such a pain in the ass at the same time," Lauren remarked.

Sarah laughed. "That statement holds true for a lot of things— pets, kids…"

Lauren chuckled. "You're not kidding."

"So," Sarah said, turning off the television.

"So," Lauren replied, dipping her head shyly.

"Shall we get ready for bed?" Sarah asked. "I can lend you pajamas, though they may be a bit baggy on you. What do you prefer, a nightshirt or flannels?"

"A nightshirt would be great."

Sarah went upstairs to get things situated for her guest. After a few minutes, she returned and found Lauren had gone to wash the dishes. She stopped short at the kitchen doorway, silently taking in the sight of Lauren busying herself at the sink. Sarah felt a pang of…she wasn't exactly sure what. Maybe it was that no one else had been here late at night, taking care of household chores, since Kris. Or maybe Sarah very much liked seeing Lauren in that position. Either way, she felt slightly unnerved.

Clearing her throat, she walked into the kitchen. "I've got everything you'll need up in the bathroom, and the daybed in the guest room has an extra blanket in case you get cold."

"Thanks."

"Thank *you* for taking care of those dishes."

"Oh, no problem," Lauren responded, rinsing the last dish, then drying her hands on the dish towel. "It's the least I could do. Thank you so much for taking me in like this, in my weather-induced time of need. I really appreciate it."

"Well, of course. What kind of person would I be if I'd let you get stranded in a ditch?" Sarah replied with a wink.

"And thanks for being there during the whole mess with Trent earlier. It really helped to have your support. Seriously, what would I do without you?"

Sarah flushed warm. "You'd do just fine. You're the strong one, remember?"

"You make me feel like I am," Lauren said softly. "You make me feel like I can do anything." The look on her face drew Sarah in like a moth to a flame, and she took a step forward.

Reverse course! Reverse course!

Sarah stopped, and acknowledged Lauren's words with a nod. "Well, I guess we'd better hit the hay," she said, her voice a little too chipper to her own ears.

Lauren frowned slightly for a second, then recovered and said, "Yep, guess we'd better." She went upstairs to get ready for bed as Sarah checked the doors, fed the cats, and banked the fire.

In the bathroom, Sarah had laid out a washcloth and towel, a brand new toothbrush still in its package, and a pink nightshirt sporting penguins in sunglasses and the words *Chill Out*. Lauren smiled at the thoughtfulness of her host, and as she readied for bed, she thought about how much she enjoyed spending time with Sarah. She had not been this comfortable around another person in literally a decade, and it felt good.

Sarah reached the top of the stairs as Lauren exited the bathroom and stopped in her tracks. Lauren realized how she must look; the pink nightshirt fell to midthigh and clung to her body, accentuating her curves. Her breasts were free from the constraints of her bra, nipples prominent through the thin fabric. Sarah's gaze slowly traveled from Lauren's feet to her flushed cheeks, and Lauren clutched her bundle of clothes to her chest self-consciously.

Sarah shook her head almost imperceptibly and said, "All set? Can I get you anything else?"

"No, thanks," Lauren replied, acutely aware of the heat Sarah's gaze had caused in her belly. "I'm good."

"Okay, then. Your room is there, opposite mine," Sarah said, pointing to a door just down the hall.

Lauren wanted badly to hug Sarah good night, but she doubted the wisdom of such a move. Sarah seemed to be having similar thoughts, because they both just stood still, looking at each other. As the tension built, Lauren could practically see the conflicting emotions waging war in Sarah's mind.

Sarah sighed and looked down at her feet for a moment, then back at Lauren. "Good night, hon. Sweet dreams," she said softly.

Lauren nodded, clutching her clothing tighter. "Good night." She went into the guest room and closed the door, then rested her forehead against it. "Good God," she whispered. Sarah had made her wet with just a look, and her arousal stunned her. She took a few deep breaths, then turned and looked around the room. A daybed, covered with a nine-patch quilt in blues and greens, was set under one window. On the adjacent wall beneath the other window was a bookcase, and gracing the corner was a tall reading lamp which bathed its companion easy chair in golden light.

She needed a distraction, and not just from thoughts of Sarah. She didn't want to let Trent and their earlier conversation creep back into her head, either. Walking to the bookcase, she perused a few titles, drawing some out to read the back-cover blurbs. Most appeared to be lesbian romances, and Lauren was intrigued. One in particular, its cover showing a snow-covered landscape, seemed appropriate after the morning she'd had. Knowing she wouldn't sleep anytime soon, she settled in the chair and began to read. By the third chapter, Lauren was deeply engrossed in the romance, which was doing nothing to temper her arousal. She imagined that she and Sarah had taken the place of the characters in the book, and as she continued reading, her hand traveled slowly down her stomach and settled gently between her legs. She closed her eyes and began to stroke herself through the damp cotton of her panties.

Sarah lay staring at the ceiling, painfully cognizant of the woman across the hall, and of how adorably sexy she had looked in her bedtime attire. She couldn't remember the last time she'd been so turned on.

Sarah had left her door ajar, and she could still see a sliver of light under the guest room door. It took all of her self-discipline to stay put with Lauren only twenty feet away. She wondered what Lauren was doing, and if she had felt the electricity between them, too. *You need to quit wondering*, she admonished herself. *You set a boundary, and you can't cross it.* Sarah sighed and closed her eyes, willing her body to settle down. Sleep took its sweet time coming.

Chapter Twenty-three

Lauren pulled into her driveway at ten thirty a.m., exhausted. She and Sarah had gotten up, had a quick bite to eat, and gone out to tackle the two feet of snow covering the cars and driveway. After an hour and a half of snow blowing and shoveling, Lauren was able to move her car. Kat had called earlier to tell her that one of their neighbors, bless his heart, had plowed out their driveway, so at least she didn't have to shovel again at home. She was sore and tired and ready for a nap, despite the early hour.

"I'm home," she called as she walked in the door. She shrugged out of her coat, kicked off her boots, and promptly collapsed on the couch.

"Hey," Kat said, as she trotted down the stairs to give her a hug. "Can you believe all this snow?"

"My back can," Lauren replied with a groan. "It's killing me from shoveling. Is Bridget still here?"

"No, she left about an hour ago." Kat sat down next to Lauren. She stared at her hands for several moments, twiddling her thumbs nervously, then said, "Dad texted me last night."

"Oh?" Lauren said, trying to sound nonchalant.

"Yeah. He asked me three times for our address," Kat replied.

Lauren's heart skipped a beat. "Did you tell him?"

"No, I didn't respond at all. Have you talked to him recently?"

Lauren sighed and pinched the bridge of her nose. "I filed for divorce, and he got the papers. He called yesterday and went off on me."

"I knew he would," Kat exclaimed. "What did he say?"

"That he's sorry he made mistakes, and he wants us to come home to work on things," Lauren replied tiredly. She wasn't about to share all the bloody details with her daughter.

Kat looked concerned. "You're not going back, are you?"

"No, honey, I'm not." Lauren looked at Kat's eyes, so like her own, and saw nothing but relief there. "I told him I was done, but he didn't take it well."

Kat wrapped her arms around her, laying her head on her shoulder. "I'm really proud of you, Mom. He needs somebody to stand up to him."

Lauren was deeply touched by her daughter's support, but she felt a bit strange that the tables had turned. "Hey, aren't I the one that should be telling *you* how proud I am?"

"You always have, Mom. Now it's my turn."

Tears sprang to Lauren's eyes, and she turned to give her sweet loving child a hug. "I love you, Kit Kat. I sure got lucky having you for my daughter."

"Ditto, Mom," Kat said, getting misty herself.

"And you know what? I think this divorce will end up being good for your dad, too. He may not be ready to admit it, but he hasn't been happy, either. This may be what we both need to move forward, instead of staying stuck in a relationship that doesn't work anymore." Lauren knew her words rang true for herself; she could only hope Trent would one day feel the same way.

"I hope you're right, Mom." Kat shrugged. "It would be nice to see him happy for a change." They both sat quietly, each lost in her own thoughts.

Needing to change the subject, Lauren broke the silence. "So, tell me," she said, leaning back on the cushions. "What did you girls do last night?"

Kat blushed crimson. "Um, not much. We mostly binge-watched stuff on Netflix." She looked everywhere but at Lauren.

Despite Kat's best efforts to hide her feelings, nothing got by Lauren's motherly intuition. "Honey, I just want you to know I really like Bridget, and I totally approve of your relationship."

"Uh-huh," Kat responded warily.

"And I just want you to be careful, to be sure you're ready, if things start moving to the next level. You know?"

"Mom, jeez," Kat exclaimed. "Is this a sex talk?" Impossibly, she had turned even redder.

Lauren flushed, too, wondering if her daughter was experiencing things she herself wanted to experience, especially after last night. "It's just that, under the circumstances, I want to be sure you feel safe."

"I'm good," Kat replied, unable to stop herself from smiling. "I always feel safe with Bridget."

"Good. That's all I care about," Lauren said.

"Well, what did *you* do last night?" Kat asked with a saucy grin.

"If you must know, we played Boggle and watched movies," Lauren responded. *And thought about kissing each other a dozen times*, she thought, flushing again.

Kat looked at her mom curiously, then said, "Bridg and I also talked about my birthday. It's coming up, you know."

"Yes, I'm well aware. I was there when you were born, don't forget. So did you make plans?"

"Well, we figured we'd go out to dinner or something, but we didn't really plan beyond that."

Lauren looked at her daughter and shook her head.

"What?" Kat inquired.

"I just can't believe you're going to be eighteen. It went by so fast, and now you're all grown up, and I'm...old." Lauren sniffed dramatically.

"Mom, you are *not* old. Natasha's parents are in their fifties—*they're* old."

Lauren laughed. "Well, that's a relief. I've got a good fifteen years, then, before I become decrepit and senile."

Kat rolled her eyes, but she was smiling. "Whatever."

Lauren stifled a yawn. "I'm going upstairs for a nap. Throw a load of laundry in for me, will you?"

"Sure," Kat replied with a smirk. "It'll be my good deed for the day, helping the elderly."

Lauren gave Kat a swat on her behind. "Brat."

❖

Lauren was at the grocery store when she got a text from Sarah. *Guess what? I won a four-pack of tickets on the radio. Call me.* After checking out and getting her groceries into the car, Lauren called Sarah at work. They hadn't spoken in the couple of days since the storm.

"Hey there," Lauren greeted when she answered. "I'm calling you, as directed."

Sarah's voice became very animated. "Oh my God, Lauren, I am so excited. I won tickets to a concert I've been dying to see. The tickets went on sale two months ago, but they were expensive, and I didn't want to go alone." She practically squealed. "I never win anything—I can't believe it."

"Congratulations. Who is it?" Lauren responded, smiling at Sarah's giddiness.

"Lindsey Stirling."

Lauren had never heard of the person. "Who's she?"

"She is an amazing violinist and performance artist, and her music is fantastic. You've gotta come with me."

Lauren laughed. "Okay, okay—when and where is the show?"

"This coming Saturday, in Syracuse."

"Oh no," Lauren said, "Saturday is Kat's birthday. I was going to take the girls out for dinner at the Japanese hibachi restaurant."

"You mean Ichiban? I love that place. Listen, I don't mean to impinge on your birthday celebration plans, but what do you say we all go to dinner, then to the concert? The girls would love it."

Lauren loved the idea. "We could surprise Kat. But wait, are you sure you don't have anyone else you'd like to take?"

"Of course not," Sarah replied. "There's no one else I'd rather go with than you...all of you, I mean."

"Well, then, it's a date," Lauren replied. "Well, sort of."

"Right," Sarah laughed. "Check out Lindsey Stirling online, and I'll see you Saturday."

❖

The rest of the week trudged by, but finally Saturday arrived. Kat knew her mom had a surprise, and she had been relentless in her efforts to figure it out.

"You'll just have to wait and see," her mom had told her.

At four thirty p.m., the doorbell rang. "I'll get it," Kat hollered, running down the stairs. Bridget was at the door, carrying a bouquet of flowers and a pink gift bag.

"Happy birthday, Blue," she said, presenting the flowers to Kat and giving her a hug.

Flushing with pleasure, Kat gave her a peck on the cheek. "Thanks. I've never gotten flowers before. They're so pretty."

"Not as pretty as you. I know, corny line, but it's true," Bridget replied sheepishly.

"Aww. Let me put these in some water. Mom, do we have a vase?" she yelled up the stairs.

"Check the cupboard next to the sink."

As Kat went into the kitchen, her mom started down the stairs. "Hi, hon," she greeted Bridget, "has Kat been driving you crazy about tonight's surprise?"

"Oh, yeah. I told her I have no idea what's going on, but she doesn't believe me. Stubborn little thing, isn't she?"

"You have no idea."

"I have ears, you know," Kat griped good-naturedly as she returned with her vase of flowers.

"Ooh, those are beautiful," her mom enthused, admiring the bouquet of daisies, carnations, and pink roses. "What a lovely gift."

Blushing, Bridget handed the pink bag to Kat. "Would you like to open your present now or later?"

"Now, of course," Kat replied. From the bag she drew out an envelope and a tiny silver box. She opened the card first, and as she read it to herself, the sentiments contained within made her heart feel close to bursting. She looked up at Bridget adoringly, her eyes moist. Clearing her throat, her mom went to busy herself in the kitchen, leaving the two young women alone.

Kat slowly removed the lid from the silver box, and she let out a gasp. Inside was a beautiful silver claddagh ring, the delicately carved hands holding a heart made of aquamarine, Kat's birthstone.

"I didn't know if you'd ever seen a claddagh before," Bridget said. When Kat shook her head, Bridget continued. "The hands stand for friendship, the heart for love, and the crown for loyalty." Bridget took the ring from the box and placed it on Kat's right ring finger, with the bottom of the heart pointed toward her wrist. "If you wear it like this," she explained, "it means your heart belongs to another."

"Definitely true," Kat whispered, holding her hand out to admire the ring. "It's perfect." She put her arms around Bridget's neck and gently kissed her. "Thank you."

Bridget responded by bringing their lips together more thoroughly.

The sound of the doorbell brought Lauren out from the kitchen and prompted the girls to quickly disengage from their embrace, faces scarlet from embarrassment at having been caught. Lauren pretended she didn't see a thing, smothering a smile at the sweetness of young love.

Sarah was at the door, and when Lauren opened it, she scooted inside, cheeks pink from the early spring air.

"Hey, everybody," she greeted. "Are we ready for our special evening out?"

"Absolutely," Lauren replied, putting on her coat, and the girls nodded vigorously.

"Can I tell you all something before we go?" Bridget asked. She looked like she was going to explode.

"Sure," Lauren said, and the others waited expectantly.

"The letter came today," Bridget said, "and I got in."

Kat let out a whoop and started jumping up and down.

Lauren looked at Sarah with a confused smile, and Sarah explained. "I believe Bridget's telling us that she's been accepted to Cornell University."

"Oh my goodness, that's fantastic, sweetie. I'm so impressed."

"Thanks. I didn't want to take the focus away from Kat's birthday, but I couldn't stand it anymore," Bridget said, beaming with excitement.

"Are you kidding? Your news is just a bonus birthday present," Kat replied. "And now we have two things to celebrate tonight."

"Well, in that case, let's move on to our first destination," Sarah said.

"You mean there'll be more than one destination tonight?" Kat asked.

"You'll just have to wait and see," Lauren answered for the hundredth time, and everybody cracked up as they piled into Sarah's car.

❖

"That was *so* good," Bridget said with a groan as they made their way to the car after dinner.

"Right? My stomach is going to explode, but it was totally worth it," Kat agreed.

Lauren laughed. "Glad you enjoyed it. We'll have to come back next time someone has a birthday."

Sarah glanced at her phone. "We'd better get downtown or we'll never find a parking spot."

Kat looked like the suspense was going to do her in. "Can you please tell me where we're going?" she begged.

"All right, all right," Lauren replied. "We're going to the Landmark Theatre in Syracuse."

"Theater? We're going to a movie?"

"Nope," Bridget said excitedly. "They have plays and concerts there. We must be going to a show."

"You would be correct, but we're not saying another word about it," Sarah said, winking at the girls.

They drove down to the city and parked three blocks from the venue. Kat linked arms with Bridget and practically skipped all the way to the Landmark's doors. Lauren and Sarah walked at a more leisurely pace, shoulders touching.

"Thanks so much for all of this," Lauren said. "I haven't seen Kat this excited in a long time."

"You're welcome. Kat's not the only one who's excited. I haven't had a night out like this in ages."

"Well, maybe we'll need to remedy that," Lauren said, glancing sideways at Sarah with a smile.

"Maybe." Sarah playfully nudged Lauren's elbow with her own.

They caught up with the girls and went inside.

The tickets Sarah had won were actually for very good seats. They were on the center aisle, thirty rows back, with an unobstructed view of the stage. Kat and Bridget talked animatedly as they waited for the opening act, while Lauren and Sarah tried to hear each other over the noisy crowd.

"This is kind of weird. I feel like I'm on a double date with my kid," Lauren said.

"This is not a date. It's a birthday celebration."

"Well, I've had a great time so far on this non-date," Lauren replied, smiling.

"Wait until the music starts—it'll get even better." As if Sarah's words were the cue, the lights dimmed and the crowd roared.

❖

"She was so amazing," Kat exclaimed, as they left the concert.

"I can't believe she can play the violin so well while she's dancing and jumping all over the stage," Bridget added.

"It really was a phenomenal show," Lauren agreed. "Thanks to Ms. O, we got to see it."

"Yeah, thanks, Ms. O. This was my best birthday ever."

"You're very welcome," Sarah said, smiling. The girls walked ahead a bit, holding hands and chatting excitedly about the show.

"You made her whole month, you know," Lauren said. "How am I going to top this next year?"

Sarah laughed. "I'm sure you'll think of something. Did you enjoy the show?"

"It was fantastic. The music was so beautiful. Really, thank you for bringing us along." Lauren tucked her hand in Sarah's elbow, and Sarah hugged it to her side. They walked along companionably, happy to be spending time together.

On the way home, they listened to the CD Lauren had purchased from the merchandise vendors, which made the ride go by quickly. They pulled into Lauren's driveway just before midnight, tired and happy after a wonderful evening.

The four women walked up onto the porch and waited while Lauren fished her house key out of her purse. As she pushed it into the lock, a familiar yet chilling voice spoke from the darkness.

"Happy birthday, Kat."

CHAPTER TWENTY-FOUR

Lauren heard Kat's sharp intake of breath and spun around, peering into the darkness to see where the voice had come from. A dark-colored truck sat at the end of the driveway, and the shadowed figure of a man approached them.

"Trent," Lauren said, trying to keep her voice calm, "what are you doing here?"

"It's my daughter's birthday," he said, slurring his words. "I always see my daughter on her birthday. What, no one's happy to see me?"

Lauren's brain went into protective mode. "Of course, Trent. We're just surprised, is all."

As Trent came closer, it became very obvious he was drunk. "I wanna come in. I need to talk to you."

"I think it would be best if you didn't. It's pretty late for a visit. Why don't we get together tomorrow?" Old feelings of panic came flooding back, and Lauren's hands started to shake.

"Oh, so these people can go in your house, but I can't?" He turned his attention to Sarah, who was standing close to Lauren. "Who the fuck are you?"

"My name is Sarah, and I'm a friend of Lauren's," she replied calmly. "We've just been out celebrating Kat's birthday."

"I know where you've been," Trent sneered, "and I think you're way too friendly with my wife. And you," he snapped at Lauren, "why are you letting our daughter parade around holding hands with…with *that*?" He spat out the word, pointing at Bridget, and Kat flinched.

Lauren caught Bridget's eye and shook her head in warning. Bridget stayed silent, but Kat found her voice.

"Dad, please. I appreciate the birthday wish, but let's just talk tomorrow, okay?"

"No. I've waited long enough for you two to come to your senses. We'll deal with this now." He slowly advanced on them, and he was moving strangely. His shoulders were twitching, and his eyes were unnaturally wide open and darting all over the place.

Lauren held up her hands, palms out, trying to placate him. "It's Kat's birthday. Let's not ruin her night by fighting. We'll talk about all this in the morning, I promise."

"Ruin *her* night? Are you fucking serious? You two are ruining my life." His voice had risen to a fever pitch. "You're not gonna disrespect me anymore, you hear me?" he raged menacingly, fists clenched. He took a step closer, and the porch light glinted off something metal in his hand.

Worst-case scenarios flashed through Sarah's mind as she watched Trent pace and mutter to himself. She glanced back and saw Lauren's key still in the lock. She slowly reached behind Lauren and turned the key, then cleared her throat to get Bridget's attention. She darted her eyes from Bridget to Kat, to the door, then back to Bridget, hoping like hell the girl was catching her meaning. The increasingly irate man was about twenty feet away. They'd only have one chance.

Sarah touched Lauren's hip, then whispered, "Move backward on three." She tapped Lauren's hip three times, then pushed open the door and pulled Lauren in. Bridget grabbed Kat from behind and shoved her through the door, then slammed it shut just as Trent reached the top of the porch stairs.

"Lock it, quick," Sarah told Bridget.

Trent was pounding and yelling, "Open this door, dammit! You can't shut me out."

Two minutes later, the faint wail of a siren coming closer could be heard over his voice. "I texted my mom to call 9-1-1," Bridget said breathlessly.

"Oh, honey, good thinking," Sarah said, and Kat burst into tears of relief.

A patrol car pulled up outside, lights flashing. Trent tried to get to his truck, but the officers intercepted him before he could get in. Lauren took a deep breath and went outside, feeling safer now that Trent was in handcuffs.

As she approached them, Trent turned to her, eyes flashing. "You bitch. You called the cops on me?"

One of the officers gave his cuffed hands a sharp jerk. "Sir, that's enough. Ma'am, do you know this man?"

"Yes," Lauren said, voice quavering slightly, "he's my husband." Everything Trent had had on his person was sitting on the hood of the pickup, and Lauren saw one of his hunting knives there. A shiver ran down her spine.

As the officers tried to put Trent in the back of the patrol car, he struggled and kicked, yelling, "I didn't do anything. We were just talking. You can't arrest me. I'm a corrections officer." Once he was safely in the vehicle, one of the officers questioned Lauren while the second went up to the house to speak to the others. Fifteen minutes later, Trent was taken away, his erratic behavior earning him charges for menacing and resisting arrest.

Lauren went slowly back into the house. Sarah met her at the door, and Lauren fell into her arms, shaking violently. "Oh my God, Sarah. He had a knife," she whispered.

"Jesus, Lauren," Sarah replied, holding her close. "It's okay now. You're safe."

Kat and Bridget were on the couch, looking stunned. Kat sat trembling in the circle of Bridget's arms, tears tracking down her cheeks as she looked to her mom for some kind of explanation.

Lauren let go of Sarah and went to kneel in front of the girls. "I'm so sorry, baby."

"Was he stalking us? Why did he come here?" Kat asked, fear still present in her eyes.

"I don't know, honey. I know he's upset I filed for divorce, but that can't be all. He was definitely not himself, even if he was drinking."

Lauren put her hand on Bridget's knee. "Thank you so much. Your quick thinking made sure a bad situation didn't get worse." She glanced up at Sarah, who had come to stand next to the couch. "And you took a hell of a risk to keep us safe. I'm so grateful you were here, but I'm so terribly sorry you both got mixed up in this."

"You have no need to be sorry," Sarah replied. "It was pretty obvious you wouldn't be able to reason with him, so we just did what we had to do. The most important thing is you're safe."

"I know they took him to jail, but I can't help feeling like he's going to come pounding on the door again," Kat said in a tremulous voice.

"He won't. Now," Lauren said, standing up, "it's nearly one o'clock. Why don't you girls go upstairs and try to get some sleep?" Another thought occurred to her. "Wait, Bridget, we need to call your mom."

"All taken care of," Sarah said. "I talked to her while you were outside. Since they arrested Trent, Mrs. James is okay with Bridget staying with Kat."

Kat stood up and threw her arms around Lauren, sighing against her neck like she used to when she was small.

Lauren hugged her tightly. "It'll be okay, Kat. I won't let him hurt you."

"He seemed like a total stranger, didn't he?" Kat said. "He's never scared me like that before."

"I agree—something is going on, and I'll find out what it is. Now you need to go rest and think about what a great night we all had together, okay?"

"I'll try," Kat said softly. Then she took Bridget's hand and they went upstairs.

Sarah watched them go, then turned to Lauren. "Are you okay?"

"Oh God, I don't know," Lauren replied, throwing her hands up. "Never in a million years would I have expected him to show up here. I never even told him our address. Maybe it was on the legal papers or something."

"You've been living here for months. He could have just Googled you," Sarah guessed.

"I don't know, but I'll tell you what—I'm going to get to the bottom of things. There's no way in hell I'm going to let him scare Kat like that again." Lauren started to pace, her protective instincts fueling her anger.

"Well, in that case, you'd better get some rest, too." Sarah moved to get her coat.

"Will you stay?" Lauren asked, suddenly feeling very vulnerable.

"Of course," Sarah said, drawing Lauren into her arms. "I'm here," she whispered into her hair, and all the emotions of the evening spilled out through Lauren's sobs.

CHAPTER TWENTY-FIVE

It was almost ten when Lauren was awakened by a very hungry Gracie. She tried to sit up and found her legs were entangled with Sarah's, who was still asleep on the other end of the couch. Lauren gazed tenderly at her sleeping face, beautiful in repose, and remembered how Sarah had gently rubbed her back last night until she fell asleep.

Very gingerly extricating herself so as not to awaken Sarah, Lauren got up and fed the cat. Then she put coffee on, and while waiting for it to brew, she went over the previous night in her mind.

She pictured how Trent had looked: thinner, unshaven, his messy dark hair longer than his typical military cut. Kat had said he'd seemed like a stranger, and it was true. Sure, they'd endured similar drunken tirades from him in the past, but something about the way he had looked at them last night was foreign and unsettling. Lauren grabbed her phone and Googled the number for the county jail. She was going to have to face Trent and find out what was going on.

A quick call confirmed Trent was still there. He would remain locked up at least until his arraignment on Tuesday. Lauren hung up her phone, then grabbed a mug of the now-ready coffee and went back out to the living room.

Sarah was sitting up on the couch, looking rumpled and adorable, albeit unrested. "Mornin'," she said quietly.

"Hey there. Coffee?"

"God, yes, please." Sarah groaned, rubbing her hands over her face.

Lauren smiled and returned to the kitchen to get another mug. She brought the steaming brew out to Sarah, who accepted it gratefully.

"Mm, hazelnut, my favorite," Sarah said, breathing in the coffee's aroma.

Lauren sat down on the arm of the couch. "Did I wake you?"

"Not really," Sarah replied. "I've been drifting in and out for the last hour or so. Did you sleep okay?"

"Actually, I think I did. The last thing I remember was you rubbing my back, and then all of a sudden Gracie was waking me up for her breakfast."

"Can't keep a kitty waiting." Sarah chuckled. "Mine are probably royally pissed off at me right now."

"Oh, I'm sorry," Lauren said, feeling bad that she'd put Sarah out.

"Nonsense. Those little fur balls will survive just fine. They have plenty of energy in reserve, believe me."

"Thanks for staying last night," Lauren said, her brow furrowing in memory. "What a crazy chain of events, huh?"

"Certainly unexpected," Sarah agreed. "I heard you on the phone earlier. Did you get any news?"

"Yeah. Trent's at the county jail, and he'll be arraigned on Tuesday. I'm going to go see him in the morning."

"Are you sure you want to go up there?" Sarah asked, concern written all over her face.

"Yes. The man we saw last night was not the Trent I know, and I need to know why." Lauren felt determined and strong.

"I know you need to do this on your own, and I'll be at work, but will you please call me if you need anything?"

"Yes, but all I need is what you've already given me. Your support means the world." Lauren met Sarah's eyes, and the connection between them was almost audible, like electricity crackling across a line.

Lauren held their gaze for one moment, two, then looked away, flustered and slightly unnerved by her feelings. The depth of emotion between them had grown substantially, and Lauren felt it like a jolt every time she looked into Sarah's eyes.

"I'd better jump in the shower," she said, needing to give herself space. "There are blueberry muffins and more coffee in the kitchen." Lauren trotted quickly up the stairs without looking at Sarah again.

In the shower, Lauren stood under the warm spray, trying to get a grip on her conflicting emotions. Truth be told, seeing Trent and Sarah in the same space last night had thrown her, like seeing darkness and light collide. She was very aware of what she felt for Sarah, and equally sure of what she didn't feel anymore for Trent. So much had changed. Hot tears threatened; Lauren leaned her back against the tile wall and let them come.

❖

At eleven o'clock the next morning, Lauren pulled into the parking lot of the county jail. She sat for a moment, looking at the imposing building and steeling herself for her visit with Trent. The man was still her husband, and she cared about what happened to him. He was facing possible jail time, and she knew if other inmates found out he was a CO, he would be in danger.

She locked her car and entered the building, then waited as a couple of other people went through check-in. Lauren had purposely worn no jewelry, and had brought in only her keys and ID, knowing it would expedite her trip through security. A few moments later, she was sitting at a table in the visiting area, looking around anxiously at the stark surroundings. A few other visitors and inmates were talking quietly.

The door opened then, and Lauren turned to see Trent being led in by an officer. He was cuffed and clothed in a standard issue orange jumpsuit and slip-on sandals. The most remarkable thing about him, though, was the haunted expression on his face. He looked horrible, broken and scared.

Trent tried for bravado when he sat down across from Lauren. "What are you doing here?"

His voice challenged her, but his eyes pleaded for something else. Forgiveness? Understanding? Lauren wasn't sure what was going through his head.

"I promised you we'd talk. I just didn't think it would be under these circumstances," she said, not unkindly.

"Yeah, well," Trent started, then just shook his head and fell silent.

"Trent, I know you weren't yourself the other night. What is going on?"

Trent's anger returned. "What do you care? You up and left me, and you didn't care then how I felt, so why now?"

Lauren felt a stab of guilt, but she didn't succumb to it like she had in the past. "I do care about you, Trent. That hasn't changed, but *I* needed a change. And I wanted you to get help."

"I don't need help," Trent barked, and the CO in the corner stepped forward and cleared his throat in warning. In a lower voice, Trent continued, "I just need my wife."

Again, Lauren didn't take the bait. "You were extremely drunk, Trent, and you had a knife. If the police hadn't come, what would you have done?"

Trent at least had the decency to look ashamed. "I really don't remember much," he mumbled, head down. Then suddenly he lifted his head and looked at her. "I didn't hurt you, did I?" It was clear by the look on his face he was pretty fuzzy on the events that had occurred.

"No, you didn't hurt anyone, but you scared the crap out of us, and that's unacceptable." Lauren looked him in the eye then, with as much kindness as she could muster. "Trent, what is going on with you?"

He met her gaze then, and after a moment, his shoulders slumped and he looked away. "My life has gone to shit, that's what," he answered sullenly.

"It's more than the divorce, isn't it?" Lauren pressed. She noted his sunken cheeks and the dark circles under his eyes.

Trent didn't answer for a long time, but finally, he quietly told Lauren the truth. "After you left, I was pissed all the time. I went out every night after work, because I didn't want to be home alone. After a while, other officers told me I was being an asshole at work, dealing too harshly with the inmates and shit. I ignored them. I guess somebody reported me, because about a week ago, my lieutenant called me in and put me on administrative leave. He said I've got sixty days to get myself into rehab because my drinking is out of control, and I need to complete at least a monthlong program if I want to keep my job."

Lauren whistled low. "Whoa."

"Yeah," he said, and for the first time, Lauren noticed tears in his eyes. All of a sudden, she caught a glimpse of the boy she once knew. "I'm scared, L. I can't go to prison—they'll kill me in there."

"Prison?" That seemed a bit extreme for what had happened. Lauren had figured they'd probably just keep him in jail until he sobered up.

"They charged me with menacing and resisting arrest," he said, "but they also found spice in my truck."

Spice was synthetic marijuana, and if Trent had used it, she had explanation for his bizarre behavior the other night. "Oh my God," she whispered.

"My lawyer says he can probably get the menacing charge dropped, and he'll try to get me a plea deal and see if the judge will send me to rehab instead of jail, since I'm a first-time offender."

"I never expected you'd spend more than a night in jail. But," she said, "maybe this is a blessing in disguise."

Trent snorted. "Some fucking blessing," he mumbled, but Lauren caught a flicker of something akin to relief on his face.

"Five minutes," the officer announced loudly, signaling the impending close of visiting hours.

"Trent, I meant what I said. We are not going to get back together, but please take this chance to get your life back on track, okay?"

He wouldn't look at her for several moments, but finally, he nodded. As another officer came to escort him back to his cell, he stood and looked at her with a new intensity. "Please tell Kat I'm sorry," he said, his voice breaking. Lauren nodded, and then Trent turned and walked away.

CHAPTER TWENTY-SIX

S arah was in the cat room at the SPCA, cleaning the cage and scratching the ears of their newest arrival, a cat that looked just like Gracie. That's all it took to bring images of Lauren rushing to mind. Sarah was so grateful, and impressed, that Lauren had weathered the recent problems with Trent as well as she had. She was thinking how great it was to see Lauren's much more frequent smiles when her cell phone rang. Speak of the devil.

"Hello?"

"I got a job." Lauren's excitement radiated through the phone.

"Another magazine shoot?"

"No, better. I applied for a position at the community college, and I got it."

"Details, woman. What will you be doing?" Sarah asked with good-natured impatience.

"I'll be teaching continuing education courses in digital photography, portraiture, and photo-editing software. They have several sessions every year, and I'm told they're popular and well-attended. Oh, Sarah, you have no idea how much better I'll feel with a more regular paycheck. Funds are running low, and freelance work is hit or miss."

"Congratulations, hon. I know you've been applying all over the place."

"I really have. There aren't a lot of jobs in my field, and I was starting to get worried. I even put in applications at the grocery stores a couple of weeks ago."

"Well, I'm thrilled for you, Lauren," Sarah said sincerely. "The new job sounds like a lot of fun. When do you start?"

"May. It doesn't pay much, but if I supplement it with side jobs, I should be okay. Someday I'd love to open up my own studio."

"That would be fantastic. You'll need to have something to keep you busy when Kat goes off to college, right?"

"Ugh, don't remind me." Lauren groaned. "In my entire life, I've never really lived alone. I don't know if I'll love it or hate it."

"It does take some getting used to," Sarah replied. "Sometimes it's great being alone with your thoughts, and at other times that's the last thing you want."

"Tell me about it," Lauren agreed.

After several silent moments, Sarah thought the call had dropped. "Lauren, are you there?"

"Yeah, just remembering when Trent told me I'd never be able to make it on my own. Guess he was wrong, huh?"

"Damn right."

"Hey, could we get together?" Lauren asked. "I…I need to see you."

Sarah's desire to be there as a friend for Lauren warred with her growing attraction, which was becoming harder and harder to keep at bay when they were together. Either way, she couldn't say no.

"I'll be done here at the shelter at one o'clock. Do you want to meet somewhere?" Sarah asked, thinking she'd be safe from her hormones if they were in public.

"Would you mind coming to my place?"

So much for that plan.

"I'll be there."

❖

Shortly after one, Sarah knocked on Lauren's door.

"Hey," Lauren said when she opened it, smiling at Sarah and making her heart beat faster.

"Hey, yourself."

"Come on in."

Sarah took in the beautiful sight as Lauren moved aside to let her pass. Dark hair fell to Lauren's shoulders in glossy waves. She wore snug jeans with an ocean-hued Henley top that accentuated her breasts and impossibly blue eyes, and her feet were bare. Sarah's heated gaze traveled back up her body, stopping at Lauren's full lips.

Sarah swallowed and looked down, then realized with embarrassment how bad she must look. Her faded jeans sported dog hair and a muddy paw print on one thigh. A tuft of white cat fur was stuck to the sleeve of her old black Kelly Clarkson concert tee, and she imagined she must smell like a kennel. When she looked back up, Lauren was closing the distance between them, an amused smirk on her lips. Lauren reached out and plucked the fur from Sarah's shirt, let it float to the floor, then wrapped her in a more-than-friendly hug.

Sarah's hands dropped to Lauren's hips, and she buried her face in the soft hair at her neck. It smelled sweet, like coconut, and Sarah groaned softly, pulling Lauren closer until their bodies touched from head to knee. "God, this is so hard, not crossing that line, Lauren."

"I know, but I feel like I haven't seen you in forever," Lauren murmured, making no move to disengage from their embrace, "and it's only been a week."

"But a crazy week for you," Sarah replied, stroking Lauren's hair. "How are you holding up?"

"I'm okay. I'm happy Trent's going to rehab, but I know he's hoping I'll change my mind about the divorce. I told him I wasn't going back, but he never listens to things he doesn't want to hear."

Sarah pulled back from Lauren. Her body was humming with desire, and she needed to create distance. Still, she ran her fingers down Lauren's arm and clasped her hand, not wanting to separate from her entirely.

"Maybe the counseling he'll get at treatment will help him understand," she said, as she led Lauren over to the couch to sit. "How's Kat handling everything?"

Lauren tucked a leg beneath her and sat facing Sarah. "She was very upset about what happened the night of her birthday. He really scared the shit out of her, and she told me she's had a couple of nightmares since then. I think part of her feels glad he's going to get help, though. He wasn't always like this. She remembers when she was little and he used to take her to movies or the park and spend time with her."

"It's hard when you love someone but hate their behavior," Sarah said. "It makes you feel so conflicted."

"Exactly. I think she doesn't really know how to feel about him. I, on the other hand, have realized quite a few things about my feelings lately."

Unsure of what Lauren was getting at, Sarah simply said, "Oh?"

Lauren nodded. "When I was a kid, I thought Trent was strong and handsome and fun. Then when we got to Alabama, he kept having his fun while I became super responsible. When Kat came along, I was irritated he didn't take parenthood more seriously, but we still did what we thought was right and got married. Living together wasn't all it was cracked up to be either, but we worked at it and were fairly happy for a while."

Lauren shifted positions and, laying her head on the back of the couch, she stared at the ceiling.

"Trent didn't finish college. He had all these dreams of being a famous sports announcer and working for ESPN, but when Kat was born, his parents told him he needed to get a job to support us. He got into corrections with his cousins and never left. I think he resents Kat and me for ruining his plans."

"That's hardly fair," Sarah said. "His parents told him to quit school, not you."

"Yeah, but we were the reason. Plus, I did get to finish my associate's degree. I think he wanted to go back to school at some point, but it just never happened, so he focused on moving up in corrections. He made sergeant after about eight years, but he was in charge of D-Block, which houses the worst of the worst inmates. It stressed him out so much, and he just started to change. He wanted to get promoted to lieutenant so he could get out of having so much direct inmate contact, but he was passed up twice. That's when his drinking escalated and things got worse at home."

Lauren sighed and remained silent for several moments. Sarah watched the emotions conjured by Lauren's memories play across her features.

"You know, I felt bad for him, tried to be understanding and supportive, but it was like I couldn't get through to him. He was so bitter, so angry, and such an asshole. I have no idea why I stayed in that mess for so long."

Sarah held Lauren's hand, rubbing her thumb in light circles over her knuckles, and just listened. She realized Lauren needed to purge, to tell this story so she could make sense of everything that had happened and move on.

"That's why Kat and I are so close. We relied on each other because Trent was so unpredictable. But I never thought he'd turn on her and hurt her like he did. Something snapped in me and I knew I was done, with his tirades, his drinking, and his bullshit. And you know what? When I was with him this week at the jail, all I saw was a weak, selfish man who never really grew up. I felt absolutely nothing."

Lauren sat up and looked at Sarah with tears in her eyes. "But when I'm with you, I feel everything. Every inch of me feels alive and happy. How did I live all these years without that?"

Lauren's words touched Sarah so deeply she couldn't speak. She knew then with certainty she felt exactly the same way, and all she could do was pull Lauren into her arms and hold her. After stumbling along for years, she was finally ready to embark on her own new path of healing.

❖

"Tell me about Kris." Lauren was lying on the couch with her head on Sarah's thigh, while Sarah played with her hair. Lauren tilted her head back to watch Sarah's reaction to her gentle demand.

Sarah closed her eyes for a moment, her lovely face suffused with that mixture of sadness and affection people often feel when remembering a departed loved one. With a sigh, she began, "Kris was my first real love. I met her during grad school. She was the graduate assistant for my favorite professor, and since I took every class I could from Dr. Gerber, I ended up seeing her a lot." Sarah smiled at the memory. "Kris was everything I wasn't—outgoing, confident, and incredibly gorgeous. I spent quite a bit of time studying her instead of paying attention in class, and she noticed. She used to say she could tell if I was nearby, even if she couldn't see me, because she could feel my eyes on her." Sarah laughed. "Makes me sound like a creepy stalker, huh?"

"Nah," Lauren replied. "I saw her picture. She was gorgeous. I bet you weren't the only one staring at her."

"Very true. Anyway, thank God she was a take-charge kind of woman, because I thought she was way out of my league and never would've made a move."

"But she did?"

"Good Lord, did she ever," Sarah replied. "She came over to me on the last day of my practicum course and said, *Sarah, we need to date.*"

"Damn. That's pretty ballsy."

"I almost fell out of my chair. Kris was magnetic. She did everything with such intensity and passion. She forced me out of my comfort zone so many times. God, I did things with her I never thought I could do. While she was adding excitement to my life, she told me she needed me in hers because I calmed her and helped her stay grounded."

"I can see that. You do have a very calming presence, and you're very good at helping others."

"Well, thanks, but I obviously couldn't help enough," Sarah replied, shaking her head. "Kris was always on. She was a beast on the softball field. She drove like a maniac. She put in crazy hours at work. Her hobby was making crafts out of inlaid wood, like the picture frame on my mantel, and each piece had to be perfect, or she'd scrap it and start over." Sarah paused for a few moments, staring off into space. "I've often wondered if the way she lived her life contributed to her death. They told me at the hospital that many people have brain aneurisms, but only a small percentage actually burst or bleed. Kris had high blood pressure, but we didn't know it. What woman thinks she's going to die in her thirties?"

"Oh, honey, you don't blame yourself, do you?" Lauren asked, obviously seeing the anguish in Sarah's eyes.

"No, not really. Wild horses couldn't have stopped her from doing things her way. It just sucks that someone so full of life could be gone so quickly. She woke up that day with an awful headache, and four hours later, she was dead." Sarah wiped away a tear and let out a huge sigh. "You know what? I haven't talked about Kris like this to anyone in years. I thought I was over it as much as I'd ever be. But you," Sarah said, stroking Lauren's cheek with her thumb, "make me feel free of it, like I don't have to carry this grief around anymore."

Lauren reached up and touched Sarah's hand. "Do you think we were supposed to meet, like life threw us together on purpose?"

Sarah smiled. "Could be. I know it sounds cliché, but I believe everything really does happen for a reason."

Lauren sat up and turned around to face Sarah. "I have to take a road trip," she said, changing the subject abruptly, "back to Alabama while Trent is in rehab. I left things behind I'd like to get, and I need to tie up loose ends. I'm thinking it'll help me get closure on the place that was my home for so many years."

"I imagine you're right. When are you going?" Sarah asked.

"I was thinking next weekend, when spring break starts."

"Good, then Kat won't miss school while you're gone."

"Kat isn't going," Lauren said flatly. "She's afraid she'll run into people she doesn't want to see. I have a list of things she'd like from her old bedroom, but she was adamant she didn't want to go. I don't feel like I can force her, you know?"

"Yeah, but jeez, isn't it an awfully long drive alone?"

"I'll manage," Lauren said. "I've got to do this now. I couldn't deal with being there if Trent was home. Under the circumstances, this is the perfect opportunity."

"Absolutely," Sarah agreed. Suddenly, a bold and impulsive thought entered her mind. Before she could convince herself she was nuts, she said, "Do you think Kat would mind watching my kitties?"

"Huh?"

Hoping she wouldn't be rebuffed, Sarah took the plunge. "I'll help you drive."

At first Lauren looked confused, then stunned as she realized what Sarah was offering. "You mean help me drive to Alabama?"

"Well, I don't have to work over break, so I could lend a hand. If you want me to," she added quickly.

"Holy shit. You'd do that for me?" Lauren was looking at Sarah like she had three heads.

"Of course." Then a logistical and somewhat saner thought occurred to Sarah. "I'm sure you'll want to stay in the house when you get there. I'll just get a hotel room nearby."

"Uh-huh," Lauren said, not really paying attention and getting more excited by the minute. "Oh my God. This'll be so much fun." She grabbed Sarah's hands and squeezed. "We'll be like Thelma and Louise."

Sarah gave her a look of mock horror. "Jesus, I hope not. Things did not end well for them, if you recall."

"Ooh, good point," Lauren said. "Okay, Thelma and Louise except for the horrible ending."

Sarah smiled at Lauren's enthusiasm, but a niggling thought made her ask, "I'm not overstepping my bounds, am I?"

"Of course not," Lauren said, giving Sarah a quick hug. "I can't tell you how much I appreciate the offer. So, we have a plan?"

Sarah nodded. "We have a plan."

CHAPTER TWENTY-SEVEN

The following Saturday, at the crack of dawn, Lauren and Sarah were headed down I-81. Kat had been left with copious instructions by her mom, who was having a hard time leaving her eighteen-year-old home alone for a week.

"Gimme a break, Mom," Kat had said. "What do you think I'm gonna do, throw a kegger and destroy the place?"

"No…yes? You'd better not," Lauren had answered, only partially kidding.

Bridget's mom was Kat's emergency contact, and she had promised to make sure the girls behaved themselves. Sarah had asked Jamie to watch her cats, both she and Lauren having decided it might be best not to let Kat know they'd be taking this trip together. Kat knew they were friends, but they weren't ready to divulge their budding relationship to her. Jamie, on the other hand, was thrilled Sarah was getting out and doing things again.

Now that Lauren and Sarah were on the road, the excitement about the trip and the time they'd be spending together was the only thing on Sarah's mind.

"This is great," Sarah said. "I've never been as far south as we're going before."

"You won't think it's so great after spending twenty hours in the car."

"Hey, as long as I have good music, good snacks, and good company, and can stop to pee periodically, I'll be just fine," Sarah insisted happily.

So they drove, and talked, and sang along to the radio, and talked some more. Before they had even left New York, they had shared their memories from high school, the favorite teachers they'd had, and what they were like as teenagers. Heading through Pennsylvania, Lauren talked about her childhood and the loss of her parents, and Sarah described the craziness of growing up with her older brothers, who had been her greatest tormentors as well as her fiercest protectors.

Sarah was ready for a break when they stopped to stretch their legs and have a quick lunch in Fredericksburg. The air was much warmer here than it had been when they left home, which compelled Lauren to shed the zip-up hoodie she'd been wearing. Underneath was a form-fitting tank top that made Sarah look twice. With her trim figure, sleek ponytail, and sunglasses perched atop her head, Lauren looked like a hot but classy twentysomething. What attracted Sarah even more was that Lauren was so unpretentious. She was usually oblivious to the admiring looks she got from men and women alike, but as she slid behind the wheel, she must've felt Sarah's gaze upon her.

"What?" she said, when Sarah didn't look away.

"I'm just wondering if you realize how gorgeous you are," Sarah replied with a slow smile.

The look on Lauren's face told Sarah the compliment was very much appreciated. "No, but I'm glad you think so."

They looked at each other fondly for another long moment, until Lauren shook herself and smacked Sarah's knee. "Now quit looking at me, or we'll never get anywhere. I need to concentrate—this car can't drive itself, you know."

"Sorry, my bad," Sarah replied with a grin. "I'll behave."

Lauren pulled back onto the interstate, and they rode along in silence while she maneuvered around several slower-moving tractor trailers. Once clear of them, she glanced at Sarah, who had her head back on the headrest and her eyes closed.

"Are you going to take a nap?" Lauren asked quietly.

Sarah opened one eye. "Nope. Just keeping my eyes to myself."

Lauren laughed. "So, we've talked about family, our childhoods, and high school. What else do I need to know about you?

Oh, I know," she said, snapping her fingers. "Tell me your coming-out story."

Sarah opened both eyes and sat up straight. "Seriously?"

"Yep. I want to know how you knew you were gay."

"Well," Sarah said, leaning her head back again and trying to remember, "I think my first clue was in elementary school."

"Really?"

"Yes, like around third grade. There was a girl who always sat with me on the bus. She'd sit on the aisle, and whenever she wanted to look out the window, she'd put her hand on my thigh and lean over me. I remember it made me feel all warm and tingly."

"Holy crap. Raging hormones in third grade?" Lauren asked, incredulous.

"I have no idea if hormones were involved. I just remember it felt good when she touched me."

"Okay, go on," Lauren said, her interest piqued.

"I used to have celebrity crushes on female actors and singers. I always paid way more attention to them than their male counterparts."

"Like who?"

"Well, I had older brothers, so I wasn't into the same music other kids were, like boy bands or Britney Spears. I was into Stevie Nicks, Pat Benatar, women like that. When other kids were going to Dave Matthews shows in the summer, I was going to Lilith Fair." Sarah laughed at the memory. "I certainly wasn't mainstream. And with actors, I had a thing for Jodie Foster and Mary Stuart Masterson, like tons of other budding lesbians, I'm sure."

"Huh. But when did you really *know* know?" Lauren persisted.

Sarah thought for a bit. "I guess, I was about seventeen. I didn't really realize all those other things might mean something until then. But two things happened junior year. Ellen came out on TV and gave me the language I needed to describe myself. And I figured out, painfully, that I was in love with Anne, my best friend."

"Whoa," Lauren said. "What happened?"

"We'd been friends since ninth grade, and I thought she was cool and pretty and smart. I'd go to her house for sleepovers, try to take the same classes in school, be around her a lot. In retrospect, I was probably too emotionally attached, too needy, but I didn't see it then. My mom thought I just needed girl time, since I only had brothers, so she encouraged my friendship with Anne."

Sarah gazed out her window, still able to remember the pain of that earlier time. After a few moments, she continued.

"In junior year, Anne started seriously dating guys, and I remember feeling like my heart had been ripped out. The dynamic between us shifted, and I was hurt and resentful. I didn't even know why—I just knew I was jealous. I teased her about something stupid one day at the beginning of senior year, and she got all upset. I tried to apologize. I remember calling and calling, but she refused to talk to me. That was it. Our friendship was over. I was devastated. Her parents and siblings wouldn't talk to me either, and the other girls in our friend group took Anne's side. To this day it still hurts to think about it. Needless to say, twelfth grade sucked, and I spent a lot of time in the counseling office."

"Oh God, how brutal," Lauren said, empathizing with the teenaged Sarah.

"Yeah. I've thought about it many times over the years. I was totally clueless back then, but I wonder if Anne sensed my feelings were more than friendship and it made her uncomfortable. Guess I'll never know."

"Is that why you became a school counselor?" Lauren asked.

Sarah shot a look of surprise at her, unnerved at her insight.

"Actually, yes, in a way. Remember Ms. Duffy? She was one of the counselors when we were in school. Well, I was a hot mess all year, and she totally saved me. I became a counselor because of her, and because I wanted to help other kids navigate the minefield of adolescence, as I call it."

"Excellent description. And thank God you had Ms. Duffy, so my daughter could have you."

"Aww, thank you." Sarah reached over to give an affectionate rub to Lauren's arm, but Lauren captured her hand and held it to her thigh. They exchanged a warm glance and a smile.

"So anyway, not long after, I finally realized I was gay, and I came out to my parents. They were concerned but supportive, just wanting to make sure I was safe and okay. My obnoxious brothers started asking me to go cruising for girls with them." Sarah chuckled with affection. "My family was awesome, God love 'em. They made it easier for me to accept myself."

Lauren squeezed Sarah's hand. "I'm so glad they were there for you." She was pensive for a while, until Sarah asked if she was okay. "I'm just thinking about my parents, and wondering how they would have reacted if I'd been like you in high school."

"Did you ever think about another girl that way?" Sarah asked.

"I've thought a lot about that lately. I don't remember feeling physically attracted to any girls back then, but the emotional part, definitely. I think I even had a crush on my French teacher."

"Mrs. Beauchamp? Oh my God, I did, too," Sarah exclaimed. "She was hot."

"She was. I do remember admiring attractive women, idolizing certain female celebrities, but it never occurred to me to do anything other than what was expected. That's why I agreed to date Trent when my friend set us up. I mean, he was cute and fun, and I did eventually love him. Then when my parents died, he was all I had. I never dated anyone else."

"None of that really means you're gay, though," Sarah said, then groaned. "Ugh, I'm sorry. That sounded rude. I don't mean to minimize what you've experienced. It's just, often there are major defining moments that make a person realize they're gay, you know?"

Lauren pulled her hand back from Sarah's with a sigh and gripped the steering wheel tightly. She didn't say anything for several moments, and Sarah felt a knot form in her stomach.

"I'm sorry, Lauren. I didn't mean—"

"I know what you're thinking," Lauren interrupted. "You're afraid I don't really know how I feel. Maybe I'm just a late bloomer, but I know what I've experienced with you feels right. Maybe *you* are my major defining moment."

"Oh, honey," Sarah said, tears threatening. She reached over and cupped the back of Lauren's neck, caressing gently. "I'm sorry if I made you think I don't trust you."

"I get it, Sarah. This is uncharted territory for me, and I'm figuring a lot of things out. Just hang in there with me, okay?"

Sarah impulsively leaned over and kissed Lauren's cheek. "Okay."

"Now quit it. I'm trying to drive," Lauren said with a smile.

❖

They made it as far as South Carolina before they were too pooped to continue. Lauren had grabbed one of those travel booklets at the last rest stop and had been calling hotels to book a room. "Damn," she said, as she ended yet another call in frustration.

"What's going on?" Sarah asked, yawning.

"Apparently there's a huge regional car show around here this weekend. I've called five hotels, and they're all booked up."

"Oh, man, that's not good. Where have you been calling?"

"I'm trying to find someplace halfway decent. Shit, even the roach motels are probably full," Lauren griped.

"Don't give up just yet. Call a few more, okay?"

With a sigh, Lauren tried again. On the third call, she got lucky. "You have one room left? Oh, it's a single king." She glanced at Sarah, who nodded vigorously. "Okay, we'll take it." She gave her credit card information to hold the room, and ended the call. "Thank God."

"Where is it?" Sarah asked, thrilled that they'd soon be getting off the road.

"Next exit down."

Half an hour later, they dropped their bags and collapsed on the bed with a groan.

"Did I volunteer for this?" Sarah whined.

"Yes, you did. Told you it was a long drive."

"How in the world did you drive the whole way by yourself before?"

"Lots of coffee. Plus, I was trying to get as far away as possible before Trent found out we were gone. That had my adrenaline pumping." Lauren rolled onto her side and looked at Sarah. "Sorry about the one bed. Nobody had any double rooms."

"It's no problem. Besides, I'm too tired to jump your bones."

"Brat," Lauren said, giving Sarah's leg a whack. "We'd better get some sleep. We've got another eight hours to go tomorrow."

"Fabulous," Sarah replied sarcastically, then went to change and brush her teeth. She came out of the bathroom in sleep shorts and a loose black tank top, feeling self-conscious about her larger-than-it-used-to-be physique.

Lauren just smiled at her. "Feeling better?" she asked.

"Infinitely. I so had to get out of that bra." Sarah immediately felt her cheeks flame. *Way to be awkward*, she thought.

Lauren's eyes had dropped to Sarah's chest, where they lingered before slowly moving back up to Sarah's embarrassed face. "I'd better get ready for bed," she murmured. She grabbed her bag and made a beeline for the bathroom.

Sarah groaned inwardly and turned on the TV. A few minutes later, Lauren emerged. Her hair was down, and she wore a sage green tank and capris pajama set. Sarah turned her gaze from the TV and stared at the beautiful woman before her. "What side of the bed would you like?" she asked nervously.

"Doesn't matter," Lauren replied.

Sarah claimed the right side and climbed under the covers, studiously avoiding eye contact. Lauren lay down on the left, as close to the edge as she could get. Sarah surfed through the channels on the TV for a bit, hoping to find a suitable distraction.

"Do you see anything you'd like to watch?" she asked.

"You mean on the TV? Not really."

"Okay," Sarah responded, reading volumes into her comment. She switched off the TV and rolled to look at Lauren. "This isn't easy, you know."

"You are the queen of understatement," Lauren replied drily, staring at the ceiling. "Incidentally, there are seventy-one days until graduation."

"Oh, good Lord," Sarah groaned. "I'm having trouble remembering why we decided to do this to ourselves."

"To make sure of our feelings, and to not make things weird for Kat."

"Right, Kat. Gotta say, though—I'm pretty sure of how I feel right now," Sarah said.

"Frustrated?" Lauren quipped, and Sarah burst out laughing.

"Something like that. We did agree not to do anything we might regret later, right?"

"Yep," Lauren said, "and we are two grown adults. Surely we can use this bed for its intended purpose and go to sleep."

"Absolutely," Sarah responded, with as much conviction as she could muster. "Good night, then." She switched off her bedside light, wriggled down under the covers and closed her eyes.

"Sarah?"

"Hmm?"

"Thanks for coming with me."

"You're welcome."

Lauren switched off her light and settled in. Sarah lay there, needing to sleep, but so maddeningly aware of Lauren it was difficult to relax. After several minutes, Sarah heard the sheets rustle. Lauren's hand came reaching across the bed, searching for hers. Their fingers touched, then entwined, and Sarah heard Lauren let out a contented sigh. Giving Lauren's hand a squeeze, she drifted off to sleep, smiling.

❖

When Sarah awoke, Lauren was already up and in the shower. With a long stretch, Sarah sat up and rubbed her eyes. She'd slept like a rock, surprisingly; she usually didn't sleep well in strange places. She remembered holding Lauren's hand before falling asleep, and she smiled.

"What are you so happy about this morning?" Lauren said cheerfully as she emerged from the bathroom, towel-drying her hair. Already dressed, she looked fresh and rested.

"Just thinking about how unusually well I slept, holding your hand," Sarah replied, her smile widening.

Lauren looked at her with a warmth that made her insides quiver. "Did you sleep well?" Sarah asked.

"Like a baby, but we've got another long day on the road, so get up, woman."

"Yes, ma'am," Sarah replied, hopping out of bed with a grin. "Let me take a quick shower, and we can be on our way."

❖

A short while later, after grabbing a couple of bagels and coffee at the hotel, they were back on the road. Sarah drove the first shift, and they picked up where they had left off, talking about whatever topic came to mind.

The morning sun was streaming in through the driver's side window, causing Sarah's hair to glow like fire. Lauren reached out and began to play with the strands on the back of Sarah's neck.

"You have the most gorgeous hair. Many an envious woman has tried to find that color in a bottle, you know."

"Thanks. I hated having red hair when I was a kid. One time I wanted to dye it black, and my mother about had a cow."

"I agree with your mom," Lauren said. "Dyeing your hair would be a sin."

"I wish you could have known my mom," Sarah said, her voice holding a note of sadness. "She was such a great lady, and she would've loved you."

"Well, if she was anything like you, I'm sure I would've loved her, too," Lauren replied, ruffling Sarah's hair. Sarah shot her a glance, then looked back to the road.

Lauren's comment had been innocent enough, but she realized she'd sort of indirectly thrown the *L*-word out there. She thought about it; were her feelings for Sarah approaching that level? She looked at the woman beside her, taking in her lovely skin, incredible hair, the adorable dimple in her cheek. At that moment, Sarah looked at her again, her warm green eyes shining, and flashed her a beautiful smile. Lauren's heart and stomach did tandem somersaults, and she once again marveled at the connection between them. For the first time in a long while, she felt hopeful about her future.

Hours later, Lauren drove them across the border into Alabama, extremely glad to be on the home stretch. Sarah was napping beside her, leaving Lauren alone with her thoughts. The enormity of her decision to permanently stay in New York was hitting her, and she was anxious about how she'd feel being back in her house. She mentally reviewed the things she needed to accomplish on this trip, trying not to think about Trent or what his reaction would be.

It was amazing how much her life had changed in ten months. What had started as a temporary getaway was now a whole new life, for her and Kat. It was like they'd both been released from an existence they hadn't even realized was trapping them, and were now free to discover and be their authentic selves. The change was mind-blowing.

❖

Sarah stirred in her seat. "Where are we?" she asked.

"We've been in Alabama for almost an hour."

"Oh, wow. Sorry, I fell asleep. Do you need me to drive?"

"Nope, I'm good. We'll be there soon." Lauren let out a long sigh.

"Are you freaked out, hon?" Sarah asked, sensing Lauren's unease.

"Yep, a little."

"Listen, whatever you need from me, just tell me, okay? I know this is a huge deal for you. I don't want to get in your way."

"Oh, sweetie, thank you. Just having you with me will help immensely." Lauren reached over to hold Sarah's hand, which seemed to have become her new favorite pastime.

"How about some music?" Sarah asked. Lauren nodded, and Sarah began searching, bypassing several country and gospel stations until she landed on an old familiar tune.

"Ooh, I love this song. It was one of my mom's favorites." Roberta Flack and Donny Hathaway were singing "The Closer I Get To You," and the lyrics suddenly took on a whole new meaning for Sarah.

Wonder if the radio gods are trying to tell me something?

Sarah looked at Lauren, who was singing along softly to the music, and her heart did a backflip. When the song ended, Lauren was smiling.

"Damn, brings back memories. My mom used to listen to those songs, too. She'd always have the radio on in the kitchen, and I can picture her making dinner and singing." She gave Sarah's fingers a squeeze. "Betcha our moms would've liked each other."

"Probably." Sarah was still thinking about the song lyrics and how they had struck a chord. *God, this woman matters to me*, she thought. *Please don't let anything screw things up between us.*

"We're only about an hour away," Lauren said. "I'm praying none of the nosy neighbors will be around. I really don't want to talk to anybody."

"Isn't there anyone you *would* like to see?" Sarah asked.

"Yeah, I'd like to go see Jane, my boss at the portrait studio. She held my job for me until I finally called and resigned back in December. She's a sweetheart. Other than her, though, there really isn't anyone I've missed all that much. Pretty sad commentary on my life, don't you think?" Lauren was trying to make light of it, but not very successfully.

"You didn't socialize much, then?"

"Not really. My main choices were the PTA moms and the other COs' wives. I didn't particularly care to hang out with either group. Too much drama and gossip for me. I did go to all of Kat's school events and even volunteered in her classrooms when she was younger, but as far as socializing beyond that, I just didn't." Lauren sighed. "I'm quite sure Kat and I have been a hot topic of gossip since we left," she said, annoyed. "I just don't want to deal with any of that crap."

"Should we sneak you into town under cover of darkness? We could launch a stealth operation to retrieve your belongings, then hightail it out of there before anyone is the wiser," Sarah teased. She started to hum the theme song from *Mission: Impossible*, then winked at Lauren.

"You're a goof," Lauren said, but her smile had returned. She had exited the highway and was now driving through a residential area. Turning down a pretty, tree-lined street, she passed several houses, then slowed. She pulled into the drive of a dark gray Craftsman-style home with white trim. The house itself was lovely, but the landscaping hadn't been tended recently, and the grass needed cutting.

Lauren turned off the car and sat looking at her house for a long while. Poignant memories flooded her mind: the first time she saw the house and fell in love with it, planting the magnolia tree in the front yard when Kat was just a toddler, the hours spent decorating her home just so. And other, more painful, memories, of fights and Trent's drunken tirades, and of the events leading up to her leaving.

Sarah put a gentle hand on Lauren's shoulder. "You okay?"

Lauren blinked back tears and nodded. "Let's get this over with."

When Lauren fitted her key into the front door, it stuck, and she fleetingly worried Trent had changed the locks. After some wiggling, the key turned, and she breathed a sigh of relief. Upon entering, the first thing she noticed was the smell. Trent must have been smoking in the house, something she had not allowed when she lived here. The air was musty and reeked of stale cigarette smoke.

"Let's open the windows and air the place out," she said to Sarah, and they set about their task. Then Lauren slowly walked through the rooms, taking stock. The kitchen looked the same, although the pantry and refrigerator were nearly empty. In the living room, a thin layer of dust coated the shelves and furniture, and the family pictures were no longer displayed where they'd been.

Sarah stayed in the living room as Lauren went upstairs. The first thing Lauren noticed was a hole in the wall of the hallway, no doubt put there by Trent's fist, and she felt her blood pressure start to rise. She slowly opened the door to her bedroom and gasped loudly. Strewn all over the unmade bed were photographs, and several had been cut in half. Lauren felt a surge of anger when she noticed her lace-covered wedding album on the floor, partially concealed by the bed. As she approached the mess, she realized all the pictures had been ruined.

"You son of a bitch," Lauren cried. Trent knew how precious photographs were to Lauren, how important her need was to document their lives in pictures. Lauren had been left with very few photographs of her parents when they died, and she never wanted that to happen to her daughter. In his childish anger, Trent had systematically removed her not only from the wedding pictures, but from several other family shots as well. Lauren was beside herself.

"Lauren?" Sarah said tentatively from the doorway.

Lauren turned to her, tears streaming down her face. She gestured widely at the destruction, unable to speak.

"Oh, honey," Sarah said, and Lauren crumpled to the floor, sobbing. She cried and cried, releasing all the anger, sadness, and frustration she'd been carrying for far too long. Feeling arms encircle her, she turned her face into Sarah's shoulder and sobbed until she had no tears left.

Lauren went from room to room, robotically sorting through books, decorative items, CDs, and clothes. She was exhausted, but at least there had been one bright moment. Among her things on the shelf of her closet, there was a box full of negatives and SD cards she'd saved from years of taking photographs. Now that she could recover the majority of her pictures, Trent's rampage on her memories no longer caused the same anguish she'd felt hours before.

"Lauren? Would you like me to start packing this stuff?" Sarah had assembled the flat boxes they'd picked up at a U-Haul store in New York, and she now stood waiting, with packing tape in one hand and a Sharpie in the other.

Lauren smiled tiredly. "How about we do that after we eat? I'm starving. Trent barely has a can of soup here. We'll have to go out somewhere."

"Are you sure? I can go grab pizza or something if you don't want to risk running into anyone."

"Thanks, Sarah, and I appreciate your thoughtfulness, but right now I don't give a rat's ass who sees me or what they'll think if they do."

Sarah grinned. "Attagirl. Let's go somewhere nice, then, my treat. You deserve it after the day you've had."

"I don't know about somewhere nice. Look at me. I'm a sweaty, dusty mess!"

"You look beautiful," Sarah said sincerely, "but if it'll make you feel better, go wash your face or something. What's your favorite restaurant around here?"

"Don't laugh, but there's a local diner in town that I love. They have awesome comfort food, and their homemade rice pudding and cream pies are to die for."

"Homemade rice pudding and cream pies. Be still my sugar-addicted heart," Sarah said dramatically.

"Such a goof," Lauren said, shaking her head with a smile.

After a surprisingly fantastic meal and two decadent desserts, which they shared, Lauren and Sarah went back to the house to continue the chore of separating Lauren's life from Trent's. Sarah busied herself packing and marking boxes, while Lauren sought the requested items in Kat's old room. By the time she finished, it was quite late.

"Let's go to bed," Lauren said, yawning. "This'll all still be here tomorrow. Will you help me make up the beds with clean sheets?"

"Sure," Sarah answered, "but where...?"

"I'll sleep in Kat's bed, and you can have the guest room. I can't stomach the idea of sleeping in my old room—plus I refuse to clean up the mess the bloody idiot made in there." Lauren scowled, remembering.

They changed the beds and then got ready themselves. Lauren stood in the doorway of the guest room as Sarah turned down the covers.

"Sarah?"

"Hmm?"

"Thank you, again, for being here and helping me deal with everything," she said, her voice cracking from the strain of the day.

"But I just..." Lauren paused, then blew out a breath. She stood there, arms wrapped around herself as if she was cold, and looked miserably at the floor.

"What is it?" Sarah asked gently, crossing the room to stand before Lauren.

"I'm just sorry I got you mixed up in all this," Lauren said, tears escaping. "You've been so amazing, so good. You shouldn't have to deal with my screwed-up life."

"Hey, now," Sarah said, as she tenderly took Lauren's face in her hands and wiped her tears away with her thumbs. "You didn't get me mixed up in anything. I'm here because I want to be here, with you, okay?" She placed a soft kiss on Lauren's forehead. "Things will look brighter in the morning, hon. You just need sleep."

Putting an arm around Lauren's shoulders, she walked with her to her bed. "C'mon, now. Climb in." Lauren was so exhausted, she could barely keep her eyes open.

"'Kay," she mumbled, snuggling into the pillow. "G'night."

Sarah's desire to lie beside Lauren and hold her while she slept was so strong, it was almost physically painful. She stood for several moments, gazing at Lauren's already sleeping face. Her pale skin made the circles under her eyes look almost like bruises, and her forehead was etched with worry lines, but even so, she was incredibly beautiful. Sarah very gently smoothed the lines on Lauren's brow, then bent to place a whisper of a kiss on her lips. With a deep sigh, she went off to her own bed, hoping sleep would come quickly.

CHAPTER TWENTY-EIGHT

Two more days in Alabama ensured Lauren had time to sort through clothes and personal items and take what she didn't need to the Rescue Mission. She also visited Jane at the portrait studio to make copies of her work, in case she needed a portfolio to show to employers. All that remained was getting everything boxed up and loaded into the SUV, which Sarah handled.

She left the majority of kitchen items, linens, towels, and household tools for Trent, as well as most of the movies and CDs. She emptied Kat's drawers and closet and packed everything, so Kat could sort through things herself. Lauren took several mementos, framed art and photos, and all of the special Christmas ornaments Kat had either made or received for the last eighteen years.

The work took a toll on Lauren emotionally. Although she was sure she was making the right decision for herself and her daughter, there was still an inevitable feeling of loss weighing on her. Sarah had been wonderful, helping her to stay positive and focused on the task at hand. She would definitely not have accomplished what she had without her help. It was at night, after Sarah had retired to the guest room, when Lauren let herself cry.

As Trent was not allowed outside contact for the duration of his stint in rehab, Lauren wrote a detailed note for him, outlining what she had taken or donated. He would be upset, surely, that she had done all this without him present, but she felt it was best to handle things this way.

Lauren had cleaned up and organized the house as best she could for him, and had even found and removed his hidden stash of booze, to give him the best chance to maintain his sobriety. At this point, there was nothing left to do but leave.

"Everything's in the car," Sarah called from the front porch. "Take your time. We'll go whenever you're ready."

Lauren looked around one last time, saying good-bye to the house she had loved. This experience had been difficult and draining, but Lauren finally felt at peace. With one last glance, she walked out the door and locked it. Turning to Sarah with a smile, she said, "Let's go home."

❖

"So, how was the road trip?" Jamie asked at school on Monday.

"It is a *very* long drive to Alabama, let me tell you," Sarah responded, "but it was great to see places I'd never been before."

"Uh-huh. Let me rephrase. How was your road trip *alone* with Lauren?"

Sarah rolled her eyes. "Fine, Jamie. She had a tough job to do. I just went along for moral support."

"So she really left her husband, huh?" Jamie asked.

"She filed for divorce, yes."

"You'd better be careful, Sarah. I know you really like this woman, but you don't want to be her rebound romance," Jamie cautioned.

Sarah knew Jamie meant well, but she was getting irritated with the direction the conversation had taken. "Listen, I'm not looking for some meaningless fling. You should know me better than that."

Jamie backpedaled rapidly. "I'm sorry. I didn't mean to imply—"

"That I don't know what I'm doing?" Sarah finished. "Believe me, I know the implications of really liking that woman, but first and foremost, she is my friend. I have no intentions of taking advantage of that."

"Okay, okay. I hear you, and I know you've probably put a lot of thought into this already. I just don't want to see you get hurt," Jamie said, clearly trying to smooth over any bruised feelings.

"So says the woman who's always telling me to get out there and take a risk," countered Sarah, softening her words with a smile. "I am taking a risk, but it's mine to take, and the consequences are mine as well. Either way, I'll be fine." Sarah didn't know if she entirely believed her last statement, but at least it got Jamie off her back.

"Gotcha. So, what do you have going on this week?" Jamie asked, changing the subject.

"AP exams start soon. I'll be proctoring three of them, so I get to read a bunch of boring directions, then sit and watch the kids take their exam for three hours. At least I can catch up on my reading or paperwork."

"Sounds exciting," Jamie replied, with a voice indicating she'd rather watch paint dry.

"I actually don't mind it. May is my quietest month. Scheduling for next year is over, college and scholarship applications are all in, and even the drama seems to settle down at this time of year." Sarah shrugged. "Everyone's counting down until June." *Only sixty days to graduation.*

"Tell me about it. Well, I'd better get to homeroom. And since you're not super busy, I expect you to join me for lunch," Jamie demanded, heading off down the hall.

"Yes, ma'am," Sarah called after her.

Jamie's comment about Lauren being on the rebound bothered Sarah more than she cared to admit. If she was honest, the same thought *had* occurred to her, but the connection between her and Lauren felt deeper. Still, a bit of anxiety had crept into Sarah's mind, and she felt uneasy.

As if psychically sensing trouble, Lauren texted her.

Hey, hon. How are you?

They had returned from their trip on Friday evening and not spoken all weekend. Sarah had taken the time to do work around the house and relax before school reconvened. She knew Lauren had to unpack all they had brought back from Alabama, as well as emotionally process the finality of the move with Kat, so she had not reached out. Now, she very much wanted to hear Lauren's voice.

Call me, she texted back. A few seconds later, her phone rang. "Hey."

"Hey, yourself," Lauren replied, in the rich, warm alto Sarah loved to hear. "After all the conversation on our trip, I was going through withdrawal not talking to you."

Sarah laughed. "I know. I wanted to give you peace and quiet from my incessant chatter."

"Oh, stop. I had a great time listening to all your stories," Lauren scolded.

"Thanks. So, how did the unpacking go?"

"Physically or emotionally?"

"Both."

"Well, Kat was initially very happy that I brought everything of hers back, but when she was going through it all, she found a lot of reminders of the people she used to be friends with." Lauren sighed. "The boy who raped her was in a few group photos."

"Ouch. How did she handle that?"

"Extremely well, I think. She got upset, but not in a fearful, panicked way. She was just pissed. She took a black Sharpie and very neatly removed just him from each of the pictures. Then she went on about her business like he never existed." Lauren chuckled in wonder. "She's a stronger person than I'd be."

"I disagree," Sarah said. "From what I've seen, she gets her strength from you."

"Thanks for saying so," Lauren replied, with a hitch in her voice, "but how can you believe that when I cry at the drop of a hat?"

"Because crying is not a sign of weakness, sweetie. It takes strength to acknowledge your emotions. You cry because you have a huge heart and you feel things deeply. There is definitely nothing wrong with that, in my humble opinion."

Lauren sniffed. "There you go again, making me feel all good about myself."

Sarah laughed. "Excellent. Now, what do you say we meet this week for dinner?"

"Kat has to work after school, so you could come over here. I'll do Mexican. You don't know this yet, but I make a kick-ass burrito."

"*Muy bien*," Sarah said. "I'll be there."

❖

After devouring the best chicken and cheese burrito she'd ever had, Sarah sat back with a satisfied groan. "I am so full, but that burrito was fantastic."

"Thanks. I found the recipe online a few years ago. They're very easy to make, actually," Lauren said, as she cleared their plates.

They moved to the living room sofa with their bottles of root beer, Sarah's contribution to dinner. Gracie immediately jumped up on Sarah's lap and began to purr.

"Look. She remembers that you rescued her," Lauren said, smiling.

Sarah stroked the beautiful cat. "She is a sweet thing, isn't she?"

"Yes, and she's been very therapeutic for Kat and me. Best gift ever."

"I'm glad. So, what's next for you?"

"Well, I start at the college on Monday. Thank God, because I had to send in Kat's deposit for Ithaca the other day. I'm very nervous. I know my way around a camera, but I've never actually explained it to anyone else before. I downloaded a few materials and activities to help, so hopefully it'll go well."

"You'll be great. You're patient, knowledgeable, and friendly, and your voice is very soothing. Hey, maybe I'll sign up for your class. You think anyone will notice I've got a thing for the teacher?" Sarah winked at Lauren with a mischievous grin.

"Oh, that won't do, not at all," Lauren teased back. "I can't possibly enter into a relationship with one of my students. Think of the gossip."

"You had to go there," Sarah countered, rolling her eyes.

"Actually, I do want to go there," Lauren said more seriously. "I need to talk to you about our agreement."

Sarah's heart sank. *Oh shit, oh shit, oh shit.* "Okay," she said, quietly.

"We gave ourselves four months to figure this out," Lauren said, motioning back and forth between them with her finger.

"Yes."

"And I imagine you might be unsure if it's a long enough period of time, given that I just recently left my husband," Lauren continued.

Sarah just stared, incredulous that Lauren had summarized all of her fears in one sentence.

Lauren read her expression. "Ah, I thought you might be worried. I tried to put myself in your shoes. If it were me, I'd be cautious, too."

Sarah was having trouble finding her voice. *Where is she going with this?*

"So," Lauren was saying, "if you need more time to be sure about us, I completely understand."

Sarah just sat there, dumbstruck.

Lauren leaned over and, with a grin, put a finger under Sarah's chin and closed her mouth. "Relax, honey," Lauren soothed. "I just want you to know I'll give you all the time you need. For the record, I'm surer about you than I've ever been about anything, but I get that you might be leery of the not-yet-divorced and used-to-be-straight chick."

Sarah's eyes grew moist. A million amazing thoughts were racing through her head, but all she could manage to say was, "You're incredible."

"Glad you think so," Lauren answered with her heart-stopping smile. "So, does this mean we're still on for our day-after-graduation first date?"

Screw caution. "It's all I can think about," Sarah said.

"Really?" Lauren's eyes widened.

"Really. I'm so glad we've taken this time to get to know each other. I mean, I was attracted to you from the moment you entered my office that first day, because, you know, you're hot."

Lauren laughed. "Go on."

"But now, though you're still gorgeous, it's who you are inside that I'm wildly attracted to. You impress and inspire me, Lauren, and I haven't felt so at peace with anyone, even Kris, in my whole life."

"Sarah," Lauren said, "you just spoke my own thoughts. How is that possible?"

Pushing her long-held fears aside, Sarah took Lauren's hand and brought it to her cheek, then gently kissed the tender skin on the underside of her wrist. "Maybe we're meant to be?"

Lauren pulled her into a tight embrace, and Sarah could feel her trembling. "I think maybe you're right."

Sarah was acutely aware that things had shifted beyond physical attraction to something much deeper, and her heart sang.

Lauren released Sarah and looked at her with eyes sparkling with emotion. "Thank you," she whispered. "Thank you for just being you."

Sarah felt the magnetic pull to kiss Lauren and couldn't help herself from slowly leaning in. Then, they heard a key in the lock of the front door.

"Kat's home," Lauren said, placing a finger on Sarah's lips with a smile.

Sarah took a step back, chagrined and relieved at the same time. "Saved by the teenager," she said with a grin. "That was a close one."

CHAPTER TWENTY-NINE

"God, this month is dragging," Kat complained. "Down South, everyone's out of school already."

"Yeah, but remember, they were going to school in August while you were still enjoying summer," her mom replied. "You're in the home stretch now. There's, what, seventeen days of school left? Plus, we have a long Memorial Day weekend coming up."

"Okay, Ms. Positivity," Kat grumbled. "I still have three finals to take, and I'm so over high school. Please allow me my mini bitch fest and pity party."

"All right, grumpy pants, sheesh," her mom said. "Finish your breakfast—you're still going to school today."

"Whatever. At least tonight will be fun."

Today was the annual Fine Arts Extravaganza, and she had been looking forward to it for weeks. In the halls outside the auditorium, art students had their best work displayed in a museum-like showing, while on stage, the choral groups and bands would be putting on a musical showcase.

As a senior, Kat had several pieces on display, including two that had won awards in the regional scholastic art show. Her vibrant watercolor seascape had earned an honorable mention, and her pencil portrait drawing, which was so realistic it looked like a photograph, had won the Silver Key award.

Kat and Bridget walked through the displays after school, admiring all the artwork. When they came to Kat's portrait in pencil, Bridget scoffed in mock indignation.

"You should have gotten the Gold Key for this one, or even Best in Show," Bridget fussed. "I mean, seriously, can they not recognize perfection when they see it?"

Kat nudged her girlfriend with her elbow. "You know you only feel that way because it's a drawing of you."

Bridget flashed a cocky grin. "Mm-hmm, and you made me look damn sexy, too."

The girls were still giggling when they were joined by Kat's mom. "What's so funny?"

"Oh, Bridget here was just admiring her portrait," Kat replied.

"As she should. It's stunning."

"See? Told you," Bridget teased.

"Kat, I am so impressed with all of your work. I was just talking to Mr. Baker, and I thanked him for helping you create such a fantastic portfolio. I think he was able to discover talent even you didn't know you had."

"Thanks, Mom. He really is a great teacher. Which piece is your favorite?"

Lauren shook her head. "I'm not sure I could choose just one. I love Bridget's portrait, of course, and the black-and-white photo you took of Gracie sleeping in her sunny spot, but your "Past and Future" painting really moved me."

She was referring to an emotionally charged piece Kat had finished just last month. It depicted a girl walking on a path, with darkness behind her and light up ahead. In the darkness, Kat had painted the letters *PAST* to resemble haunting, agonized wraiths. The letters *FUTURE*, conversely, burst forth boldly from the other side of the canvas like rays of the sun. The girl held one hand up behind her, as if holding the wraiths at bay. With her face turned forward, her other hand reached out toward the promise of her future. The painting was an artistic rendering of Kat's journey, her catharsis, and it was very powerful.

"Hey, we'd better go find seats," Bridget interjected. "The concert's about to start."

With Lauren's blessing, the girls went off to join their friends. She entered the auditorium and stopped a few feet up the aisle, waiting for her eyes to adjust to the dimness. She let out a yelp when a hand grabbed her wrist.

"Are you trying to give me a heart attack?" she scolded, looking down at Sarah's impish grin.

"Of course not. Just thought you might need a seat," Sarah replied.

"Thanks. I didn't know you were going to be here," Lauren said, scooting past Sarah's legs to sit down.

"Jamie roped me into working the concession table with her tonight. My shift is over, so I thought I'd stay for the show."

"Well, I'm very glad to see you," Lauren said quietly, giving Sarah a flirtatious smile.

Sarah winked. "Ditto."

As the house lights dimmed further, Lauren discreetly moved her hand into the narrow space between their seats and was pleasantly surprised to find Sarah's hand already there, waiting. Linking their fingers, they glanced at each other with a smile and settled back to enjoy the music.

After the show, they stayed in their seats, chatting while the crowd dispersed.

"So, Kat's abandoning me to go camping with her friends this weekend," Lauren pouted. "Guess this will be a trial run of how it'll be once she goes to college."

"Well, that's perfect, actually. Jamie just told me she and her husband are putting their boat in the water on Saturday, since the weather's supposed to be so warm. She invited us to join them."

"Us? As in you and me?" Lauren asked, surprised.

"Yep. Jamie is dying to meet the woman who has me all dreamy-eyed, as she puts it."

"Wow. Are you sure you want to be seen out and about with me?" Lauren teased.

"Don't see the harm. After all, we're *just friends*," Sarah replied, making air quotes and winking.

"Then I accept. It'll be great to have a reason to put on my swimsuit again."

"Oh, my," Sarah replied, waggling her eyebrows, "thanks for the visual. I'll be looking forward to seeing that in person."

"Behave yourself," Lauren scolded. "Now, I need to go find my kid and get home. I've got notes to finish for my class tomorrow."

Sarah rose from her seat. "C'mon, then. I'll walk you out."

CHAPTER THIRTY

The next three days seemed to move in slow motion, but finally, Memorial Day weekend arrived. Sarah had four days off, and she was looking forward to relaxing before the final push at work, when she'd be busy checking final exam grades, registering kids for summer school, and adjusting course requests for the coming year.

She spent Friday frantically looking for a swimsuit, since her old one had seen better, and slimmer, days. After searching three department stores without any luck, she hit the jackpot at the outlet mall. Her purchases included black swim shorts and a matching tank, rubber-soled swim shoes, and a hooded white cover-up. Confident that she'd look at least halfway decent on the boat tomorrow, she headed home.

The next morning, Sarah swung by to pick up Lauren on the way to the marina. By midmorning, it was already seventy-five degrees and was promising to be a gorgeous day.

When she pulled into the driveway, Lauren came bounding down her front steps, a look of excited anticipation on her face. She was adorable in cutoff jean shorts and a pink T-shirt, with her ponytail pulled through the back of a white baseball cap and a beach bag slung over her shoulder.

"Hi," she said, as she got into the car. "I have so been looking forward to this. I'm excited to get out on the lake."

"Me, too," Sarah replied, grinning at Lauren's exuberance. "Looks like we've got perfect weather for it."

They met up with Jamie and Jay on the dock next to their cabin cruiser. Jay was loading coolers onto the boat and waved when he saw the women approaching.

"Jamie, they're here."

Jamie quickly emerged from below deck and came to greet them.

"Hey, girls. Ready for a little fun in the sun?" she asked, holding out a hand to help them aboard.

"Definitely," Sarah and Lauren answered simultaneously, then laughed.

"Hi, Lauren. I'm Jamie Gibson," she said, shaking Lauren's hand. "I really didn't get to meet you properly the night of the dance. Glad you could join us."

Lauren's smile faltered for a second at the mention of that awful night, but she recovered her composure quickly. "Thanks for inviting me. I've really been looking forward to this."

"You ladies ready?" Jay called.

"Yep," they answered. Jamie hopped onto the walkway to un-tether the boat, then quickly jumped back on board as Jay idled out of the slip.

They headed out on Owasco Lake, Jay cruising at a leisurely pace. The women sat on the deck, enjoying the breeze and waving at passing boaters.

"Did you remember the right kind of sunscreen this time, Sarah?" Jamie asked, as she stripped down to her swimsuit and began to apply lotion to her arms.

"Of course," Sarah replied. "Don't want to go through that again." To Lauren, she explained, "Last summer, when we were out on the boat, I brought spray-on sunscreen. It was breezy and the stuff didn't cover me enough—I burned red as a lobster. Lesson learned. I now use only lotion, and I spread it on thick." Sarah reached into her bag and produced an economy-sized bottle of sunscreen.

"That ought to cover you," Lauren laughed.

Sarah removed her T-shirt and shorts to reveal her new swimsuit. "Would you mind putting some on my back?" she asked, handing the bottle to Lauren.

"It would be my pleasure," Lauren murmured with a smile. She squeezed the lotion into her palm and began to slowly spread it across Sarah's fair, freckled skin. She ran her hands lightly over Sarah's back and shoulders, then down her arms, massaging the lotion in and lingering longer than was necessary for the task. When she was finished, she handed the lotion back to Sarah.

"Now do me," Lauren said, with a flirtatious grin. She stepped out of her shorts and pulled off her T-shirt to reveal a royal blue one-piece suit that fit her like a glove.

Sarah tried unsuccessfully not to stare at the vision before her. Lauren looked so sexy, Sarah felt the attraction in her groin. Lauren gave her a knowing smile, then turned to present her back. Sarah slowly applied the sunscreen to Lauren's velvety, sun-warmed skin, nearly moaning from the contact.

"So, girls, would you like a drink?"

Jamie's question startled Sarah, who had momentarily forgotten they weren't alone. "Sure," Sarah replied, reluctantly removing her hands from Lauren's skin. "What have you got?"

"Bottled water, hard cider, and soda," Jamie responded, pointing to a red cooler. "And yes, there's root beer."

"Ah, you're the best. Lauren, what would you like?"

"I'll have a root beer, too—if I'm allowed, that is," Lauren replied teasingly.

"I suppose I can share." Sarah went to the cooler, where Jamie was already getting herself a Pepsi.

Leaning close, Jamie whispered, "Holy shit. She's a hottie."

Sarah shushed her. "I know," she whispered back.

Jamie winked, then went up to the cockpit to bring Jay a drink.

Lauren had stretched out on a reclining deck chair and had her eyes closed, face to the sun. Sarah came and sat beside her, leaning back on the rail and wishing she had an excuse to touch her again.

"Kris was right," Lauren commented quietly, without opening her eyes.

"Huh?" Sarah said, startled at the mention of Kris's name.

"I said Kris was right. I can feel your eyes on me, too."

Sarah flushed with heat at Lauren's words. "I can't help it. You're so damn beautiful."

Lauren smiled and looked at Sarah tenderly. "I've never felt as beautiful as you make me feel. How do you do that?"

Sarah shrugged. "I'm just telling the truth."

"Well, from you I believe it."

Jamie came back from the cockpit then and settled into a chair, interrupting the moment. "So, girls, what's new?"

❖

Lauren was having an excellent time. Jamie and Jay were fun, and Sarah was relaxed and smiling as she helped Jamie prepare their lunch. Jay had dropped anchor, and the boat was gently rocking on the waves. Lauren pulled her camera out of her bag and began taking candid shots of them all as they chatted, unaware. Sarah was laughing at something Jamie had said, and as Lauren zoomed in for a close-up of her dimpled smile, Sarah turned and caught her. The look that passed between them could've set the boat on fire, and Lauren nearly dropped her camera.

"Jamie, I think I'm going to jump in and cool off before we eat," Sarah said, eyes never leaving Lauren's face.

"You sure about that? The water's still pretty cold," Jamie replied.

"That's okay. I'm feeling a bit overheated."

Lauren watched as Sarah draped her towel over the back of the boat, stepped onto the swim platform, and dived into the water. She emerged with a whoop, shaking her hair out of her eyes.

"It's cold, but it feels good."

Before she could think better of it, Lauren took off her sunglasses and jumped in. She came up sputtering to Sarah's delighted laughter.

"Holy crap, that's a shock," she said, moving close to Sarah in the water. "Was this your idea of a cold shower?"

"How'd you guess?" Sarah said, catching Lauren's hand under the water.

"Because I was a little overheated, too."

They gazed into each other's eyes, grinning like fools, until Jamie called, "Hate to break up your polar bear plunge, you two, but you're gonna freeze if you don't get back out."

❖

Sarah helped Jamie bring the remains of their lunch down to the galley. As soon as they were alone, Jamie pounced.

"Girl, you got it bad."

Sarah played dumb. "What do you mean?"

"Oh, please. The way you two look at each other, it's plain as day. You're falling in love, aren't you?"

Whoa. Love. The word flowed over Sarah like warm honey, soothing rather than scaring her. "She's pretty amazing, isn't she?"

"Yes, she's great, and you didn't answer my question."

"Oh, Jamie. I think maybe I am."

Jamie gave Sarah a huge bear hug. "Woo-hoo, girl. I approve."

"Well, jeez, thank goodness for that," Sarah said, rolling her eyes.

"I'm excited for you, honey. She looks good on you."

Sarah couldn't stop smiling. "I'm happy, Jamie."

"Good. You deserve it. Let's head back up, so I can watch you get all dreamy-eyed again," Jamie teased.

"Don't you embarrass me, Jamie Gibson," Sarah warned, swatting Jamie on the arm.

"Wouldn't dream of it."

Sarah climbed the galley steps and took a seat on the deck chair next to Lauren's. She stretched out her legs with a contented sigh.

"Jamie just winked at me," Lauren said. "What were you two talking about down there?"

Sarah leaned over and whispered, "She likes you. And she likes *us*, together."

"That Jamie is one smart woman," Lauren replied, looking pleased.

"Yes, she is." Sarah looked Lauren in the eye. "I told her you make me happy."

Lauren's face lit up. "Do I?"

Sarah nodded, then took Lauren's hand in hers and lay back in her chair. *I'm out on the lake, soaking up the sun, and holding hands with the most beautiful woman I know. Yep, I'm happy.*

CHAPTER THIRTY-ONE

Graduation day dawned bright and sunny and was fore-casted to stay that way, ensuring the ceremony would be held outdoors in the high school stadium. Kat and Bridget had gone out for a late breakfast, then spent the day together up at the lake. It was a big day, and they were both excited and nervous. Though they were ready to leave high school behind, the next phase of their lives loomed large.

"What do you think college will be like?" Kat asked, as they sat sunning themselves on a blanket and watching the ducks at the water's edge.

"I don't know, but it'll definitely be way different than high school."

"No doubt. It'll be weird having a roommate. That's kind of freaking me out. What if we end up with people we can't stand?"

"Well, the housing questionnaire they made you fill out is sup-posed to help match you to someone compatible. Guess we'll have to wait and see," Bridget said with a shrug.

"Do you think we'll be able to see each other much?" Unspoken was Kat's fear that, since they'd be on different campuses, Bridget would find other activities, or girls, to occupy her time.

"Our campuses are only five minutes apart, but unfortunately, I think I'll be living at the library twenty-four-seven." Bridget groaned. "I've heard the students at Cornell are pretty intense about their academics. I'll probably have to bust my ass on the daily just to keep up."

"You'll be fine. You got into Cornell for a reason, and I'm sure I'll be spending tons of time in the art building myself. I'm not gonna lie, though, Bridg. It'll be tough not seeing you every day." Her anxiety was evident in her voice.

"We have two months to go before we have to think about it," Bridget soothed, "and there's always Skype. I agree, though. College will definitely be an adjustment."

Kat was trying hard not to seem too needy, but her anxiety won out. "What if you meet someone else?"

"Oh, baby, is that what you're worried about?" Bridget took Kat's hand in hers.

"Well, yeah. I mean, you're so amazing, and you're going to meet so many new people…"

"Don't you think I've thought the same thing about you? You're gorgeous and talented and sweet. I bet tons of girls, and guys, will be checking you out." Bridget squeezed Kat's fingers. "It scares me, too, you know. We can't predict what'll happen down the road."

Kat shrugged and stared at the blanket, trying to hold back her tears.

"Baby, look at me," Bridget demanded gently.

Kat met Bridget's eyes and saw that they, too, shimmered with unshed tears.

"All I know is I can't imagine finding anyone who is more perfect for me than you are, and I have no intention of even looking. I love you so much, Kat—you must know that."

Kat, not caring who might be nearby, launched herself into Bridget's arms, nearly knocking her over. "Oh my God, I so needed to hear those words," she whispered into Bridget's ear, "because I feel exactly the same way. I love you, too."

They put each other's fears to rest with the most deeply emotional kiss they'd yet shared. When an approaching group of noisy picnickers reminded them of their surroundings, Bridget stood and pulled Kat up with her.

"C'mon, Blue. It's graduation day. Let's go get ready for one of the most important moments of our lives."

❖

As the seniors lined up waiting for the processional to begin, Kat fidgeted with her cap and tassel. She was nearly giddy with nerves and excitement. She couldn't believe she was graduating; what a year it had been.

Kat thought back to her first day. She could never have guessed how much her life would change. She was the happiest she'd ever been, and a feeling of deep gratitude swept over her. Kat turned to find where Bridget stood, farther back in the line. Bridget caught her eye, winked, and mouthed, "I love you." Kat flashed a brilliant smile in return and blew her girlfriend a kiss. Just then, the dignified notes of "Pomp and Circumstance" reached the graduates' ears, and they slowly began to file into the stadium.

As she walked, Kat searched the stands for her mom. She soon found her, frantically waving her arm at Kat and beaming from ear to ear. This was a huge day for both of them. Tears came to Kat's eyes, and she was overwhelmed with happiness.

The ceremony began. Student leaders spoke to their peers, sharing memories and offering congratulations on their collective growth and accomplishments. Then the superintendent and principal spoke, each dispensing words of wisdom and extolling the virtues of hard work, good character, and compassion for others. The principal also spoke about overcoming obstacles, assuring the students they all had the strength to handle whatever life would throw at them. Kat listened intently and felt a flash of pride, believing that, at least for her, his words rang true.

Finally, the time came for the students to receive their diplomas. Sarah approached the podium with Joan Hayden to perform their roles in the ceremony. As the line of students reached the podium, Sarah's job was to take the name card from each student, check for correct pronunciation, and hand the card to Joan, who announced the student's name. Sarah loved having the opportunity to do this every year. She got to calm nerves, give hugs, and congratulate each student as they crossed the line from high school teen to young adult, and it was extremely gratifying.

As they got to the *E*s, Sarah could see Kat nervously approaching. *Jason Earle...Tricia Edwards...Shaniqua Ellison...*

Then it was her turn. Sarah could see the moment was deeply emotional for the young woman. She smiled, and Kat suddenly reached out to give her a huge hug.

"Thank you for everything, Ms. O," she whispered.

"Oh, honey, I'm so proud of you. One more step, and then you're off to college. Ready?"

Kat stepped back and nodded. Then she leaned in again and whispered, "When I go, take good care of my mom." Mrs. Hayden announced her name, and with a wink, Kat moved on.

Oh my God, she knows? Sarah was flabbergasted, but she had to recover quickly; the next student was waiting.

As the ceremony ended and gaily flung mortarboards sailed through the air, the crowd of well-wishers flooded the field. Kat wove through the throngs of people, trying to find her mom and Bridget. Bridget found her first. Swinging Kat around in a giant bear hug, she hollered, "Woo-hoo!"

Kat giggled. "Put me down, you goof."

"We did it, Blue. High school is officially over." Bridget glanced over Kat's shoulder. "Here comes your mom."

Turning, Kat nearly collided with her mom's outstretched arms.

"My baby, a high school graduate," her mom said, squeezing Kat tightly. "I'm so proud of you."

"Thanks, Mom."

Her mom and Bridget exchanged hugs, too, then Kat took a selfie of the three of them. She could never have imagined a year ago that she'd be at her graduation, with her *girlfriend*, feeling happy and whole again. Kat was infinitely grateful, and like the principal had said in his speech, her future looked very bright. She turned to smile at Bridget, seeing so much love in her eyes. "Happy graduation, baby. We did it."

A few minutes later, they began to make their way out of the stadium. Lauren repeatedly scanned the crowd, looking for Sarah. They had nearly made it to the parking lot before she caught sight of her, laughing with a couple of students and their parents. Lauren's heart leapt with pleasure.

"You go on," Lauren said to Kat. "I'll meet you at the car."

She walked toward Sarah, taking in the details. It was a warm evening; Sarah had removed her black faculty robe and master's hood and had them draped over her bare arm. She wore a sleeveless black V-neck blouse with creamy white pedal pushers and black sandals. Her bright hair gave the outfit a splash of color, and when those warm green eyes caught sight of Lauren approaching, she was treated to a pulse-quickening smile.

She waited for Sarah to disengage from her conversation, which didn't take long. Sarah motioned for Lauren to join her under a nearby tree, where fewer people were milling about.

"Hey there, beautiful," Sarah greeted quietly, giving Lauren a discreet once-over.

"Hey. You're looking pretty fabulous yourself. Lovely ceremony, wasn't it?"

"Yes, it was. Kat seemed very happy."

"She's been so excited all day. I'm thrilled for her," Lauren said. "What did she say to you down there? You got a funny look on your face."

Sarah's eyes widened. "You won't believe it. She said, *Take good care of my mom*, and winked at me."

"Shut up. She did not."

"Swear to God," Sarah said, crossing her heart. "So much for discretion, eh?"

"Kat's a smart cookie. Not much gets by her, but damn."

"I know, right?" Sarah chuckled. "It's all good."

"Yes," Lauren agreed, "it is. I just wanted to tell you that tonight is all about Kat and her accomplishments. But tomorrow," she said softly, brushing Sarah's hand with a fleeting touch, "will be all about us."

Sarah's lovely face flushed and her eyes darkened. "Until tomorrow, then," she whispered.

Lauren gave Sarah a quick hug and hurried off to celebrate with her daughter.

CHAPTER THIRTY-TWO

S arah had just gotten out of the shower when her phone rang. Running naked and still dripping into her bedroom, she snatched it up on the second ring.

"Hello?" she said, a little breathlessly.

Lauren's throaty laugh came over the line. "Morning, sunshine. Did you just run a marathon or something?"

"Like that would ever happen. I just got out of the shower," Sarah replied, holding the phone in one hand while trying to towel dry with the other.

"Mm," Lauren said flirtatiously. "So, I'm calling to confirm the plans for our first date."

"Excellent. If you'd still like to, we can drive over to Skaneateles and putter around in the shops, then have dinner at the Sherwood Inn. I made reservations."

"Sounds lovely," Lauren replied.

"Pick you up at two o'clock?"

"Yes. I can't wait to see you," Lauren said, her voice dropping lower. "Wear something sexy."

Good Lord…no pressure there.

After Sarah hung up, she perused her closet for a long time, trying desperately to find something that would qualify as sexy. She had never in her life thought the adjective could apply to her, and she was at a loss.

She tried imagining the types of outfits she found attractive on women, but that was a bust. No little black dresses had ever graced the hangers in *her* closet. Sarah flopped on her bed and groaned. She needed to have her outfit laid out before she left for her shift at the shelter, and she was running out of time.

Sarah sighed. *You're trying too hard. Just be yourself.* After a moment, she got up and found her newest pair of black capris and her favorite forest green sleeveless silk blouse. She laid them on her bed and nodded, as satisfied as she was likely to be.

Suddenly, thoughts of Kris entered her mind, and although Sarah felt a pang of loss, it was nothing like the sharp pain she used to feel.

You always said I looked pretty in green, Krissy. What do you think? Sarah closed her eyes, and an image of Kris flashed before her. Disbelieving tears sprang to Sarah's eyes when she heard Kris's voice, with crystal clarity, say, *You're ready, babe. Go and be happy.* In her mind's eye, Sarah saw Kris smile and nod, then blow her a kiss.

Overwhelmed with love and gratitude, Sarah cried, cleansing away her fear and replacing it with hope. She knew in her heart that she had just received Kris's blessing and that her grief would no longer hold her back. As she dried her eyes, she thought of Lauren, and her heart soared.

❖

Lauren felt like she was going to bust out of her skin with excitement and nervous energy. She and Sarah had survived their four-month waiting period, and for days, all Lauren had wanted to do was get Sarah alone and kiss the daylights out of her. It wasn't helping matters that she now had an addiction to lesbian romance novels. The more she read, the more her inner lesbian romantic wanted to get down to business.

Sarah would be here in half an hour, and Lauren was still second-guessing her outfit and hairstyle. She finally settled on a long skirt, patterned with tiny forget-me-nots in blues and greens, and a fitted white top with three-quarter sleeves and a generous V-neck. She accessorized with a matching necklace and earrings in sterling silver with lapis gemstones.

After pulling her hair into a loose braid, Lauren applied just a touch of mascara and lip color, then stepped back to appraise the result. It had been years since she had gone to these lengths to make herself look good for someone, and she hoped Sarah would like what she saw.

Lauren slipped into her shoes and got downstairs without a moment to spare. The doorbell rang, and Lauren opened it to a smiling Sarah.

"Hi there," she said, letting her eyes travel the length of Sarah's body and back again. "You look fantastic."

Sarah had given her a simultaneous head-to-toe perusal, and her eyes shone with admiration. "Damn, Lauren, you're gorgeous."

Lauren flushed with pleasure. "Thank you. Ready to go?"

"Most definitely."

When they got into Sarah's car, Lauren immediately grabbed her hand.

"Why do I feel like a sixteen-year-old right now?"

"Maybe because it's been so long since either of us has done this," Sarah replied, entwining their fingers and stroking the back of Lauren's hand with her thumb.

"Now that our first date is here, I'm nervous," Lauren admitted. "I haven't dated in twenty years."

"I know what you mean. Let's take the word date off the table, then. This is just you and me, spending time together. No script, no expectations—okay?"

"Agreed."

They drove down to Skaneateles and luckily managed to find a place to park. Since it was graduation weekend and the weather was beautiful, the lakeside village was bustling with people.

Sarah couldn't keep her eyes off Lauren as they strolled along the main street. "Did I mention you look incredibly beautiful today?"

"I believe you did, though I certainly don't mind hearing it again," Lauren replied, with a smile that made Sarah's mouth go dry.

They meandered along, stopping in shops along the way and showing each other treasures they'd found. In the Irish store, Lauren bought a silver claddagh pendant, since she'd admired Kat's ring so much. Sarah purchased a silver ring with a Celtic knot design. The pet boutique yielded new bell collars for their kitties, and they thoroughly enjoyed browsing the myriad knickknacks and collectibles in the gift shops.

Sarah was incredibly tuned in to Lauren's body near hers. Every touch of Lauren's hand on her back, every brush of fingertips down her arm, made Sarah's body tingle with arousal.

Good Lord, do you think you'll actually make it through dinner in the state you're in?

Sarah acknowledged that she might very well explode before dessert, but she didn't care, damp panties notwithstanding. Lauren looked at her then and gave her a slow, sexy smile. Obviously she wasn't the only one who was turned on.

"Let's walk down by the lake," Sarah suggested, suddenly needing to move to dispel the tension.

"Great idea," Lauren agreed.

As they strolled along the waterfront, they passed an elderly couple seated on one of the park benches.

"Come, my love," the old gentleman was saying. He tenderly helped his tiny, fragile-looking wife to her feet, murmuring encouragement. She smiled up at him brightly, and they slowly made their way across the grass, hand in hand, faces awash with love for each other.

Lauren caught Sarah's eye and smiled, the sweet moment touching them both. They sat down on the bench the old couple had vacated, and Lauren sighed contentedly.

"This is such a beautiful spot," she said. "So peaceful."

They sat in silence, watching a couple of sailboats skimming the water in the distance. A light breeze blew off the lake, and the afternoon sun warmed their faces. Sarah sat with her arm along the back of the bench, her fingers gently tracing circles on Lauren's shoulder.

Lauren leaned close and whispered, "If you keep touching me like that, I might make a scene."

Sarah grinned. "Really? What kind of scene?"

"Perhaps an inappropriate public display of affection, which would be unwise, since there are children present." Lauren nodded toward a group of youngsters on the shoreline, who were throwing bread to the ducks.

Sarah stilled her hand but did not remove her arm. "I'm not sure I can stop touching you for long," she warned. "Jeez, where's a broom closet when you need one?"

Lauren laughed. "You want to ravish me in a broom closet?"

"Well, it wouldn't be my first choice, but it would do in a pinch," Sarah replied cheekily.

Lauren stood suddenly and removed a compact digital camera from her purse. "I want to take pictures of you. May I?"

Sarah groaned. "I suppose, but I don't know why you want so many pictures of me. I'm not very photogenic."

"Nonsense," Lauren admonished. "I think you're beautiful."

Lauren's first shot captured Sarah's flushed cheeks and surprised smile. Delighted, she rapidly took several more.

"Can we go over by those flowers?" she asked, pointing to a colorful bed of gerbera daisies and late-blooming tulips. She positioned Sarah in front of the flowers, with the lake in the background. After snapping several photos, she gave the camera to Sarah so she could see them.

"Not photogenic, my ass. Look at you," Lauren gushed.

Embarrassed but pleased, Sarah whispered her thanks into Lauren's ear, then stayed close, breathing in her lavender perfume.

"You smell amazing," she said softly, and it was Lauren's turn to flush with pleasure. "Our dinner reservations—"

"Are not until six thirty," Lauren finished breathlessly.

"A whole hour from now."

"Mm-hmm," Lauren murmured, looking intently into Sarah's eyes.

Sarah swallowed, hard. "C'mon, let's go back to the car." She grabbed their packages and Lauren's wrist.

"Where are we going?" Lauren had to walk quickly to keep up with Sarah's determined stride.

"Somewhere more private."

Once in the car, Sarah drove out of the village toward what quickly became open countryside. She took a left down a winding road and drove on a minute or two more, then slowed. Up ahead was an old abandoned barn, surrounded by rolling fields of alfalfa. She pulled over onto a narrow dirt path beside the barn. There wasn't a soul in sight.

Turning off the engine, Sarah turned and looked at Lauren, whose expression told her that she, too, knew what was about to happen.

"Four months is a really long time to wait," Lauren said, her voice husky and low.

Sarah closed her eyes and took a deep breath, needing to say what was on her mind. "You are my best friend, and I don't want to jeopardize that," she said, then opened them to look at the beautiful woman beside her. "But God, I want more. I need to know you are sure about this, because once I kiss you, there's no going back."

Lauren reached out and cupped Sarah's cheek in her hand. "You are my best friend, too, which is exactly why I *am* sure. And if you don't kiss me right this minute, I am going to lose my mind."

Sarah got out of the car and quickly went around to the passenger side. Opening the door, she took Lauren's hand, then led her around to the back of the barn, out of sight of the road.

Tenderly taking Lauren's face in her hands, Sarah trembled with anticipation. Lauren ran her hand through Sarah's short, soft hair, then cupped the back of her head and erased the last few inches between them. The first touch of their lips was whisper soft, but the kiss quickly became more intense, driven by need.

Lauren moaned as Sarah's tongue met hers, and she leaned back against the rough, weathered barn wall. Sarah followed, pressing her body firmly against Lauren's and covering her jaw with kisses. She moved her mouth feverishly from lips to throat, unable to get enough. Lauren dipped her head to recapture Sarah's lips, and they kissed long and deep.

Pulling back to catch her breath, Lauren looked at Sarah, her eyes hooded with desire. "And I thought our first kiss was amazing."

"There's a lot more where that came from," Sarah promised, and claimed Lauren's mouth once again. She ran her hands down Lauren's sides, thumbs brushing the sides of her breasts, then gripped her hips and pulled her closer still. When Sarah pressed her thigh to Lauren's center, Lauren gasped and nearly cried out.

"Are you thinking what I'm thinking?" Sarah asked, breathing hard.

"Depends. Are you thinking our dinner reservations can wait for another day?"

"Mm, yes," Sarah answered, as she nibbled on Lauren's ear.

"Then take me home."

Sarah barely got her key in the lock before Lauren attacked her. They fumbled through the door, and as soon as Sarah got the door closed, Lauren had her pressed up against it.

Lauren couldn't remember when, if ever, she had been this aroused. She ached from wanting; how would she be able to stand it when Sarah finally touched her?

Sarah grasped the hem of Lauren's blouse and searched her eyes for permission. Lauren nodded, and Sarah drew the blouse over her head. Gazing reverently at Lauren's lace-covered breasts, she cupped them in her hands, rubbing her thumbs over the taut nipples beneath the fabric. Lauren groaned, and Sarah bent her head to kiss the swell of each breast, her lips lingering. She brought her hands to Lauren's shoulders, and with excruciating slowness, pushed the straps down her arms.

"I'm dying here," Lauren said breathlessly.

Sarah smiled. "Don't rush me, baby. I want to remember this."

She gently removed Lauren's bra and tossed it to the floor, then reached behind her to lower the zipper on her skirt. It slid easily to Lauren's feet, and she stepped out of it, kicking the garment to the side. Sarah stood perfectly still, gazing at Lauren, nearly naked before her.

"You are incredible," she whispered, her voice breaking with need. She covered Lauren's breasts with her hands, palming the nipples until they hardened like pebbles. Lowering her head, she took one nipple between her lips, then bathed the swollen tip with her tongue.

"Oh," Lauren breathed, shuddering from the exquisite sensation. Her knees nearly buckled, and Sarah caught her with an arm around her waist. "Upstairs…please," she whimpered.

Sarah took her hand and led her to the bedroom, stopping halfway up the stairs to kiss her again. Once inside the room, she reached for Lauren, but was stopped by a firm hand on her chest.

"I am at a distinct disadvantage here. Gotta level the playing field," Lauren murmured, fixing Sarah with a sultry look.

Sarah groaned and bit her lip.

Reaching for the buttons on Sarah's blouse, Lauren slowly undid them. She pushed the silk off her smooth, freckled shoulders, then made quick work of her bra. Touching a fingertip to Sarah's lips, she ran it slowly down her throat, through the valley between her breasts, and down her belly to her waistband. She quickly unfastened the button and zipper and ran her hands inside the back of Sarah's pants to cup her bottom. Stifling Sarah's moan with a kiss, Lauren nipped her bottom lip, then blazed a trail of kisses down to her belly.

"Off," she demanded, pushing Sarah's pants down her legs.

"God, Lauren, are you sure you haven't done this with a woman before?"

"I haven't, but I feel inspired by you. How am I doing so far?" Lauren replied, placing a wet kiss in the center of Sarah's belly.

"A masterful job, but I wonder, what else have you got in store for me?"

"Whatever you need, love, whatever you need," Lauren replied, capturing Sarah's lips for a soul-searing kiss. She caressed the back of Sarah's head, pulling her close and reveling in the exquisite softness of her body. Sarah's groan of protest when she broke the kiss was replaced by a whimper of pleasure as Lauren sucked first one nipple, then the other. She hefted Sarah's full breasts in her hands and lavished them with attention, until Sarah collapsed backward onto the bed.

They quickly removed the remainder of their clothing and lay facing each other, every possible inch of their bodies touching. As they kissed, Sarah worked Lauren's braid loose with her fingers and ran her hands through the dark waves. Lauren rolled Sarah beneath her without breaking their kiss, and settled her body on top, her legs straddling Sarah's thigh.

"I've dreamt of this," Sarah murmured, "but you're even more beautiful than my dreams."

"And you," Lauren replied, as her hips began moving of their own volition, "make me want more than I ever thought possible. Please, Sarah, make love to me."

Even if she tried, Sarah could not have made this moment more perfect. She pressed her thigh to Lauren's core, causing Lauren to rock against her. Massaging her breasts, she took the nipples into her mouth, sucking them into hard peaks. Lauren's eyes closed as her breathing grew ragged. When she opened them to watch Sarah's ministrations, they had darkened to indigo from her desire. Lauren's hips began moving faster, her arousal coating Sarah's thigh.

"Not yet, baby," Sarah whispered, rolling Lauren onto her back. She let her gaze roam over every inch of Lauren's body beneath her, and her hands followed the same velvety path. Lauren's chest heaved, her pale skin flushed with pleasure. Sarah stroked Lauren's belly, tickling a circle around her belly button before reaching lower. She spread Lauren's thighs apart, bending one leg at the knee and caressing the back of her thigh with slow teasing strokes. With every pass of her hand, she moved closer to Lauren's center, tickling the curls on either side but not touching where Lauren needed her most.

Lauren threw her head back onto the bed as the pressure built. She whimpered with need, her belly trembling.

"Shh, it's okay," Sarah soothed, ending the torturous wait. Dipping a finger into Lauren's arousal, she began to stroke her.

"So wet," she whispered, spreading the warm silk. She drew circles around Lauren's clit, bringing her close, then retreating to slip her fingers inside. Sarah repeated this once, twice, and twice again until she felt Lauren stiffen beneath her.

"Come for me," Sarah demanded softly, as she brought Lauren to the precipice and, with one final thrust, sent her over.

Lauren cried out, her body quaking from the power of her orgasm. When the tremors subsided, she lay spent, tears mixing with the sweat that darkened the hair at her temples.

Sarah stroked her all over, soothing her trembling muscles. "Are you okay?"

"More than okay. I have never felt anything so intense in my life." Lauren laughed softly. "I always thought people were exaggerating when they said they could see fireworks, but I just did. It was like the Fourth of July when you made me come."

Sarah smiled and kissed her. "I'm that good, huh?"

"Oh yes, you are that good." Lauren cupped Sarah's cheek, then rubbed her thumb over her full lips. "I can't believe how amazing you just made me feel."

"It was easy. You're so incredibly responsive," Sarah replied, running a gentle finger over Lauren's nipple and making her twitch.

"Stop it." Lauren swatted at Sarah's hand. "I need recovery time—you just shattered me. Besides," she said, pushing Sarah onto her back, "it's my turn."

She began by nibbling at Sarah's lips with her own, then deepening the kiss until neither of them could breathe. Moving lower, she tickled Sarah's full breasts with her hair and rubbed her cheek on their pillowy softness.

"I rather enjoy these," she said, massaging Sarah's breasts and stroking her nipples to attention. "They're lovely."

Shifting from fingers to tongue, Lauren worshipped Sarah's breasts until she was writhing beneath her.

"You have to touch me," Sarah said, gasping.

"My thoughts exactly." Lauren ran her fingertips slowly, teasingly along a meandering path to Sarah's core.

Lauren's first touch, the silky heat of it, astounded her. She dipped her fingers into the well of Sarah's opening and spread the wetness over her swollen flesh, marveling at the wonder of a woman's arousal and feeling very powerful to have caused it.

Sarah moaned and rolled her hips, aching for more. Lauren explored Sarah's soft lips, then centered on the most sensitive part of her. Noting which movements made Sarah more responsive, she began a steady rhythm and watched the sensations play over Sarah's face.

"Please, I need you—inside me," Sarah begged.

Lauren continued stroking with her thumb, but glided two fingers to her entrance and slid inside. Sarah sighed and began to thrust her hips against Lauren's hand. Synchronizing with Sarah's motion, Lauren quickly became enamored with the feel of being inside another woman. The molten walls of Sarah's sex were smooth and slick, then rippled as her throbbing muscles clenched Lauren's fingers.

Lauren stroked and circled, then leaned down to once again take Sarah's nipple into her mouth. The combination of sensations sent Sarah speeding toward the point of no return. She cried out, her rigid thighs holding Lauren inside of her until the aftershocks subsided.

"Oh my God," Sarah breathed, unable to move her limbs for several moments. "How did you know how to do that?"

Lauren grinned, pleased at Sarah's reaction. "I don't know. I just...felt what you needed."

"You're unbelievable," Sarah replied softly, pulling Lauren down beside her. Lauren snuggled in, laying her head on Sarah's shoulder and entwining their legs beneath the covers. Pulling the sheet up to their breasts, she sighed in utter contentment.

"Hell of a first date," Lauren remarked drowsily.

Sarah chuckled as she stroked Lauren's back. "Colossal understatement."

For several moments they were quiet, then Lauren suddenly lifted her head. "Babe?" she said, looking into Sarah's eyes.

"Hmm?"

"This is probably not what one generally hears on a first date, but I have to tell you something."

"What's that?"

"Aside from the birth of my child, I think this has been the most amazing experience of my life, hands down."

Sarah's eyebrows arched in surprise, but Lauren's finger on her lips prevented a response.

"You were already my dearest friend, and now you are my lover as well. I feel so blessed. I don't think I could be happier if I tried."

Tears sprang to Sarah's eyes, and Lauren stroked her cheek tenderly.

"I just want you to know how much I love you," Lauren whispered, her own eyes moist.

"Oh, Lauren," Sarah replied, voice breaking with emotion, "I love you, too."

Lauren had drifted off to sleep, and Sarah held her close, her heart nearly bursting with happiness. The enormity of Lauren's words washed over her, and she had to pinch herself to be sure it hadn't been a dream.

As she held the woman she loved, an incredible sense of peace settled over Sarah, and she sent a prayer of thanks to the heavens. Lauren stirred in her arms, and she placed a lingering kiss atop her dark head. It had been a long road, and it had taken many baby steps to get to this moment, for both of them. Sarah now knew with certainty that the journey was always meant to bring her here. True love had claimed her heart once again.

About the Author

Erin McKenzie has been a lover of words since she first learned her ABCs, sparking a lifelong passion for reading, writing, and of course, word games! She is a professional school counselor, mom to her three young children, partner to her wife of fifteen years, chief dishwasher and laundry folder, soccer mom and homework checker. She and her family live in the Finger Lakes region of New York State and share their home with several furry friends.

Where Love Leads, Erin's debut novel, has been a long-time labor of love. She hopes you enjoy the story!

Books Available from Bold Strokes Books

Complications by MJ Williamz. Two women battle for the heart of one. (978-1-62639-769-9)

Crossing the Wide Forever by Missouri Vaun. As Cody Walsh and Lillie Ellis face the perils of the untamed West, they discover that love's uncharted frontier isn't for the weak in spirit or the faint of heart. (978-1-62639-851-1)

Fake It Till You Make It by M. Ullrich. Lies will lead to trouble, but can they lead to love? (978-1-62639-923-5)

Girls Next Door by Sandy Lowe and Stacia Seaman eds. Best-selling romance authors tell it from the heart—sexy, romantic stories of falling for the girls next door. (978-1-62639-916-7)

Pursuit by Jackie D. The pursuit of the most dangerous terrorist in America will crack the lines of friendship and love, and not everyone will make it out under the weight of duty and service. (978-1-62639-903-7)

Shameless by Brit Ryder. Confident Emery Pearson knows exactly what she's looking for in a no-strings-attached hookup, but can a spontaneous interlude open her heart to more? (978-1-63555-006-1)

The Practitioner by Ronica Black. Sometimes love comes calling whether you're ready for it or not. (978-1-62639-948-8)

Unlikely Match by Fiona Riley. When an ambitious PR exec and her super-rich coding geek-girl client fall in love, they learn that giving something up may be the only way to have everything. (978-1-62639-891-7)

Where Love Leads by Erin McKenzie. A high school counselor and the mom of her new student bond in support of the troubled girl, never expecting deeper feelings to emerge, testing the boundaries of their relationship. (978-1-62639-991-4)

Forsaken Trust by Meredith Doench. When four women are murdered, Agent Luce Hansen must regain trust in her most valuable investigative tool—herself—to catch the killer. (978-1-62639-737-8)

Her Best Friend's Sister by Meghan O'Brien. For fifteen years, Claire Barker has nursed a massive crush on her best friend's older sister. What happens when all her wildest fantasies come true? (978-1-62639-861-0)

Letter of the Law by Carsen Taite. Will federal prosecutor Bianca Cruz take a chance at love with horse breeder Jade Vargas, whose dark family ties threaten everything Bianca has worked to protect—including her child? (978-1-62639-750-7)

New Life by Jan Gayle. Trigena and Karrie are having a baby, but the stress of becoming a mother and the impact on their relationship might be too much for Trigena. (978-1-62639-878-8)

Royal Rebel by Jenny Frame. Charity director Lennox King sees through the party girl image Princess Roza has cultivated, but will Lennox's past indiscretions and Roza's responsibilities make their love impossible? (978-1-62639-893-1)

Unbroken by Donna K. Ford. When Kayla and Jackie, two women with every reason to reject Happy Ever After, fall in love, will they have the courage to overcome their pasts and rewrite their stories? (978-1-62639-921-1)

Where the Light Glows by Dena Blake. Mel Thomas doesn't realize just how unhappy she is in her marriage until she meets Izzy Calabrese. Will she have the courage to overcome her insecurities and follow her heart? (978-1-62639-958-7)

Escape in Time by Robyn Nyx. Working in the past is hell on your future. (978-1-62639-855-9)

Forget-Me-Not by Kris Bryant. Is love worth walking away from the only life you've ever dreamed of? (978-1-62639-865-8)

Highland Fling by Anna Larner. On vacation in the Scottish Highlands, Eve Eddison falls for the enigmatic forestry officer Moira Burns, despite Eve's best friend's campaign to convince her that Moira will break her heart. (978-1-62639-853-5)

Phoenix Rising by Rebecca Harwell. As Storm's Quarry faces invasion from a powerful neighbor, a mysterious newcomer with powers equal to Nadya's challenges everything she believes about herself and her future. (978-1-62639-913-6)

Soul Survivor by I. Beacham. Sam and Joey have given up on hope, but when fate brings them together it gives them a chance to change each other's life and make dreams come true. (978-1-62639-882-5)

Strawberry Summer by Melissa Brayden. When Margaret Beringer's first love Courtney Carrington returns to their small town, she must grapple with their troubled past and fight the temptation for a very delicious future. (978-1-62639-867-2)

The Girl on the Edge of Summer by J.M. Redmann. Micky Knight accepts two cases, but neither is the easy investigation it appears. The past is never past—and young girls lead complicated, even dangerous lives. (978-1-62639-687-6)

Unknown Horizons by CJ Birch. The moment Lieutenant Alison Ash steps aboard the Persephone, she knows her life will never be the same. (978-1-62639-938-9)

Divided Nation, United Hearts by Yolanda Wallace. In a nation torn in two by a most uncivil war, can love conquer the divide? (978-1-62639-847-4)

Fury's Bridge by Brey Willows. What if your life depended on someone who didn't believe in your existence? (978-1-62639-841-2)

Lightning Strikes by Cass Sellars. When Parker Duncan and Sydney Hyatt's one-night stand turns to more, both women must fight demons past and present to cling to the relationship neither of them thought she wanted. (978-1-62639-956-3)

Love in Disaster by Charlotte Greene. A professor and a celebrity chef are drawn together by chance, but can their attraction survive a natural disaster? (978-1-62639-885-6)

Secret Hearts by Radclyffe. Can two women from different worlds find common ground while fighting their secret desires? (978-1-62639-932-7)

Sins of Our Fathers by A. Rose Mathieu. Solving gruesome murder cases is only one of Elizabeth Campbell's challenges; another is her growing attraction to the female detective who is hell-bent on keeping her client in prison. (978-1-62639-873-3)

The Sniper's Kiss by Justine Saracen. The power of a kiss: it can swell your heart with splendor, declare abject submission, and sometimes blow your brains out. (978-1-62639-839-9)

Troop 18 by Jessica L. Webb. Charged with uncovering the destructive secret that a troop of RCMP cadets has been hiding, Andy must put aside her worries about Kate and uncover the conspiracy before it's too late. (978-1-62639-934-1)

Worthy of Trust and Confidence by Kara A. McLeod. Agent Ryan O'Connor is about to discover the hard way that when you can only handle one type of answer to a question, it really is better not to ask. (978-1-62639-889-4)